ARMAGEDDON

A James Acton Thriller

Also by J. Robert Kennedy

James Acton Thrillers

The Protocol	*The Riddle*	*The Nazi's Engineer*
Brass Monkey	*Blood Relics*	*Atlantis Lost*
Broken Dove	*Sins of the Titanic*	*The Cylon Curse*
The Templar's Relic	*Saint Peter's Soldiers*	*The Viking Deception*
Flags of Sin	*The Thirteenth Legion*	*Keepers of the Lost Ark*
The Arab Fall	*Raging Sun*	*The Tomb of Genghis Khan*
The Circle of Eight	*Wages of Sin*	*The Manila Deception*
The Venice Code	*Wrath of the Gods*	*The Fourth Bible*
Pompeii's Ghosts	*The Templar's Revenge*	*Embassy of the Empire*
Amazon Burning		*Armageddon*

Special Agent Dylan Kane Thrillers

Rogue Operator	*Death to America*	*State Sanctioned*
Containment Failure	*Black Widow*	*Extraordinary Rendition*
Cold Warriors	*The Agenda*	*Red Eagle*
	Retribution	

Templar Detective Thrillers

The Templar Detective	*The Sergeant's Secret*	*The Code Breaker*
The Parisian Adulteress	*The Unholy Exorcist*	*The Black Scourge*

Kriminalinspektor Wolfgang Vogel Mysteries

The Colonel's Wife	*Sins of the Child*

Delta Force Unleashed Thrillers

Payback	*The Lazarus Moment*	*Forgotten*
Infidels	*Kill Chain*	*The Cuban Incident*

Detective Shakespeare Mysteries

Depraved Difference	*Tick Tock*	*The Redeemer*

Zander Varga, Vampire Detective

The Turned

ARMAGEDDON

A James Acton Thriller

J. ROBERT KENNEDY

For those who didn't make it.

ARMAGEDDON

A James Acton Thriller

"A fearful explosion. A frightful sound. I am writing this blind in pitch darkness. We are under continual rain of pumice-stone and dust. So violent are the explosions that the ear-drums of over half my crew have been shattered. My last thoughts are with my dear wife. I am convinced that the Day of Judgement has come."

Captain Sampson
British vessel Norham Castle
August 27, 1883

"She lies almost completely intact, only the front of the ship is twisted a little to port, the back of the ship a little to starboard. The engine room is full of mud and ash. The engines themselves were not damaged very much, but the flywheels were bent by the repeated shocks. It might be possible to float her once again."

Member of the rescue ship that discovered the Dutch gunship Berouw one month after the eruption, carried miles inland by a wave estimated to be over 120 feet high.
September 1883

PREFACE

It was the loudest sound ever heard by humankind. On August 27, 1883, the volcanic island of Krakatoa erupted with such violence, the power output was estimated to be over 200 megatons of TNT, equivalent to 13,000 times the nuclear bomb dropped on Hiroshima.

Over 36,000 died.

There were four terrific explosions, the loudest detected by barographs around the world. However slight it eventually became, the shockwave circled the globe four times before becoming undetectable, and was described by one scientist as the "quite impossible occurrence of an earthquake in the air!"

The resulting devastation wasn't limited to that of the explosion and the continuing eruptions of multiple volcanoes. The shock also resulted in numerous tsunamis, triggered in part by earthquakes resulting from the pressure shift.

It was just such an earthquake that formed the 2004 Boxing Day Tsunami resulting in the death of over 225,000 surrounding the Indian Ocean.

An earthquake that originated in the same region our intrepid professors now find themselves.

The Blessed Land

Present Day

Jara peered intently at the beach revealed by the low tide, his expert eye seeking the slight dimple in the wet sand indicating a crab might be just below the surface. He spotted one and jabbed his stone spade into the sand, pushing it deep, then shoved down on the wood handle, popping the sand onto the surface. His hand thrust into the turned pile and squeezed, grabbing the crab that was revealed and tossing it into his woven basket sitting nearby, already half-full.

It had been a successful day, the gods granting him a bountiful harvest that would have him heading home early. He could return to collect more, but that would be wasteful. One basket was all he needed to help feed his village for the evening meal. The sweet, succulent meat was always a pleasant addition. He'd be back tomorrow to get more, and because he hadn't been greedy today, there would be plenty left.

His people had learned long ago to never take more than was necessary, otherwise you risked there being none when you needed it next. He scooped out another crab, tossing it expertly into the basket, and moved on to the next dimple in the sand, happily humming.

Something flashed on the horizon and he rose, staring out over the water, toward where the Outsiders called home, and prayed whatever he was looking at didn't signal another attempt to invade the realm granted exclusively to his people by the gods.

The horizon quickly darkened, and it sent a chill up his spine as whatever it was grew. A crack of thunder, louder than anything he had ever heard, forced him backward as he gripped his ears, his chest physically reacting to whatever had caused the sound, and as quickly as it had started, it was over.

He tentatively removed his hands from his ears, confirming the sound was gone, then found himself struggling to control his pounding heart. It had been the most terrifying experience of his young life, and he wasn't sure what to make of it.

But something else was happening now.

He stared out at the water. Something was rapidly approaching, a fog that obscured the horizon. He stood tall, peering toward it, struggling to comprehend what he was looking at, when the ground started to vibrate, a sound building, drowning out the waves crashing on the reef.

And he knew this had nothing to do with the Outsiders, but was a message from the gods.

He ran.

Shiraz Hall

Chennai, India

Two Days Earlier

Archaeology Professor James Acton adjusted the knot of his tie slightly, giving himself an extra quarter-inch of play as the fashion accessory dug at his neck. He wasn't a fan of suits. They should be reserved for politicians and businesspeople, not scientists. Whenever he was invited to an event, if it said Black Tie, he would try to find some reason to get out of it, but too often there was simply no way to avoid it.

Like tonight.

His wife, Archaeology Professor Laura Palmer, discreetly stepped in front of him, straightening his mangled tie then giving him a gentle kiss on the cheek. "Maybe next time you should wear a clip-on."

He grinned. "Consider it done."

"With our track record over the past few years, our luck is eventually going to run out. Do you really want to be caught dead with a clip-on?"

5

He chuckled. "If you die with me, then I don't give a shit how they find me, but if you don't, I know you'll take care of it."

She patted his cheek. "You can count on it. While we're on the subject, should I make sure you have clean underwear on as well?"

His eyebrows bobbed suggestively. "What if I'm not wearing any?"

She leaned in and a hand cupped the boys. A squeeze had him grunting. "I don't know who I'll miss more, you or him."

Acton cleared his throat, adjusting his tie once again as he eyed the room packed with scientists, dignitaries, and local high society. "Who are you talking to?"

She let go. "I'll never tell."

He shrugged. "I don't care. Either way, I come off great. And if you're planning on touching my balls or anything else again, I'll have to warn you that Ritesh is heading our way."

She took a step back and took his breath away as she always did. She was gorgeous, to him the most beautiful woman he had ever seen. And every moment he spent with her made him realize just how lucky he was. He had resigned himself to a life alone, his lifestyle not conducive to a long-term relationship, what with gallivanting around the globe for months at a time. But that lifestyle was her lifestyle, and she understood it and participated in it with equal enthusiasm. They were a match made in Heaven. Some people said opposites attracted, but they were anything but opposites.

"Jim, Laura, so happy you two could make it."

Laura turned, beaming a smile at Professor Ritesh Jannarkar. "Well, we could hardly ignore the invitation after missing the past two years."

Jannarkar laughed. "I was beginning to take it personally."

Acton shook the man's hand. "I can assure you, whatever excuses we made were genuine, and we're happy to be here to support the cause."

"Yes, you've been quite generous with your donations, even when you don't attend to take advantage of our hospitality."

Laura smiled. "We've been fortunate in life, and preserving historic buildings is a cause dear to my heart. All history should be preserved. It's only through understanding and remembering our past that we can learn from it."

"I agree wholeheartedly. Tearing down the past because one is offended by it today, means that those former remembrances are no longer in the public eye so they can be discussed and questioned. If history is hidden away because of offense, then so is the reason for that offense, and then one can no longer learn."

"Wise words, my friend." Acton's eyes scanned the room. "I thought your wife was going to be with you tonight."

Jannarkar threw up his hands. "She was supposed to be but got called away. Apparently, the Barren Island volcano is acting up, so she's leading a team to investigate. The timing is fortuitous, since I'm heading to the area in two days with a team. A local villager discovered something, and I'm taking some of my students to see what it might be."

Acton perked up at the mention of a new discovery. "Any clues? Pictures?"

"I believe it's an old naval vessel, mid-to-late nineteenth century."

"Interesting, though hardly unusual."

"No, not if it were found on the shore."

Now Acton's curiosity was piqued. "What do you mean?"

"I mean, it was found buried several miles inland."

Laura's hand gripped his. "That could mean only one thing. A tsunami."

Jannarkar smiled. "The two of you are the best archaeologists I've ever met, and together you're unstoppable. That's exactly the conclusion that I came to, though not within five seconds."

Acton's pulse quickened. "Wait a minute. Mid-to-late nineteenth-century vessel carried inland by a tsunami. Are you thinking what I'm thinking?"

Laura stared at him, her eyes wide. "It has to be Krakatoa. Where was it found?"

"You're not going to believe this. The Andaman Islands."

Laura's jaw dropped. "You're kidding me! That far west?"

Acton squeezed her hand a little tighter. "There were multiple tsunamis that occurred over days, if not weeks, that wiped out entire islands. It's definitely possible."

Jannarkar cleared his throat. "There's more."

They both turned to their host, Acton ready to burst from the anticipation. "Out with it, man, you're going to give me a stroke."

Jannarkar laughed. "It was found on the *west* coast."

Acton's eyes narrowed, doubting himself. "How far from the east coast is that?"

"It was found a little less than ten miles from where the tsunami would have hit on the eastern shore."

Laura's hand darted to her mouth. "I've heard of tsunamis making it that far inland, though those events were unprecedented." She stared at both men. "Could it be possible for a ship to have been carried that far inland, almost to the other side of the island?"

Acton squeezed the back of his neck with his free hand. "There's only one way to find out."

Jannarkar stared at both of them with a wide smile. "You're welcome to join us if you wish."

One glance at Laura and Acton knew her answer. "Try to stop us!"

On board the Norham Castle

Northwest of Krakatoa

August 27, 1883

Captain Sampson sat in his cabin, recording yet another fairly routine log entry, though perhaps not entirely routine. Since they had arrived in the area, a volcano had been acting up on the horizon, though it was far enough away to be of no concern. He, of course, had heard of volcanoes, though had never seen one himself. It was fascinating, and most of the crew, when not on duty, were up on the deck watching what was likely a once in a lifetime experience for all of them.

This was why he had become a mariner. He had wanted to see the world, as his father had, and his father before him. He wasn't sure how far back in his lineage the sea went, but he was certain he had saltwater running through his veins. He loved this life, though he loved it a little less since he'd been married and the first of his children had been born.

He missed them dearly every day, and the farther into any voyage, the worse it became.

He was near his destination now, their incredibly valuable cargo soon to no longer be his responsibility. Yet it would be a long journey home, and he'd be counting down the days until he was reunited with them. He had decided this would be his last long-haul voyage. It was simply too difficult, and not fair to his wife, now that they had three young children. While expeditions like this paid handsomely, especially as Captain, it was simply too painful to justify the extra pay. There were plenty of captaincies that would keep him close to Europe, where instead of seeing his wife once or twice a year, he'd see her once or twice a month. It would mean he'd have to work longer before he could retire, though work never scared him. It was the time away that tormented him now.

He finished off his entry then blotted the page, folding shut the ship's log then locking it away. He leaned back in his chair and stretched his arms, then leaned forward, resting his elbows on his desk as he laced his fingers behind his head and gently stretched his neck forward. The sound of the ocean was amplified by his hands and wrists over his ears, magnifying the source of his pain. He pressed the palms against his ears, shutting out the sound, leaving only the pounding of his heart, a heart broken a little more each day as he thought of his wife back home, fending for herself.

Suddenly a terrific noise overwhelmed him, a sharp crack, as if a cannon had been fired right next to his ear. The sound was so terrific, it hammered his lungs, and he could feel its effects in every fiber of his being. He bolted to his feet and could hear the cries of his men on the deck. He rushed from his cabin to see what had happened, and as he came out into the open, he found his men lying on the deck, screaming in agony, blood flowing from their ears. As he struggled to figure out what had happened, he finally noticed what he couldn't believe he had missed.

The volcano that appeared so far in the distance earlier, filled the horizon.

Fiery lava ejected into the air sending red-hot burning embers in all directions as black ash spewed forth, rapidly turning the sky dark. The black cloud threatened to blot out the sun as a frenzy of lightning bolts crackled among the mass. It was unlike anything he had ever seen, and prayed he never would again, and as he peered into the distance at the hellish fury unleashed upon God's earth, he spotted something that terrified him even more than what he had already experienced.

"Brace yourselves!"

Outside Wandoor, Baratang Island

Andaman Islands, India

Present Day

James Acton continued to sketch as Professor Jannarkar's students, along with Tommy Granger and his girlfriend, Mai Trinh, efficiently excavated what was definitely a ship. The timbers used in its construction were rotting, some to the point of crumbling when touched. He feared there would be little chance of preserving the ship itself, though the contents were another matter. Two intact skeletons had already been retrieved and Jannarkar was examining them nearby. Beyond the human tragedies, scores of artifacts had been recovered. Some everyday items, some part of the standard equipment of a ship of the era, others personal trinkets.

Including the all-important ship's log. It was too fragile to risk examining here. It would be taken back to a lab and scanned in a strictly controlled environment. To him, nothing else they had found so far compared. The ship's log, maintained by the Captain, would reveal the man and perhaps whatever tragedy had befallen them, if he had time to make a final entry.

They were two miles inland from the west coast of the narrow Andaman Islands, over 1000 miles northwest of where Krakatoa had erupted. They were far enough inland that Acton was convinced a tsunami had carried the ship, the crew helpless to prevent it. It would have been sudden, and there likely would have been no time for an entry. However, if this all did indeed occur during the events surrounding the eruption of Krakatoa, there might be valuable entries about those days, for Krakatoa wasn't a moment-in-time event. There were multiple eruptions and explosions, earthquakes, and tsunamis. It was an unprecedented disaster that could happen at any time, anywhere.

For this ship to have been carried inland, they would have had to be near the islands at the time—no tsunami would carry them over 1000 miles. He was dying to read the log, to discover the mysteries it might reveal surrounding the ordeal this crew must have gone through.

"I found it," said Laura, holding up her phone triumphantly. "The Norham Castle, presumed lost in 1883 during the eruption of Krakatoa when they didn't arrive as scheduled in Burma. All hands lost. Captain was a man named Sampson." She brought up a drawing of the ship and he compared his sketch.

"Definitely looks like her."

She eyed him. "There was doubt?"

He laughed. "While I'm fully aware the log had the name of the ship on the cover, I was hoping my expert drawing skills would have helped identify it should that log not have been found."

She patted his cheek. "I'm sure it would have, dear." She continued scanning what she had found on her phone. A quick inhale then her hand darting to her mouth had him concerned.

"What is it?"

She stepped closer, lowering her voice. "It says here it was a gold transport."

His eyebrows shot up. "A gold transport?"

"Yes. They were transporting gold to pay the troops in India."

"How much?"

"They don't know the exact amount, but there's an entry here that says they estimate it would be equivalent to twenty-five to fifty million dollars today."

He whistled. "That's a lot of coin."

"Do you think it's still in there?"

He shrugged, turning to stare at the find as the students continued their work. "I can't see why it wouldn't be, unless someone else found this years ago and liberated the gold."

She grabbed his arm. "Remember what happened in Eritrea when we found that ghost ship with all that gold from Pompeii?"

"That was different. That was billions. Countries that poor would be willing to go to war over those amounts. Fifty-million isn't going to have anybody invading."

She looked about them. "War isn't what I'm worried about."

"What do you mean?"

She tilted her head slightly toward the locals gathered around the perimeter, held back by half a dozen armed guards that appeared to be no more than local gang members. "Look at how poor these people are. That kind of money might not be worth going to war over, but it would certainly be worth killing over."

He chewed his cheek. She was right. If the gold were indeed on board, and the wrong people found out, they could find themselves in grave danger. He eyed the SUVs that had brought them here from the coast. He and Laura had their travel agent rent a yacht while in Chennai, intending to enjoy a week's vacation after the charity function with their young friends, Tommy and Mai, both of whom they had become close with over the years. Mai had saved their lives in Vietnam, and as a result, had been forced into exile in the United States. She had recently gained her American citizenship and eagerly accepted the invitation for a vacation. Tommy, a computer genius if there ever was one, had met her at Acton's university, and the two had fallen in love, both becoming members of his and Laura's extended family. He and Laura thought of them as their adopted adult children.

And this new revelation meant they were in danger.

Everyone was in danger.

Laura flashed a smile at a waving Mai, who appeared to be having the time of her life. "We need to stop this dig and go in there ourselves to see if we can confirm whether the gold is there."

Acton agreed and flagged down Jannarkar. "Ritesh, can we have a moment?"

Jannarkar looked up from the bones then stood, stretching his back with a groan before walking over to them, his huge smile evidence of how excited he was. He held up his hands, covered in mud. "I can't tell you how much I've missed this."

Acton smiled and leaned in close. "We might have a problem," he said, his voice low.

There was no forcing Jannarkar's smile from his face. "What kind of problem?"

"We've identified the ship."

"Yes, the Norham Castle. We know that from the log."

Laura explained. "Yes, but we've actually found reference to her. She was a gold transport for the British Army. Estimates suggest twenty-five to fifty million dollars' worth of gold might be in her hold."

Jannarkar's eyes widened. "Seriously?"

"Yes, and you see how that can be a problem, don't you?"

Jannarkar glanced around, observing the same things they had. His jaw dropped slightly. "We have to stop the dig," he muttered.

"Professor Acton! Professor Palmer! Look what we found!"

They all spun toward Tommy's excited voice and Acton cursed at the sight of the young man triumphantly holding a gold bar over his head.

And with the collective gasp of the crowd surrounding them, any hope of suppressing what this find might hold was lost.

Acton strolled quickly toward Tommy, delivering as stern an expression as he could, but saying nothing. Mai picked up on it first and reached from behind her boyfriend, pulling his arm down so the gold bar would no longer be on display. Tommy glanced over his shoulder at her,

17

puzzled, and she whispered something. His eyes darted toward the crowd murmuring in excitement, and he paled.

Acton reached them, forcing a casual smile. "What have you found there?" He held out his hand and Tommy placed the gold bar in it. The heft was impressive, but he twirled it around and spun his wrist several times in an attempt to make it appear light. He pinched it between his thumb and finger, wagging it in the air, then turned toward Laura and Jannarkar. "Sorry to disappoint everyone, but it's not gold. It's just a painted brick." He tossed it back into the hold with a loud metallic thud.

Jannarkar repeated the message in Hindi, and a groan of disappointment rippled through the crowd, many of whom drifted away, the deception at least partially successful.

"Come with us," said Acton to the young couple, and they stepped away from the wreck. "Everybody, just pretend we're having a normal conversation, all smiles." Tommy and Mai both wore fear on their faces, and the forced smiles made them appear even more unnatural. He gave Tommy a look. "Let's get rid of the smile. You look like Heath Ledger."

Laura snorted. "He does, doesn't he."

Tommy wiped the smile from his face and Acton grinned. "Why so serious?"

Tommy chuckled. "Okay, okay, I get it. So, why are we lying about the gold bar?"

"Because according to what we just found on the Internet, this ship might be carrying anywhere from twenty-five to fifty-million dollars' worth."

Tommy's eyes shot wide then he realized his mistake and forced a laugh. "So, just how much is a gold bar like that worth at today's prices?"

"Well over half a million."

Tommy turned his head away from the crowd. "Holy shit! Well, from what we found in the hold, I'd say that fifty-million estimate is probably right, if I'm doing my math correctly."

Mai agreed. "I think he's right. There were about a hundred bars, held in two strong boxes."

Acton turned his back to the crowd and faced Jannarkar. "We need to get that gold out of here now."

Jannarkar agreed. "I think you're right, but how?"

"We could take it out slowly, one bar at a time," suggested Laura. "Put it into our vehicles and then get someplace secure."

Acton scratched his chin as he did the math in his head. He wasn't overly concerned about the locals, he was concerned about the local gangs. If they got wind of this, there'd be no stopping them. One gold bar would be worth killing for. One hundred would be enough to justify killing everyone here so they'd have the time to take it all. Though his subterfuge might have been partially successful, curiosity might still be piqued, especially if anyone had heard how heavy that so-called painted brick sounded when it hit the deck after he tossed it. He should have just handed it back to Tommy, but he'd been stupid. Now he'd have to live with his mistake.

He quickly counted the number of students then eyed the guards who he still thought might be members of the very gangs that concerned him.

He turned to Jannarkar, hoping to assuage his doubts. "Do you trust these guards?"

"Not for a moment."

Acton cursed. "If we try to take it out a bar at a time, and somebody drops one or says the wrong thing, this crowd is going to know that there's gold on this ship and a lot of it, and one of three things will happen. They'll storm us, our guards will storm us, or word will get out to the local gangs, and they'll storm us. I don't like any of those options."

"Neither do I." Jannarkar's eyes widened. "What about this? We send the guards away."

"Won't that raise suspicions?" asked Laura.

Jannarkar shook his head. "No. We'll just announce that there's nothing of value here beyond scientific curiosity, and the guards are no longer needed as there's nothing worth stealing."

Acton smiled at the brilliant simplicity of it. "That's just crazy enough to work. Here's what I suggest. You do that, pay them double what they would have earned for the job so they go away happy, then we do one rapid push. We get all the gold out as fast as we can into our two SUVs, and then we get the hell out of here."

"Where should we go? The nearest place I would consider safe would be Port Blair, but it's fifteen kilometers from here. That's a long way to go if something goes wrong."

"What about our boat?" asked Laura. "It's only three miles from here. We could be there in a few minutes, unload the gold, then head for safe harbor."

Acton liked her plan and turned to Jannarkar. "What do you think?"

20

"I think it's the best idea I've heard so far, and it gets us out of here and my students safe. As long as we're on the roads, we could be attacked."

Tommy cleared his throat and indicated to look behind them with a nod of his head. Acton turned and saw one of the guards standing a little too close with an ear cocked in their direction. Jannarkar snapped at him in Hindi and the man scurried away.

"How long was he there?" asked Acton.

Tommy shrugged. "Not sure. I was so wrapped up in what we were talking about, I wasn't paying attention."

Acton cursed. "Neither was I. Okay, I think our secret's about to be outed. Let's put this plan in action fast. Ritesh, you make your announcement as pleasantly as possible, pay off the guards, and hopefully everyone will lose interest. Send the students into the hold and start bringing the gold where we can easily access it, but out of sight." A motorcycle engine roared and everyone spun toward the sound, a lump forming in Acton's throat as the eavesdropping guard roared away. He turned to the others. "Okay, we've only got minutes before I suspect all hell is going to break loose."

"What do we do if they get here first?" asked Mai, her voice trembling.

"We get in our vehicles and head for the boat. We're not dying to protect gold."

On board the Norham Castle

Northwest of Krakatoa

August 27, 1883

In Sampson's days in the Navy, he had seen explosions, some demonstrations performed simply to impress the elite of British society, some to terrify the enemy. He had been close enough at times to feel the effects of what the experts called a "blast wave," but what they had just experienced went far beyond that. The blast wave from the massive eruption of the volcano had hit the ship with a force not unlike a rogue wave. Their vessel had been shaken horribly, but fortunately, there were no further injuries. He and those who had been below, their ears not as affected as those who had experienced the initial sound of the explosion on deck, scrambled to assist the stricken, which was most of his crew.

The ship's doctor, Smithers, hurried over to him.

"What's happened to them, Doctor?"

"Their eardrums have ruptured."

His eyebrows shot up. "Their eardrums?"

"Yes."

"Will they regain their hearing?"

Smithers shook his head. "With the extent of the damage, I doubt it. You're just fortunate you were below decks like I was, Captain, otherwise this would be your fate too."

"Is there any further risk to them?"

Smithers eyed the injured men lying on the deck. "You should try to set into port to have them properly treated."

Sampson stabbed a finger toward the volcano behind them, the cloud already overhead, the sun losing the battle, day turning into night in a most horrifying manner. "You propose we head into port with this calamity almost upon us?"

Smithers shrugged. "I'm telling you as a doctor what these men need. You're the Captain."

Sampson pulled at his hair. "Will they die?"

"They shouldn't."

"Well, we all might, should whatever that is overtake us."

Rain began to fall. Sampson ignored it at first until he saw the drops stain Smithers' shirt. He held out his hands, the heavy drops quickly filling his cupped palms with a thick, dark gray fluid. He rubbed his thumb and forefinger together.

"What fresh hell is this?"

Outside Wandoor, Baratang Island

Andaman Islands, India

Present Day

Everyone was scared. Jannarkar had dismissed the guards in front of the crowd of onlookers, paying them all handsomely. They had left without hesitation, the explanation of the wreck being purely a scientific find rather than a lost treasure ship disappointing the crowd, most dispersing within minutes. They were mostly alone now, unguarded, though perhaps they always were. If the guards, provided by a local official, were as untrustworthy as Jannarkar had said, then their dismissal made no difference from a safety standpoint.

All that mattered now was time, and Acton feared they had a little of it. He eyed the gold piled just inside the broken hull of the ship. One of Jannarkar's students, Amit, emerged from below with another gold bar. "This is the last one."

"Good." Acton turned to Jannarkar. "Does everyone know what to do?"

Jannarkar nodded. "All of my students speak English, but I've made sure they understand exactly what's going on."

"Then let's get this rolling. This took way too long. If our eavesdropper is getting his buddies, they could be here any minute. We'll pull the vehicles down." Acton and Laura headed for the SUVs parked up on the road. He pointed to a route he had already scouted. "We should be able to get through here, no problem."

Laura agreed and climbed into the second vehicle. He hopped in the first, fired up the engine, then carefully guided it down the gentle slope and into the dig site. He turned around and backed up to the opening in the ship's hold, then reached over and pressed the button to pop the rear hatch.

"Let's go!" he ordered, and immediately the students formed a line, the gold bars quickly emerging from the hold as Laura pulled in beside him, a second line created. He scrambled over the seats and began organizing the gold as it was tossed inside. The pile rapidly grew and he assumed the same was happening in Laura's vehicle. If the counts matched, he estimated they were at least halfway toward their goal. He glanced over his shoulder at the road above, a few of the locals that had remained behind now excited, some with their cellphones out. If their secret hadn't already been revealed, it was now. "We have to hurry!" he yelled, Jannarkar repeating his plea in Hindi.

But it didn't help.

The students were terrified now, and it wasn't fair. They were putting their lives at risk just to save gold. They should just walk away now, but they were so close, and in the back of his mind he was telling himself it wasn't his call, it was Jannarkar who should be making the decision.

He was just a guest here.

But that was an excuse. Jannarkar was blinded by the find, as were he and the others. He had to call it. "Professor, I think we've got enough. It's too dangerous."

Jannarkar, still inside the hold, replied. "We're almost done! Sixty seconds!"

Acton cursed. Sixty seconds sounded like nothing, but could be everything. He heard an engine whine in the distance, the distinct sound of a motorcycle approaching. "We've gotta go now!" He yelled. "I can hear them coming!"

The students were hurling the gold bars inside now, desperate to finish the task their professor had given them.

"That's the last one!" shouted Jannarkar. The trunk slammed shut on Laura's vehicle then his own.

"Everybody get in a truck now!" ordered Acton as Jannarkar emerged from the hold. It didn't need to be translated as he climbed back into the driver's seat, starting the engine. Doors opened and closed on both vehicles, and Laura, the better driver of the two of them, had hers heading up the slope and onto the road before he was even in gear. He followed her out, the whine of multiple engines now unmistakable. Whoever was coming was coming in numbers, and it had his heart pounding as they gained speed, heading toward the coast and their yacht.

Crowds of locals rushed from all directions toward the dig site, word now out from the few stragglers. He reached his hand back toward one of the students. "Give me a gold bar." One of them slapped the heavy metal into his hand. He rolled down his window and tossed it out. It clanged along the rocky road and scores of villagers rushed toward it, a fight ensuing, the road effectively blocked.

"Give me another one." Another was quickly delivered.

"What are you doing?" protested Jannarkar. "Do you realize how much that's worth?"

"It's worth nothing if we can't get it out and onto the yacht. We need to delay them, and if you've got a better idea, I'm all ears."

Jannarkar cursed then reached his own hand back, and the two of them tossed out another half-dozen bars as they continued toward the small port where their boat was moored. The street was filled now for as far back as he could see in his rearview mirror, and Acton felt horrible. People were fighting each other, beating each other over the gold that could change lives. He just prayed nobody was hurt too severely, or worse, killed. The only good news he could take from it was that there were no motorcycles in sight.

"There!" pointed Jannarkar. Acton tore his eyes away from the rearview mirror and spotted the water ahead. Laura had already arrived and the students were offloading the gold as he pulled in beside her.

"Let's go, people! We've got minutes!"

Once again, a line was quickly formed and the gold was rapidly handed off, their load a little lighter this time. He pointed at Laura. "Get her ready to go. The moment we see one of them, we're out of here. I don't give a shit if the gold is offloaded or not."

She headed for the wheelhouse as Acton supervised the operation. "Just toss it on the deck. We'll put it below later!" he yelled when he spotted Jannarkar handing the bars below decks. Jannarkar gave him a thumbs-up and ordered the two students below decks out of the hold, adding more hands to the line.

The whine of a motorcycle engine in the distance had Acton pausing, though only for a moment. The students had heard it as well, and the gold bars flew even faster. With the added sense of urgency, the boat's engine roared to life as Laura prepped them to get underway. He hopped back onto the dock and cleared the mooring lines, tossing them back up on the deck as multiple motorcycle engines now roared toward them.

"We have to go now!" he shouted at Jannarkar.

Jannarkar said something in Hindi and two students replied, one from each vehicle as Acton swung over the gunwale and onto the deck. "We're almost done!"

Acton turned toward the road and spotted half a dozen motorcycles heading toward them, each doubled up, AK-47s and several variants held high in the air.

This was over.

"Everybody on the boat now, or we're leaving you behind!"

Any gold bars in hand were feverishly thrown onto the deck as the students raced along the gang plank and onto the boat. The moment the last foot cleared, Acton turned to Laura. "Get us out of here, now!"

She shoved hard on the throttle and the engine roared as they accelerated away at an excruciatingly slow pace, the water churning as the propellers spun. Gunfire ripped the air behind them and Acton spun to see their pursuers racing into the small port.

He pointed toward the starboard side of the superstructure. "Everybody get on the other side and stay down!"

Everyone scrambled out of the line of fire as he joined Laura in the wheelhouse, putting himself between her and any potential gunfire. The boat continued to pick up speed and she gently turned them away from the pier and into the open water. He glanced over his shoulder to see the lead bike racing down the dock toward them, the rear passenger extending his assault rifle in front of him and squeezing the trigger. The first couple of rounds impacted the boat, but the kickback forced the inexperienced arm up and to the right, the rest of the bullets passing harmlessly overhead. As they cleared the end of the pier, the motorcycle came to a screeching halt.

Giving the gunman a chance to properly aim.

"Everybody down!" he shouted.

Cries erupted from the students on the other side of the bulkhead as he and Laura crouched, their speed continuing to increase. They rapidly put some distance between them and the end of the pier where motorcycles collected, ridden by what he assumed were local gang members their eavesdropper was affiliated with. Gunfire tore into the rear of the boat and Laura swerved to port then to starboard, forcing the cluster of hostiles behind them to re-aim and reposition on the narrow end of the pier. She kept the throttle at full the entire time as she continued to zig-zag, and soon the guns behind them fell silent.

As they cleared the small port, Jannarkar joined them.

"Where should we head, Professor?" asked Laura.

"We won't be safe anywhere along the coast," he replied. "We need to get out to sea where a small craft can't reach us."

Acton regarded him. "Really? Shouldn't we just head for Port Blair? We should be able to outrun pretty much anything in this thing."

Jannarkar shook his head. "No, you don't understand. These gangs are all connected, and because we threw those gold bars out, they know we're carrying a massive stash. Every cellphone between here and Port Blair has already received a message telling them of us. Boats are going to be launching all along the coast to intercept us. Our only hope is at sea. Let's head south and go around the islands. It's our safest option."

Acton frowned but agreed. " I guess we have no choice."

Laura adjusted their heading, aiming them directly south. "We've got company," she said as she checked over her shoulder. They all turned and Acton's heart sank as several boats emerged from the harbor, giving chase.

"I wish we were armed."

"So do I," agreed Laura.

A sound unlike anything he had ever heard, as if every gun in the world had been fired at once, the sound he would imagine the entire planet would hear if the moon fell into the earth, nearly knocked him off his feet. He spun toward it as he instinctively pressed his hands against his ears. His eyes widened as several of the students screamed in terror.

"What the hell is that?"

On board the Norham Castle

Northwest of Krakatoa

August 27, 1883

Sampson closed the ship's log, each entry he made more depressing than the last. Whatever was happening was no ordinary volcano. He had heard the stories, but none were like this. This was biblical. This was the wrath of God or the fury of the Devil unleashed upon mankind. As he stepped out onto the deck, everywhere he looked the sky was black, the entire horizon covered. There was no sunlight, the only light provided by the flashing yellows and oranges of the underworld regurgitating onto the land far behind them, or the fires burning on the shores of the islands they passed. Fireballs shooting through the air had pummeled the islands they sailed through, fires burning out of control, some doused by the mud-laced rain, others too large to quench.

This was terrifying, and he wondered how far around the world it would spread.

"Captain, look!" One of his crew pointed to their starboard side. He peered at the shore of a town, a town he had passed before on several occasions. Nothing remained. Everything was coated in the thick mud they now battled to remove from their decks lest they become top-heavy and capsize. Scattered fires burned in the forest, but the blast wave that had hit them had also hit these islands, and almost every tree was down, every structure flattened, and the only people he saw were half-buried in the mud.

Nothing moved.

This was indeed the end of times, the Armageddon written about in the Book of Revelation. Eventually, this contagion would sweep across the entire globe, blotting out the life-giving sun, killing all the plants and animals, leaving humanity to starve to death for its sins.

And all he could think about was how his wife and his children would suffer alone in their humble home, wondering why he wasn't there with them to face the end of times as a family.

"Captain, something's happening!"

He stared at the shore, his eyes narrowing as the water drained away, then a rumble sounded behind them. He turned and gasped, then closed his eyes as he recited the Lord's Prayer.

Off the coast of Wandoor, Baratang Island

Andaman Islands, India

Present Day

"Hard to starboard, now!" ordered Acton.

Laura didn't question him, cranking the wheel to the right, banking the boat hard. Several of the students cried out as he gave her a new bearing with a pointed finger. "As fast as you can! Stop for nothing!"

"What's going on?"

He grabbed the wheel. "Look behind you." She glanced over her shoulder and her eyes bulged as her jaw slackened.

"Oh my God!" She took back control as Acton stepped out onto the deck, the others noticing the catastrophe behind them.

Tommy turned to him. "Professor, what do we do?"

"Everybody get below decks, now!"

The students scrambled in their rush to safety, shoving beginning as the competition to get through the narrow opening emerged.

34

Acton yelled at them. "Get control of yourselves! One at a time! If you keep fighting like children, you'll all die." He pointed at one of the larger students. "Amit! You take charge!"

Amit held out an arm, blocking the rush, then began pointing, each student he selected dropping through the hole. Acton gave the young man a thumbs-up and a grin was flashed. He motioned for Tommy and Mai to join the group.

"We want to stay with you, sir," protested Tommy.

There was no time to argue. What could only be described as a blast wave was racing toward them, and anyone on the deck would be swept overboard. He jerked a thumb over his shoulder toward the wheelhouse. "Get in there with Laura then get down." They rushed inside as he waited for the last student to disappear below deck. "Where's Professor Jannarkar?" he asked Amit.

"Already down below, sir."

"Okay, get your ass down there!"

Another grin was flashed then Amit dove into the hole, pulling the hatch closed behind him. Acton stared at the approaching blast wave, the half-dozen boats in pursuit rapidly overtaken as the entire horizon behind them blackened with thick billowing clouds.

"James, get inside!"

He tore himself away from the sight and stepped inside the wheelhouse, closing the door behind him. He stared out the window. The blast wave was almost upon them now. "Everybody get down!" Tommy and Mai were already in the corner, Tommy's body draped over Mai's. Laura crouched, keeping one hand on the wheel as he stepped over and shielded her with his own body, then reached up with his free hand to provide extra strength on the wheel.

The roar of the shock wave grew and was soon overwhelming. "Everybody hang on!" The boat was picked up from the rear end, pressing him and Laura against the control housing. He reached out and grabbed Tommy by the shirt as he tumbled, letting go of the wheel to resecure himself. Tommy's foot shot out and he braced against the bulkhead as the boat continued to tip forward. They were almost on-end now, their prow low in the water as a fury of sound continued to disorient them. Wind whistled and howled, water pounded the vessel like a solid wave in the worst rainstorm imaginable. They were pressed into the decking now, experiencing noticeable G-forces as they were propelled forward at a near-vertical angle. He reached up and uselessly grabbed the wheel. They weren't in control anymore, their rudder no doubt out of the water as the shock wave carried them along with it.

And then it was over.

The boat abruptly dropped level again, though still bobbing violently, and Mai's screams ceased, screams he hadn't heard until now. He slowly rose, helping Laura to her feet. "Are you okay?"

"I think so. You?"

"Yeah, I'm fine, though I think from now on when we leave the house, I'm wearing Depends."

She laughed then returned her attention to the boat as he turned to Tommy and Mai. "Are you two okay?"

Tommy lay on his back, gasping for breath. "You might have been joking about wearing adult diapers, but I seriously think I'm going to need a genuine hosing off."

Mai collapsed on top of him, her chest heaving. "Me too."

Acton stared out behind them and cursed as he spotted several of their pursuers still afloat. Laura eased off on the throttle when he turned to her. "They're still after us. Keep it floored."

"Where the hell are we going to go?" she asked, eying the continuing disaster unfolding behind them.

"What's our fuel situation?"

"I had them fill it when we arrived."

"Did they?"

She checked. "Yes. Full tank."

"So, we can reach India if we have to."

"No problem."

"Well, there's no way those guys after us can, and besides, that eruption could get far worse. Any semblance of law enforcement will either collapse or be too busy trying to deal with the disaster to be able to protect us and millions of dollars in gold." Thumping from below deck had his eyes bulging. "I forgot about the others!" He rushed out onto the deck then opened the hatch. Half a dozen faces stared up at him. "Is everybody okay down there?" A lot of head bobs accompanied by whimpering and crying. "Ritesh! You still with us?"

"Yeah, Jim. I'm okay. I whacked my head pretty good, though. What the hell happened?"

"It looks like... " Acton stopped, finally putting the pieces of the puzzle together. And it gutted him. "You better come up here and see for yourself," he said, his voice subdued.

The students shuffled out of the way and Jannarkar emerged up the ladder and onto the deck.

"Ritesh, I don't know how to say this, so I'm just going to show you." He pointed behind them. Jannarkar turned and gasped, grasping the implications immediately.

"Sushma," he whispered.

Acton put a comforting hand on the man's shoulder at the mention of his wife. "We don't know for sure."

Jannarkar's shoulders slumped and his head drooped. "Just look at it, Jim. No one could survive that."

"Your wife's the best at what she does. You know that if they saw evidence it were about to erupt, they would have left. Don't give up hope yet."

Jannarkar gripped the rail at the stern of the boat, his head sagging between his shoulders as his body shook. "Just give me a minute, would you, Jim?"

Acton patted him on the back. "Of course." He turned to see the students standing behind them, all in shock, some with tears streaking their faces, the private conversation overheard. Though he had provided words of comfort to his old friend, he didn't believe them. If there had been enough warning, they would have heard something. Local officials would have announced the threat. He feared this was a sudden, violent eruption that caught Sushma and her team by surprise. The only comfort would be that their deaths were likely instantaneous.

Gunfire erupted behind them, barely heard over the roar of the engine. Three boats were still in pursuit, the others nowhere to be seen, hopefully torn apart by the blast wave that had overtaken them all. They were out of range for the moment, and would remain so as long as nothing happened to their boat. They had far better range, and if nothing else went wrong, he was confident they would be safe.

The question was, what would happen with the volcano? From what he could see behind them on the horizon, it was a massive eruption, as big as anything he had ever seen video of. The initial shockwave could be but the first danger they would face. They were heading directly west now, toward India and hopefully safety, but it would take about 30 hours at their current speed, which they wouldn't maintain after losing their pursuers—he didn't want to risk the engine.

Birds overhead had everyone staring up. His eyes widened at the sight of thousands upon thousands filling the air, all headed in the opposite direction of the volcano. Tommy walked up beside him then pointed.

"Professor, what the hell is that?"

Acton stared in the direction the young man was pointing and a lump formed in his throat. "Oh my God!" The island behind them was engulfed in what appeared to be a mist, blotting out the land.

Yet it wasn't a mist.

It was something far more horrifying.

"James, something's happening!" shouted Laura from the helm. "What do I do?"

"Try to put as much distance between us and that!" he shouted over his shoulder.

The boat tilted slightly as she adjusted their course, though it wasn't by much, as they were already heading directly away from the island.

"What's happening, Professor?"

Acton stared at the devastation behind them. "It's a tsunami."

St. Paul's University

St. Paul, Maryland

Dean Gregory Milton sat in his office rubbing the small of his back, the pain he suffered the result of bullets he had taken to the area years ago, then a vicious beating a couple of years later. His doctors had initially thought he might never walk again, but he had proven them wrong. Though when a piece of shit mercenary had discovered his weakness and exploited it, he had once again feared he might be confined to a wheelchair for the rest of his life. Thankfully, he had recovered for the most part. The pain was getting better, though the progress was slow, and sometimes, when in a funk, he could convince himself it was getting worse.

But he kept journals recording his level of pain, recording the spasms. And if he charted them over time, there was no doubt he was still getting better. He stared at the handheld massager charging in its cradle, cursing himself for having forgotten to plug the device in when he left yesterday.

He glanced at the clock. Fifteen minutes. Surely that was enough to buy him some relief. He grabbed the device and unplugged it from the charger, then turned it on and cranked it to max, leaning forward in his chair as the device thumped relief where his fingers had failed. He groaned in pleasure as there was a double-knock at the door before it opened. He didn't bother looking up. Only his assistant, Rita Perdok, would enter without waiting.

"Oh, sorry to interrupt."

He waved his free hand at her. "Don't worry about it. What is it?"

She stood in the doorway, hesitating. He twisted his head so he could see her, and she appeared concerned. He sat up and turned off the massager, his back already dramatically better.

"What is it, Rita?"

She sighed. "Well, it might be nothing, but you know how you have me set up Google Alerts every time Professor Acton goes somewhere?"

Milton tensed at the mention of his best friend and most troublesome professor's name. Far too often, when Acton went somewhere, trouble found him. Sometimes the fool would charge into it willingly, other times he was an innocent victim. It wasn't in his friend's nature to run away. If he found himself in a situation where people needed to be helped, he was the type that wouldn't hesitate, even if it meant risking his own life. And somehow, the sonofabitch had found his perfect match in Laura Palmer.

And married her.

Between the two of them, they had seen more action than most career military, and it had taken ten years off his own life through worry.

42

He had heard of Google Alerts before, but it wasn't until Tommy Granger had made a joke at a dinner hosted by Acton that he came up with the idea of setting them up for his friend. The alerts weren't just searching for their names. Since then, every time Acton would go somewhere, he or Rita would create alerts for the destination country or region, and she would skim through them. They never turned up anything that wasn't already obvious, as most of what his friend would be involved in was only newsworthy after the fact.

Yet he had never seen Rita troubled like this. "Yes."

"Well, you know how you told me to update the alerts for the Andaman Islands because Professors Acton and Palmer were heading there?"

He leaned forward. "Did something show up?"

"There's been a massive volcanic eruption there. There are only initial reports. It just happened minutes ago. The news is probably not even covering it yet, but reports are coming in on Twitter, and it looks bad."

Milton gulped then turned to his PC, pulling up the folder where the alerts were automatically sent. He clicked on one of the most recent and brought up a series of pictures showing a city devastated, with the caption "Shockwave Flattens City." He brought up several more as a pit formed in his stomach and his mouth filled with bile. This was where his friends were. He reached for the phone as he pulled up a map of the area. Acton was supposed to be on the western coast of the main island, a few miles inland, and the volcano was less than 100 miles to the northeast on the opposite coast.

But it was a narrow island, barely fifteen miles wide at this point.

He dialed Acton's satellite phone. It rang several times before it was finally answered. All he could hear was a roar. "Hello, Jim, is that you?"

"Greg? Listen! We're about to be hit by a tsunami! We're about five miles west of the port near Wandoor, heading directly west in our boat with Professor Jannarkar and eight of his students. I don't think we're going to make—"

Screams had him flinching then the line went dead. He dropped the phone and it clattered on his desk as his eyes burned. He stared up at Rita, his mouth agape.

"What is it?" she asked, gripping her chest, her voice barely a whisper.

"I think I just heard my best friend die."

Off the coast of Wandoor, Baratang Island

Andaman Islands, India

"Greg!" Acton shouted into the phone then checked the display. The call had been dropped. He turned to the others, scrambling into the hold, once again seeking cover from Mother Nature rather than armed hostiles. Jannarkar was the last to go in this time and gave his friend a thumping hug.

"I'm sorry to have gotten you into this."

Acton slapped him on the back. "This isn't your fault. Now get inside, and we'll talk about how wrong you are later." He flashed the man a smile and it was returned. Weak. Jannarkar descended the ladder, helped by his students as the roar of the approaching wave overwhelmed everything. Acton tossed the satellite phone into the hold then slammed down the hatch. The lock fell into place and he prayed he hadn't just sentenced Jannarkar and the students to death by putting them below. But on the deck was certain death, and the small wheelhouse barely held the four of them.

There had been no choice.

"James!" cried Laura, her voice pleading for him to get inside. He took one last glance over his shoulder at the massive wave approaching, and experienced a moment of satisfaction as it tossed their pursuers like matchsticks. He rushed the few feet to the wheelhouse and stepped inside, pulling the door shut behind him and locking it in place as the wave hit. The power behind the wall of water was incredible, shoving them all into the rear bulkhead as the boat was propelled forward. His head smacked against the unforgiving metal and he was overwhelmed by a blinding light as pain seared through his body.

And as he slowly lost consciousness, the only comfort he could find were the screams of his loved ones, meaning they were still alive.

Though not for much longer, he was sure.

St. Paul's University

St. Paul, Maryland

Gregory Milton sat in stunned silence. He redialed the phone, but it just rang, unanswered. He turned and stared at two of the few photos he kept at his office, one of him and his friend after having completed the New York Marathon when they were much younger, and another of the two families together at the wedding Milton had never thought would happen for his friend. Tears rolled down his cheeks and his shoulders shook. A comforting hand was on his back within moments, and he looked up to see Rita staring down at him, her own cheeks stained.

"What did he say?"

"He said they were about to be hit by a tsunami."

She gasped, her fingers running through her hair, tugging on the strands. "That doesn't mean he's dead though, right? People survive that."

Milton sighed then sucked in a long, slow breath. He held it for a moment, steadying his nerves before nodding curtly. "You're right. This is Jim and Laura we're talking about. If there's anyone who could survive this, it's them. They wouldn't panic. They would do exactly what they needed to do. And if there's any hope that any of them survived, it could be up to us to save them."

"But what can we do?"

"*We* can't do anything, but they have friends." He opened his contacts list on his computer, then dialed the first person he could think of who would not only want to know what might have happened to his friends, but might actually be able to help.

Reading Residence

Whitehall, London, England

Interpol Agent Hugh Reading woke to his phone vibrating on his nightstand. He cursed as he reached over and turned off his CPAP machine then tore the mask off. He hated using the device, but it was saving his life and giving him back the energy missing for at least a decade. His afternoon naps were now for pleasure as opposed to a necessity to get him through the rest of the day. He grabbed his phone and peered at the display.

And his heart leaped into his throat.

There was only one reason for Acton's boss and friend, Gregory Milton, to be calling. He swiped his thumb then put the call on speaker as he reached for the bedroom light, his blackout curtains effectively doing their job. "Hello, Greg, what's wrong?"

There was silence at the other end of the line, and he thought he had missed the call somehow, but he finally heard a sniff. Milton was, or had been, crying.

"Greg, what's happened?" he asked gently.

A heavy sigh resulted in a burst of static, then there was a sharp inhale. "Sorry, Hugh, I'm still trying to come to grips with this. I just talked to Jim not five minutes ago. He and Laura, along with some others I assume include Tommy and Mai and some local students, were just caught in a tsunami. A volcano has erupted near where they are. It's a massive eruption, apparently."

Reading scribbled notes in the pad he kept by his bedside. "Are you sure they were caught in it?"

"I heard the screams before we were cut off." Milton's voice cracked and Reading took over.

"Here's what you're going to do. You're going to send me an email with everything you know. I need to know what number you called, exactly what he said and what you heard, where their last known location was, why they were there, who they were with. Send me everything you can as quickly as you can."

"I'll do that, Hugh. I tried calling him back, but it just rings and then cuts off."

"Okay, I want you to stop doing that."

"What?"

"Stop doing that. It might be the only way for us to locate them, and we don't want the battery dying. I'm going to contact our *friend* and see if he can have his people locate the satellite phone. If you hear anything else, let me know, but get me that info as fast as you can."

"I'll do it right away. Goodbye"

"Goodbye."

The call ended and Reading sat on the edge of his bed in shock. If his friends had indeed been caught in a tsunami, the chances of survival were slim. A single sob racked his body that threatened to turn into more, but he fought it off. He had lost count of how many times he thought one or both of them were dead, yet they always managed to pull through. But this was a natural disaster. How many hundreds of thousands had died in the tsunami in 2004? Depending on the size of the wave, there might be no surviving it, but until he saw their bodies, he was treating them as if they were alive. These were the best friends he had ever had, and they were friends who would go to the ends of the earth to find him if the situation were reversed.

His phone vibrated with the email from Milton. He opened it and scanned the information then went against his own advice. He dialed the satellite phone and it rang until it finally cut off. He took his notepad and phone into the living room and turned on the TV. A breaking news alert about the eruption and the tsunami warning was on, but due to the location's remoteness, they had very little information and returned to their regular news.

He launched the secure app on his phone that Acton's former student, CIA Special Agent Dylan Kane, had given him if they ever needed help. He attached the email that Milton had sent plus his own comments, then sent off the message, praying Kane was in a location where he could receive it. Sometimes the reply was instantaneous, and other times it could take days if he were on an operation where his communications were limited. He prayed this wasn't one of those times. He pulled out his laptop and searched for information about the eruption, regretting it immediately as he found video clips posted from survivors showing the devastation. He squeezed his burning eyes shut.

If they survived that, it's a miracle.

Karachi, Pakistan

CIA Special Agent Dylan Kane stared in the broken mirror, a myriad of cracks spreading out like a spiderweb, giving him a fractured view of his wounded shoulder. He had been outed by a dog. There had been reports of a senior Al Qaeda leader visiting a known sympathizer in Karachi. He had been sent in to confirm the reports and eliminate the man. Unfortunately, a neighbor's dog had sniffed him out from his hiding place and barked. He had torn open a protein bar and tossed it to the animal, but it was having none of it.

Next time I bring beef jerky.

The barking had drawn the guards' attention, and as he had shuffled back, they opened fire. He caught one in the shoulder, though managed to make his escape. It was just a graze. He'd survive, but it would be yet another scar he'd have to explain the next time he had a shirt off in bed with a woman. That was usually the love of his life, Lee Fang, who would find it intriguing, though sometimes, as part of his job, he had to bed other women while playing the role of an insurance investigator from Shaw's of London.

Despite his relationship.

It was harder to explain gunshot wounds when you were supposed to be some innocent investigator searching for fraud on large claims, though Langley had plastic surgeons that could alter the appearance of the particularly obvious ones. He poured the iodine over the wound and winced, cursing the necessary evil—there was no way he wanted to get an infection in a hell hole like this.

He leaned closer to the largest fragment of intact glass. If he were near civilization, he would get the few stitches he needed, but Karachi wasn't civilization, and an American with a gunshot wound would be immediately reported. He grabbed some gauze from the medkit his local contact had provided him when he arrived, and slapped it on the wound.

His phone vibrated on the table and he glanced at it. A message had arrived through his private network, something he had set up years ago in case the world fell apart or he had been disavowed. It was a network he had personally set up, few knew about, and was completely secure. He activated the encrypted app on his phone, holding it up to his retina. The message decrypted and displayed. His eyes widened as he finally had an explanation for what had sounded like several artillery shots in the distance while conducting his surveillance.

He pushed the message from Reading to his best friend, CIA Analyst Supervisor Chris Leroux, asking for him to action Reading's trace request, then fired back a reply.

Can't help personally. C will be contacting you shortly. Good luck. D

He killed the app then grabbed a roll of gauze. He wrapped it around his arm and tied it off with his teeth. He tucked the excess under the wrapping, retrieved a fresh shirt from his suitcase, and moments later was heading toward the compound housing his target, though not before hitting a street vendor to purchase several kabobs as a peace offering to the neighborhood pets.

Leroux/White Residence, Fairfax Towers

Falls Church, Virginia

CIA Analyst Supervisor Chris Leroux stared up at the vision that straddled him. Sherrie White was a CIA agent, first assigned as part of a honeypot trap to test his loyalty and how well he could resist the temptations of someone so gorgeous. He had passed the test, something everyone had thought impossible, but during that brief time together, they had fallen in love, and his life had changed for the better.

He was a different man now, though he would never describe himself as confident or an extrovert. He still preferred to be alone or with his very few friends, but he now led a team of ten at the CIA, and he was good at his job. He had the respect of everyone he dealt with, the love of a woman he still thought of as way out of his league, and he had a few good friends that he could count on. Life was good, and through his job, he did good things. He saved lives. He helped protect his country.

But at the moment, he could barely think straight. Sherrie had just returned from an op, and whenever she did, he was always in for several days of one hell of a good time. The sexual energy she always released the moment she walked through that door was teeth chattering, and he just held on for the ride. Shouts, screams, and entreaties to God along with various other strings of curses erupted as they both collapsed into a post-coital bliss, gasping for breath. Sherrie rolled off, flopping onto the other side of the bed.

"Oh my God, that was amazing."

He rolled onto his side, facing her with a smirk. "A bit narcissistic, isn't it, to rate your own performance?"

Her head lolled to the side and she stared at him. "Huh?"

"*You* were amazing. I just lay there. I don't know if I even moved a muscle."

She grinned at him. "Oh, you moved a muscle all right." She reached down and squeezed Little Leroux. "Next time I go on an op, I'm taking him with me."

He laughed then reached down, patting her. "Or you could leave her behind."

She gave him a look. "Where's the fun in that for me?"

He shrugged. "It can't always be about you." His cellphone vibrated on his nightstand and he reached over, recognizing the pattern as something that had to be paid attention to immediately. He grabbed the phone and logged into Kane's secure app, his eyebrows slowly rising as he read the message from his best friend, and then the forwarded message from Interpol Agent Hugh Reading, whom he had come to know over the years.

"What is it?" asked Sherrie, still splayed out on the bed.

"It looks like there might have been some sort of volcanic eruption in the Indian Ocean, and the professors might be caught up in it."

She rolled over onto her side to face him. "Are you kidding me? Somebody should put forward a motion at the UN that those two be locked down in some unpopulated area."

He grunted. "Well, I'll say one thing. If I ever hear that an asteroid is going to impact the Earth, I'm finding out where the hell those two are then going to the opposite side of the planet."

She laughed then nodded toward the phone. "So, what's going on?"

"Apparently, Dean Milton was on the phone with Acton when he said they were about to be hit by a tsunami. Milton called Reading, Reading contacted Dylan, and Dylan pushed it on to me."

"How nice of him."

He gave her a look. "You know he's on an op."

"I know, I know. But what can we do about it?"

"He wants us to see if we can get a location on the satphone that Acton had with him. Apparently, it's still ringing, which means it's functional, but nobody's answering it."

"And what if we find it?"

He shrugged. "Then we have a location to send the rescue team."

She grabbed the remote and turned on the TV in the bedroom, flipping over to BBC World News, both of them having given up on the American news networks. The lead story was about a massive eruption and a tsunami warning that had gone out across the entire Indian Ocean region, reminiscent of 2004 when so many had died.

He climbed out of bed and retrieved his laptop from the living room, then returned and sat cross-legged on the bed. He logged into the secure device then pulled up satellite footage of the area. He zoomed in on the Andaman Islands and cursed. "Look at this."

Sherrie tore her eyes away from the television screen, then gasped. The live images showed a mass of black cloud covering the area, the ash from the volcano heading in all directions, explosions flashing repeatedly indicating a massive ejection was still underway. She pointed at some bright white flashes. "What are those?"

He shrugged. "Looks like lightning to me."

"Is that normal?"

"I'm not sure. I don't know much about volcanoes, except that I don't want to be near one when it goes off."

She pointed at the cluster of islands. "Do we know where they were?"

"According to the email, Acton said they were five miles west of Wandoor. Let's see what kind of damage there is." He tapped a button and an overlay appeared, showing the population centers. He zoomed in on the capital of Port Blair, near the southern tip of the main island, but opposite from where Acton was supposed to be. His jaw dropped at the devastation. Flooding extended deep inland, and he could count on one hand how many structures still stood.

Sherrie's hand darted to her chest and her eyes glistened. "Those poor people. If this happened on land, there's no way the professors survived at sea."

Leroux picked up his phone, dialing the office. "There's only one way we're going to know."

Operations Center 2, CIA Headquarters
Langley, Virginia

CIA Senior Analyst Sonya Tong smiled at the call display before being struck with a tinge of jealousy. Her supervisor and friend, Leroux, had taken two days off after his girlfriend returned from an op. Everyone knew why. It was a running joke in the office. Sherrie would be gone, then she would return, Leroux would take two days off, then come back to the office with a smile that lasted a week.

The tinge of jealousy turned to an overwhelming wave. To say she had a thing for him would be putting it mildly. She didn't know why. He was out of reach. She couldn't compete with Sherrie. There was no way. Sherrie was gorgeous, an agent, funny, outgoing, everything she wasn't. Yet Leroux equally wasn't.

But she had missed her chance. She had been too shy to make a move, and once Sherrie became involved, it was too late. But how the hell could she have ever guessed that someone like Sherrie would be interested in someone like him? She had to get over him, though it was hard. Working with someone you had feelings for, seeing them day in and day out for hours on end was incredibly tough, yet she was coping. She could transfer to another team, but she loved the people she worked with, and Leroux was the best of the best, despite being the youngest analyst supervisor in the building. She wanted to be in this room with these people, doing the job she loved, protecting her country from threats its citizens knew nothing about.

She picked up the phone. "I wasn't expecting to hear from you."

Leroux chuckled. "Well, somebody let the professors out of the country."

Her shoulders slumped. "Not again. What is it this time?"

"Have you heard about the volcano erupting in the Indian Ocean?"

She glanced up at the massive displays that curved along the front of the state-of-the-art operations center, one of the quadrants devoted to satellite footage of the eruption. "Don't tell me they were there."

"Yes. Check your encrypted email. Dean Milton was talking to Professor Acton on his satellite phone when he said they were about to get hit by a tsunami. If you call the phone, it just rings. I want you to see if you can get a location on it."

"Are we going to be sending in a rescue team?"

"I don't know. I just looked at some images of the population centers in that area, and I think the locals are going to have their hands full."

Randy Child, the team's wunderkind, spun in his chair then pointed at another image he had just brought up. "We're getting reports of a tsunami hitting Myanmar and Malaysia."

Tong cursed. "Tsunamis are hitting the coastlines now."

Leroux sighed. "If that's the case, then there's no way in hell they're going to send a rescue team for a couple of professors."

"Sometimes the needs of the many outweigh the needs of the few, or the one." She could almost hear him smile through the phone.

"Great Star Trek reference! I knew there was a reason I wanted you on my team."

A cozy warmth flowed through her body. She input the phone number and dialed. A few seconds later, the system showed the first ring pinging back over the satellite network, and with each ring, it triangulated the location, but nobody answered. On the fifth ring, she tapped a button that sent an override, forcing the phone to pick up, the exact GPS coordinates appearing on her screen. She put the audio on speaker and everyone in the room stopped to listen.

"What is that?" asked Child.

"Waves?" suggested Marc Therrien from the rear of the room.

She agreed. "It's waves crashing on a shore, like washing up on a beach."

Leroux cut in. "What's going on?"

"I've overridden the phone. We're listening to the audio from it now. It sounds like waves crashing on a beach or a shoreline. Let me put you on speaker so you can hear." She tapped a button.

Leroux agreed with their assessment. "Sounds like waves to me, and you don't hear those at the bottom of the ocean. You're recording it?"

"I am."

"Do you have coordinates?"

"Exact."

"Okay, hang up. We don't want to waste the battery on that thing. Where are they located?"

She disconnected then pulled up the coordinates, showing them to be on the eastern coast of an island to the west of the major landmass. "It's called North Sentinel Island."

"Why does that sound familiar?"

Child attacked his keyboard then muttered a curse before throwing up a Wikipedia entry on the main displays. "This might be why."

"Why?" asked Leroux.

Tong filled him in. "According to this, it's a forbidden island. There's an uncontacted tribe that lives there, and it's illegal for anybody to go there. The last time there was any contact was when an American went in to intentionally make contact. The locals killed him. When they went in to try to recover the body, the team was attacked. There's a five-nautical-mile no-go zone around the entire island. These people don't like outsiders and will attack and kill anything that tries to say hello."

Child groaned. "What are we going to do? There's no way the locals will go in just to see if some survivors might be there. Not when there are hundreds of thousands of people on the Andaman Islands that need help."

"I'm coming in," said Leroux. "Review the satellite footage of the area. See if you can spot the boat they were on. Maybe we can catch sight of any survivors so we can offer proof of life."

"I'm on it," said Tong. The call ended and she dove into her assignment, wanting to have everything she could find ready for him when he arrived, and part of her a little giddy at the idea she was getting to see him today.

And that Sherrie wasn't getting to enjoy him as much as she usually would.

She closed her eyes for a moment.

You're a terrible person.

On board the Norham Castle

Northwest of Krakatoa

August 31, 1883

By some miracle of God, they had survived the massive wave. Several of the crew had been washed overboard, but Sampson had managed to get the rest, including himself, below decks. They had been tossed violently, but she was a sturdy vessel. The government didn't entrust cargo like they carried to just any ship. They had to be seaworthy, strong, capable of surviving rogue waves and violent storms. He patted the bulkhead. She was a fine vessel and she had come through for her crew.

He smiled as the sails once again deployed overhead, the mainmast broken when they were hit by the wave, his crew once again proving their worth. Fortunately, enough of its experienced members had been below decks when the initial blast had occurred, so their hearing was intact. When the wave had hit them, they were shielded by part of the island they had been sailing past, so were only caught by a weakened part of it. If the wave had hit five minutes earlier, they would have all certainly died.

It was indeed a miracle, God deciding they should survive this ordeal.

The question was, what did it mean? That they were cursed to spend their remaining days on a hellish Earth while God chose the worthy to join Him in heaven? Or was this perhaps not the end of days as he feared, and merely a natural calamity that people of this region would suffer through, and no one else?

"Captain, you have to see this!"

He rose from his chair and headed up onto the decks. The mud-laced rain continued to fall, though it appeared to be easing up slightly. His men had successfully kept the decks clear enough that the vessel hadn't capsized, though they were exhausted from the efforts and couldn't keep it up for much longer.

"What is it?"

The lookout pointed ahead.

He made his way to the prow of the vessel and stood, peering into the distance, wondering what had caught his man's attention.

Then his jaw dropped.

Unknown Location

Present Day

Acton awoke to his entire body aching. He forced his eyes open then blinked several times, finding them dry. His mouth was salty, and as he winced, his face revealed itself to be caked with dry salt water. He was lying against the starboard bulkhead, the boat still and tipped on its side. He remained still for a moment, listening, but all he could hear was the crashing of the waves.

Yet he was alive.

And he shouldn't be.

He stretched out his arms, wiggling his fingers, then did the same thing with his legs and toes. He took a deep breath, testing his ribs, then gently rocked his head back and forth. Nothing seemed broken. He pushed up into a seated position, and as he did so, discovered he was lying on someone. He rolled over, bracing with one hand against the bulkhead, and gasped at the sight of Laura wedged in behind him.

He resisted the temptation to roll her toward him. Instead, he leaned in, listening for her breathing, but he couldn't hear anything over the pounding of his heart and the surf outside. He checked for a pulse on her neck, not finding one at first, fueling his panic. He moved his fingers slightly and found it, strong and steady. His shoulders slumped in relief. He quickly performed an assessment, feeling over her entire body for any broken bones, then gently running his fingers through her hair, searching her scalp for any bumps.

He found none.

He gently rolled her toward him. She groaned, but rather than wake her, he let her come to on her own.

"Professor?"

He spun toward the sound to find Tommy struggling to his feet behind him. "Are you okay?"

"I think so, but I think I'm going to be black and blue tomorrow."

Acton grunted. "You're not the only one." He pointed at Mai, still lying on the floor. "Check her. Be gentle."

"I'm okay, Professor," said Mai. "Just really sore."

"James?"

Acton returned his attention to Laura, her eyes fluttering open. "Wh-what happened?"

"We got hit by that tsunami and then I don't really know. I got knocked out. I think we all did."

She held out a hand. "Help me up." He pushed to his feet and helped his wife to hers.

And he gasped. "The students!"

He pushed along the bulkheads to the closed hatch. Most of the windows were shattered and he pointed at the glass on the floor. "Everybody watch yourselves. There's glass everywhere." He unlatched the door and pushed it aside. It slammed against the bulkhead on the opposite side. He struggled along the deck toward the access hatch for the hold. It was still closed, which he took as an ominous sign.

Surely someone below would have opened it if there were any survivors.

The back end of the boat was still in the water. The bow was low, suggesting she was no longer seaworthy and that the hold might have flooded. The thought had him leaping for the hatch. He attempted to unlatch it, but it wouldn't give. He tried again, pulling with all his might, and finally it budged. Slightly. He braced against the gunwale and yanked hard, the warped hatch finally letting go. He swung it aside and water poured out. He fell back on his haunches, his shoulders shaking at the horror.

Then a hand appeared.

He reached out and grabbed it, praying it wasn't the hand of a corpse. The fingers wrapped around his wrist and he yanked. One of Jannarkar's students gasped for breath as her face broke the surface. Her head and torso came through the opening and he yelled over his shoulder. "Tommy, get out here and help me!"

"Yes, sir!"

He pulled the young woman onto the deck as another set of desperate hands appeared. He held her hand and let her gently slide toward the railing before letting go. He pulled the next student out and then another and another, Tommy now helping him. Another hand appeared and he grabbed it, crying out in relief as Jannarkar's head emerged from the hold. He and Tommy pulled him out.

"Are there any others?" asked Acton, counting the survivors on the deck.

Jannarkar shook his head. "No, I'm the last one."

Acton looked at the six surviving students. "Didn't you have eight students?"

Tears filled Jannarkar's eyes. "There wasn't enough room for us all to breathe once it flooded." His voice cracked. "I tried to sacrifice myself. Oh, God, Jim, please believe me, I tried. But they wouldn't let me. Two of them let themselves drown." His shoulders slumped. "Their deaths are on my hands."

Acton understood the man's grief, perhaps more than anyone else could. He had been forced to stand by and watch his students get slaughtered in Peru. There was nothing he could have done to prevent it, and intervening would have only meant he'd be dead now. While he'd be okay with that, at the time, he was attempting to save one of his other students named Robbie. He had ultimately failed, Robbie sacrificing himself in an attempt to save his professor.

The memories were soul-crushing.

Tears flooded his eyes at the self-sacrifice and bravery of the young man who had blamed himself for what had happened.

"I understand."

Jannarkar glanced at him briefly, his eyes burning red. "How could you possibly understand?"

"Peru." Acton's voice cracked as he said the single word, and Jannarkar's jaw sagged slightly.

"Oh, Jim, I'm sorry, I forgot all about that. You're right, of course, you do understand."

Acton wrapped an arm over his friend's shoulders and gave him a squeeze. "Now, I know this is going to sound heartless, but there's no time to grieve now. You have six other students that are counting on you."

Jannarkar sighed heavily, staring at them. "Jim, I don't even know where to begin. I can't think straight. Two of my students are dead, my wife is dead." His voice cracked as he squeezed his eyes shut and sniffed hard, gripping the railing as he struggled to control his emotions. "I'm a mess. I need you to take over."

Acton patted him on the back. "You take a few moments. I'll take care of everything."

"Thank you," gasped his friend, and Acton left him alone to grieve. He turned to the others.

"Okay, first things first. Is anybody injured?" Heads shook. "Good. Now, I tossed a satellite phone into that hold just before the tsunami hit."

One of the students held up a hand. "I saw it."

"Your name?"

"Daivik."

"Okay, Daivik. Are you willing to go in and look for it?"

Daivik hesitated before nodding. "Yes, sir." He disappeared into the hold containing the bodies of two of his friends.

Acton pulled out his cellphone, finding the screen a splintered mess. "Does anybody have a cellphone that works so we can get some GPS coordinates and find out where exactly we are, and where we have to go to get help?"

Phones were retrieved and several of them worked.

A young woman raised her hand. "I've got coordinates, Professor." She flashed a smile at his inquisitive look. "Nandini." She stared at the screen then gasped, her hand gripping her forehead. "Oh, no!"

Acton tensed. "What?"

"I only have the basic maps installed, but I think we're on the eastern coast of North Sentinel Island."

Everyone became nervous except for Tommy and Mai.

"What?" asked Mai. "Is that bad?"

"This is a forbidden island," said Nandini.

"Forbidden? What do you mean? Like a private resort?"

Tommy grinned. "Or is it owned by Dr. No's grandson?"

The young man hadn't grasped the seriousness of the situation, and Acton held up a hand, cutting him off from any more inappropriate jokes. "There's an uncontacted tribe that lives here. They're extremely hostile to outsiders. They've been known to attack and kill anyone who attempts to land here."

Tommy cursed as he held Mai and stared at the tree line several hundred feet away. "What are we going to do?"

Acton took Laura aside and lowered his voice. "Under normal circumstances, we could expect to be rescued, but if there's a regional

73

catastrophe, any rescue parties are going to be focusing on the population centers."

"There's another problem."

His eyes narrowed. "What?"

"The emergency beacon isn't working."

He had forgotten all about the fact they had one. "Are you sure?"

She nodded. "It's dead. It doesn't look damaged, so it may have never worked."

He cursed. "Remind me to mention it on TripAdvisor."

"Even if it did work, we'd still be facing authorities prioritizing between the mass casualties that could be out there, and an unverified signal."

She was right, and dwelling on the disappointing discovery was a waste of time. "Then let's forget about it and instead figure out our options."

Laura scanned the tree line then the water. "Wait, you were talking to somebody on the phone."

Acton's eyes narrowed then shot wide. He had forgotten that Milton had called just before the wave hit. "That's right! Greg called just before we were hit. I told him where we were, and that we were about to be hit by the wave. He would have tried to call again, and when he didn't reach us, he would try to get help."

Laura shook her head. "Even if he contacted the State Department, they're not going to spare any resources to come here. They'll probably presume we're dead."

"Would he go to the State Department?"

74

"Why wouldn't he?"

"Because he'd probably assume the same thing you did. I think he'd contact Dylan."

She inhaled excitedly. "You're right, he would, or at least he'd do both. But if he contacted Dylan, would the CIA be able to find us?"

"Given enough time, possibly."

Daivik poked his head out from the hold. "I'm sorry, Professor. I can't find the phone. There's a big hole in the side here. It might have washed out."

Acton cursed. The phone would have been key to their survival. "Well, there's one thing for sure."

"What's that?" asked Laura.

"We can't stay here. If the natives spot us, they'll attack. We need to survive until Dylan and his friends can save us. Agreed?"

"Agreed."

Acton turned to the group. "As you all know, this is a very dangerous place and a great catastrophe has hit the region, so no one would normally be looking for us. But I was on the phone with a friend of mine only moments before the wave hit, and we"—he indicated Laura—"have some very, shall we say, *special* friends. The person I was talking to will have contacted them, and they will have been able to trace where that phone call came from. That means we have powerful people that will be looking for us, but it's going to take time. We have to survive until they rescue us, and that means we can't be found by the natives. Now, we have supplies on this boat, including fresh water and food." He pointed at the four surviving male students and Tommy. "Tommy, you show them where the supplies are and get a chain gang going. I want all the food and water and emergency supplies in a pile on the beach as quickly as possible. Anything useful."

"Yes, sir."

"Now, did anybody have the presence of mind to actually download this region into their Maps app before they came here?"

Tommy tossed him his phone. "You know me, Doc. It's all there."

Acton handed the phone over to Laura. "Take a look. See if you can figure out where we might be able to hide and where the local populations are that we need to avoid. My understanding is the estimate is anywhere from fifty to five-hundred that might actually still live here." He pointed at the trees nearby, many knocked down. "This island's been hit, which means they could be affected as well. Let's hope that has them heading west, away from where the wave would have hit."

"I'm on it," said Laura.

He turned to the two young women and Mai. "I need the three of you to watch the tree line and up and down the beach. If you see anything, anything at all, you let us know right away."

A terrified Mai nodded. "You can count on us, Professor."

Acton returned to the wheelhouse and began opening every cabinet, searching for anything they might need, anything they could use as a weapon. He grabbed the flare gun and its three cartridges off the wall along with the fire extinguisher. He tossed both onto the beach, cursing at himself the entire time for having thrown the satellite phone into the hold. He had assumed if anyone were to get swept overboard, it would be those above deck. At the time, he had thought putting it into the closed hold would be the safest place for it, then if anyone survived below decks, they could use it to call for help.

His gamble had failed.

"Professor Acton?"

It was Mai, and he could hear the fear in her voice. He leaned out one of the broken windows. "What is it?"

She pointed. He redirected his eyes and his chest tightened at the sight.

Smoke.

They weren't alone.

Operations Center 2, CIA Headquarters

Langley, Virginia

"I think I found them," said Child as he spun in his chair, jabbing a finger toward the displays.

"Sir, stand by. We might have something," said Leroux into his headset, on the line with his boss, National Clandestine Service Chief Leif Morrison. He looked up at the display as Child zoomed in, the image resolving into a shipwreck on the shore. Child pulled up a map with a red dot showing the location.

"It's on the eastern coast of North Sentinel Island. Maybe a couple of hundred meters at most from where we traced the satellite phone." Leroux spotted movement. "Get in closer. Are those survivors or locals?"

Child zoomed the image in and Leroux counted at least ten people moving. "What are they doing?"

"It looks like they're unloading supplies," replied Tong.

"Why wouldn't they just stay put?" asked Marc Therrien.

"What's going on?" asked Morrison in his ear.

"We've got survivors, sir. And it's confirmed, they're on the eastern coast of the forbidden island."

"Okay, I'll let the State Department know and see if they can arrange a rescue, but I'm not very optimistic. The reports keep coming in. It looks like the entire rim of the Indian Ocean has been devastated once again. They're going to be low priority."

"I understand, sir. Perhaps mention should be made about the natives and how hostile they are? Maybe that might prioritize them?"

"I'll mention it, but I doubt it will help."

Morrison ended the call and Leroux removed his headset. He watched the image as the angle changed with the position of the satellite overhead.

"Could they know where they are?" he asked the room in general.

Tong shrugged. "If the satellite phone is still functioning, then maybe some of them have cellphones or tablets that work."

"But they'd have no internet connection or a cellular connection," said Therrien.

"True," replied Child. "But the GPS technology is independent of that. If one of them has a phone working, they would be able to get GPS coordinates, and if one of them had the presence of mind to download the maps to their phone before they left on their trip, they could know exactly where they are."

A smile crept up from the edge of Leroux's mouth. "Tommy Granger."

Tong turned to him with a smile of her own. "If anyone would do that, it would be him. And that could explain why they're offloading the supplies. If Acton knows they're on North Sentinel Island, he knows exactly what that means. He's going to get them off that boat and into hiding as quickly as he can before they're discovered."

"Sir, you have to see this." Child tapped at his keyboard, sending an image from his workstation onto the main display. Dozens of targets were circled, slowly moving.

"What am I looking at? How many?"

"At least a couple of dozen."

He squinted at something else on the image. "What's that on the coast to the north of the wreck?"

Child highlighted a segment. "Do you mean this?"

"Yeah, zoom in on that."

Child complied and a moment later, the image cleaned up and muttered curses rippled through the room. Three other boats were on the shore, swarming with survivors.

Tong folded her arms. "Well, that's good. Maybe the Professor's group can join up with them. Strength in numbers and all that."

Leroux didn't reply as he rose from his workstation and walked down the steps toward the displays. He pointed. "Get in as tight as you can on these three."

Child highlighted the area and it filled the display.

"Now, what does it look like they're all carrying?"

Tong was the first to vocalize what everyone in the room knew. "Looks like AK-47s or some variant."

Leroux cursed. "Something tells me these aren't friendlies that the professors can count on." He turned to Tong. "Get me Dean Milton. I need to know exactly why they were there."

Reading Residence

Whitehall, London, England

Interpol Agent Reading ended the call, struggling with the mix of emotions that now flowed through him. According to Milton, the CIA had located Acton's boat with survivors, but they were on a forbidden island with a hostile native tribe known to kill anyone who attempted to land, and apparently natives were moving in on their position.

There were also possibly hostile survivors too close for comfort. His friends had been on an island to the east to examine an old wreck they had believed might be from the eruption of Krakatoa. He flashed back to the events a few years ago surrounding the Roman gold ship from Pompeii, and how two countries had nearly gone to war over the treasure discovered.

If this boat contained anything of worth, it might have attracted the attention of the criminal element on the island. He had quizzed Milton, and from what he had gleaned from the little that was known, his friends had arrived that morning at the dig site where an old ship might be located. For them to already be on their boat just a few hours later, suggested one of two things. Either they had found nothing and left, or they had found something and had been forced to flee.

He knew his friends. They didn't get excited over gold, they got excited over history. Even if the ship they were there to excavate was empty, they would've thrilled over the entire experience for days if not weeks. There was no way they would arrive and leave the same day because they hadn't found something exciting. Spotting a timber from the hull would have had their hearts racing.

No, the only way those two left was because they were forced to leave. And his friends weren't the type to leave archaeological discoveries to be destroyed or stolen by criminals. He pinched the bridge of his nose, squeezing his eyes shut as he sighed heavily. They had found something, moved it to their boat to protect it, and were chased by whoever they were protecting it from.

He cursed. "When will you two ever learn?"

But it was all conjecture. All he had to offer to anyone who might listen were theories based upon his experiences with his friends. It wouldn't be enough to justify taking precious resources away on some wild goose chase when such a massive tragedy had taken place. If what he knew about North Sentinel Island were right, the natives that lived there wouldn't hesitate to kill the survivors. And that was if the gangs he was now convinced were pursuing them had also survived and didn't get to them first.

There was only one way they were making it out of this, and that was if their "friends" got involved.

He sighed then sat in front of his laptop and cracked his knuckles.

And put his theory in writing so he could send it to Kane.

Karachi, Pakistan

Kane gently squeezed the trigger, his target in the crosshairs of his gunsight. His watch pulsed, indicating another priority message, and he muttered a curse as he eased up on the trigger briefly. This was a long-distance shot, security now increased at the residence his target was staying at. It was evident the terrorist was preparing to leave, and this was the only chance there would be to take him out.

The man emerged from the front door of the house and into the walled courtyard. Kane had only moments before the target would be in a reinforced vehicle. He adjusted his aim slightly and squeezed the trigger. The target dropped in a heap, setting off a flurry of activity. Two of the guards dragged the body back inside as the rest desperately hunted for the source of the shot, some randomly firing over the walls.

Kane slowly crawled backward and out of sight, then packed up his weapon, stashing it for later retrieval by his local contact in the trunk of a notorious British sportscar, its stripped shell having been abandoned in the alley years ago, likely days after the warranty expired.

He made his way back to his hotel and checked the message on his watch. It indicated another secure email had arrived from Reading. That wasn't good. Leroux was supposed to be handling things, but obviously Reading wasn't happy with the results. There was no way it had anything to do with his friend's capabilities—Leroux was the best at what he did, bar none. If Reading weren't happy, it was only because Leroux's hands were tied.

The CIA wasn't his former professor's personal security detail. Unless there were national security implications, this was a rescue operation after a natural disaster. There was no way they would be prioritized, not when millions were affected, including Americans. But Reading would know that, so why he was contacting him a second time had him puzzled.

He entered the hotel room, locking the door behind him, then did a quick sweep to make certain he was alone and no one had been there since he left. He pulled his laptop out from under the mattress and logged into his secure email, quickly scanning the message from Reading, his chest tight the entire time. Reading was right. The professors would never leave a dig site they had just arrived at unless they were forced to do so.

His jaw slowly dropped as he leaned back in his chair, folding his arms. Reading had indicated his information came from Milton, and Milton had been briefed by Leroux. But that briefing was incredibly detailed, including the intel about the other group of survivors armed with machine guns. He smiled slightly. Leroux had known exactly what would happen once he told Milton this information and that there was nothing they could do beyond put a request into the State Department.

His friend would know that Milton would call Reading, and Reading would contact him. It was Leroux's way of sending him a message in a round-about way, that a favor needed to be called in.

He fired a quick reply back to Reading.

I'll see what I can do. No promises.

The Andaman Islands were Indian territory, so it was their responsibility to take care of this. He had been involved in an op a few years ago where he had saved the children of a senior Indian official, who had promised him anything Kane wanted as a thank you. It was time to call in that favor. He quickly typed a message to his contact in New Delhi with the pertinent details, then hit Send. Hopefully, the man would be true to his word.

And capable of delivering.

Shouts from the street below had him darting to the window and peering through a slight gap he had previously left in the curtains so he wouldn't have to move them. A Pakistani security patrol was unloading from their transport, and it was evident they meant to come inside.

And that could mean only one thing.

He had somehow been traced back here.

It was well known that the Pakistanis had elements within their security apparatus that protected senior Al-Qaeda members, not the least of whom was the late Osama bin Laden himself. Someone was obviously pissed because they had just lost their protection money.

He had only seconds. He grabbed his bag, still packed, and stuffed the laptop inside before slinging it over his shoulder. He left the room then headed for the roof and his preplanned escape route. He pulled out his phone and sent a 911 text message to his local contact. He needed rapid exfiltration, which wasn't unusual, though it did mean he wouldn't know if his favor was delivered upon, and his old college professor and the others were saved.

Yacht Wreck

North Sentinel Island

Andaman Islands, India

Acton cursed at the sight of the smoke. It could be anything. The beginning of a forest fire, a campfire. Whatever it was, it was too close.

"Okay, everybody off the boat now," he ordered.

Tommy disembarked immediately but Jannarkar, who had been helping offload supplies, just stared at him. "But we haven't finished."

"There's smoke only a couple of miles from here. It could mean a village. We need to get off the beach as quickly as possible. If they find us, you know what will happen."

Jannarkar's face slackened slightly before he nodded. He smacked his hands together. "Everybody off." His students complied, and within moments, everyone had disembarked. If they were to survive in hiding, fresh water was the most important thing. The island obviously had it, as there were inhabitants, however, fresh water sources were the most likely locations for any settlements.

Acton pointed at several bags. "Load up as much water as you can. Tommy, grab the flares." A thought occurred to him and he scrambled back up onto the deck. He went below into their sleeping quarters, grabbing the blankets and sheets off the beds before reemerging outside. He tossed them down. "Let's use them as makeshift bags. Toss everything we can inside then tie up the corners."

The students went to work and his eyes narrowed as he saw something tossed into the mix.

"What the hell is that?"

Amit glanced over his shoulder at him. "I found it below. It's a spearfishing gun. I thought it might come in handy if we have to defend ourselves."

Acton gave the young man a thumbs-up. "Good thinking. And make sure we've got that flare gun and that fire extinguisher." He jumped down as a strange sound emerged from the forest. Everyone froze and a shiver ran down his spine. The sound resembled a horn, which suggested a warning signal or a call to arms had just been issued.

"Where did that come from?" asked Laura.

Tommy pointed to the right, into the forest. "I think it came from that direction."

"Okay, everybody, let's go!" hissed Acton. "And keep quiet. If we can hear them, they can hear us. We need to get to the tree line."

The blankets were folded up and everyone headed for the trees. Acton brought up the rear and cursed at what was revealed. Dozens of footprints in the sand.

"Everybody, single file."

He was met with confused stares until he pointed at the sand. A single line was quickly formed with Laura in the lead. He grabbed a broken branch off the ground, the area littered with debris from the wave. He retreated back to the boat, then brushing the leafy branch over the ground, he obscured their footprints as best he could. Yet he was merely hiding their numbers. It was difficult to tell how far the tide came in here, what with it having been swept over by the wave, but none of that would matter if the inhabitants of this island were to arrive before high tide.

Another call echoed from the forest. It sounded closer, but he couldn't be sure. He glanced over his shoulder to see that Laura was already at the edge of the tree line, beckoning the others to hurry. He continued with his efforts, praying they weren't futile.

The call trumpeted again, but this time was cut short, merely a brief bleat. He continued at his task as he wondered what had happened. Why would they cut off the call to arms? And, in fact, if it were a call to arms, why would they sound one? It would reveal their position, warning those they were after that they were about to come under attack. It made no sense. If he and the others had been spotted, it would be better to get help silently than ambush them.

But if it were a distress call, then not only did it make sense, the last interrupted call suggested something had gone wrong. It had him wondering if perhaps it were merely somebody injured in the tsunami.

And part of him wanted to help.

A brief burst of gunfire from an automatic weapon cracked through the fading light from farther down the shoreline. He bolted upright, his question answered. It had been a distress call.

And they weren't the only survivors.

The Blessed Land

Jara sprinted through the forest as the sounds of his pursuers grew louder behind him. Yesterday, he could have left them behind with ease, for he knew his entire home like the back of his hand. He had spent his entire life here, learning the ways of the land, of his people, but the path of destruction in front of him was utterly unfamiliar. He was a boy when a similar wave had devastated their home years ago. Many had died, but they had rebuilt and were thriving once again.

Today's wave had appeared every bit as devastating, with half the trees along the shore knocked down. After getting caught up in it while searching for crabs, he had been carried inland then knocked out. He had come to, battered and bruised, but alive. He had to make it back to his village to check on his family and friends, and had decided the shore might be the quicker route with so many trees down. It was then that he had stumbled upon the Outsiders, three of their boats wrecked on the shore.

It had been a long time since any of the evil ones had attempted to breach their shores, the gods having protected his people from the conquerors. But today, the gods' mighty wave had failed. At least several handfuls had survived, and he had to warn the others.

If there were any left.

Someone had shouted and pointed at him, and he had ducked back in the woods. He pressed his horn to his lips and blew hard, sounding the call, indicating Outsiders were on their shores. He made his way as quickly as he could, then cried out as he twisted an ankle as a felled tree's rotted core gave way and his foot fell through. He yanked free and sounded his trumpet once again as the crashes of his pursuers neared.

He glanced over his shoulder and spotted two of them. He was desperate now. He ran as fast as he could, but the sounds behind him fueled a panic that clouded his mind. He raised his horn to his lips and drew another deep breath, blasting out another warning, another call for help, but tripped, slamming hard into the ground. He rolled over onto his back as two of the Outsiders overtook him. He reached for his knife when one of the men raised some sort of stick, and the loudest sound he had ever heard before the devastating one that had preceded the wave, erupted from it.

Near the Viper Chain Gang Wreck

North Sentinel Island

Andaman Islands, India

Pritam grabbed the scrawny little creature by the throat and lifted him into the air. The young man had nothing on but a simple belt around his waist and leather bands around his upper arms. He had a yellow band around the top of his head like a halo, but little else. Pritam had expected something more grotesque—if this kid had shorts and a t-shirt on, he might blend with the street urchins back home.

He had, of course, heard of these people, this forbidden tribe, and they didn't scare him. He had almost two dozen members of his gang with him, and they all had weapons. This so-called vicious tribe would have never encountered heavily armed men with no compunctions about killing them. Any attempt to attack would be met with violent opposition.

Though they did have a problem.

They were on a forbidden island where no rescuers would be searching for survivors. The best they could hope for would be weeks or months from now, a plane or a drone might be sent over the area by scientists interested in discovering whether the people here had survived the tsunami. He had been a teenager when the one in 2004 had hit. It still gave him nightmares to this day.

He had lost his family and had been forced onto the streets. It was the Viper Chain Gang, named after the notorious British prison on Viper Island used to jail his freedom-fighting ancestors, that had taken him in, fed him, clothed him, and gave him a purpose. And after so long of being alone, fending for himself, he had relished in the camaraderie, in the brotherhood, and of no longer being so alone, so scared. And now, all these years later, he was a leader in the gang, only a couple of rungs from the top. He had his own crew, and if he had managed to get his hands on the gold that one of his men had reported, there would have been no stopping him.

He would have ruled the entire island.

He had no desire to leave. It was his home. It was the only thing he knew and cared to know. Besides, these days, anything you wanted could be brought to you for a price. And with even just one of those gold bars thrown onto the road, he could have had anything. Food, drink, women, power, everything a real man craved.

But that opportunity was lost at the bottom of the sea, and he was shipwrecked on an island populated by blood-thirsty natives and absolutely no way to contact home. They would have to survive somehow until one of those drones or planes arrived. And to last for as long as he thought they might have to, they would need resources, resources these natives either already had or knew how to access.

He glared at his prisoner. "Where is your village?" he asked in a futile attempt to communicate. The young man merely stared at him, terror in his eyes, his entire body trembling. There was no comprehension there. He eyed the horn the kid had been sounding. It was obviously some sort of distress call, and if they just waited, what they needed might come to them. Again, there'd be no way to communicate with them verbally, though perhaps there was a chance visually.

A twig snapped ahead. Everyone turned, obviously having heard it as well. The young man screamed something and Pritam squeezed his hand hard around the kid's throat, silencing him as his prisoner's hands grasped at Pritam's, attempting to break the hold. He flailed for a few more moments before falling limp. Pritam tossed him on the ground, then readied his weapon as more sounds approached. "Spread out. Nobody fires until I give the order."

His men spread out to either side, everyone taking up position behind trees either lying on the ground or those few that had survived the disaster of only hours ago. He squinted into the forest, the light fading. Something moved slightly to his left then something to his right. The shadows coalesced into a group of natives, at least half a dozen strong. One of them raised a spear, followed by the others.

"Fire!" He squeezed the trigger and bullets erupted from his weapon, the muzzle flashes lighting the area directly in front of him. A dozen other weapons joined, sending a wall of lead at the seriously out-classed enemy. Several of them cried out, others simply dropped in silence, then all the movement stopped within seconds. He released the trigger. "Cease fire!"

The guns fell silent and he slowly advanced toward their fallen foes. One writhed on the forest floor then reached for a knife. Pritam put two bullets in the man's chest. Seven were down, but more would be coming, of that, he had no doubt.

And they'd be ready for them.

"Pritam, he's gone!"

"What?" He spun on his heel then cursed. The young man they had captured was nowhere to be seen. This, unfortunately, could change things. The kid would reveal their location, their numbers, and warn of their weaponry.

The next attack might not be so easy to fend off.

Yacht Wreck

North Sentinel Island

Andaman Islands, India

Acton finished his obfuscation job as best he could with the time he had, which was little. The gunshots meant only one thing. There were other survivors. But it also likely meant something else. That the natives he was so worried about had encountered their pursuers.

The enemy of my enemy is my friend?

He wasn't so certain that would apply here. All that he was certain of was that it provided an opportunity. He reached the tree line and regarded his handiwork. And wasn't impressed. While there might not be obvious footprints anymore, there was a clear line scratched into the sand. He'd have to pray that the locals were more concerned with those farther down the beach.

The initial burst of gunfire lasted for only a few seconds, then the second longer, perhaps thirty, before the guns fell silent. It gave him enough time to determine that whatever was going on was about a mile north of their position. Gunfire like that had to mean those pursuing them had survived the tsunami, and were either attacking or defending themselves against the natives of this island. Either way, it meant the natives would be preoccupied, as would their pursuers, meaning they had an opportunity to seek shelter and wait for the proverbial cavalry to arrive.

Most of the students were whimpering now, and at the moment, only he and Laura appeared in control. He raised a hand, drawing everyone's attention. "Listen carefully. Everybody has to be quiet. Whatever is going on over there doesn't involve us, but we can use it to our advantage. Obviously, since it's gunfire, it means that at least some of those who were pursuing us also survived, and we know there are hostile natives that live here, so there's obviously an encounter going on between the two of them. That means they're both distracted. We're going to go find a place to hide while we await rescue. Understood?"

Heads bobbed around the group.

"Okay, I'm going to take point." Puzzled looks. "It means I'm going to take the lead." He turned to the group. "Who has that speargun?"

Amit held up his hand. "I do."

"Let me have it."

The bundled blanket was lowered to the ground and opened, the speargun handed over. Amit held up several spears. "How many do you want?"

"Just the one. If I have to shoot a second one, it'll be too late."

The young man's eyes widened with understanding. Acton fit the spear in place and checked the mechanism to ensure he knew how it worked as Amit retied his blanket of supplies.

"Okay, everybody, watch where you're walking. We don't want to make any more sound than necessary, and we don't need any twisted ankles. Keep your eyes and ears open. If anybody sees anything, raise your fist in the air like this"—he demonstrated—"and everybody stops. If anyone raises their fist, you all stop and drop to a knee. If you see or hear somebody, point to where it came from, and we'll figure out what to do."

"Umm, Professor?" It was Tommy, his voice dripping with fear. "What do we do if they're coming for us."

"Who? Those gang members?"

Tommy shook his head. "I'm not really worried about them. The gold is sitting on the beach. They can have it all as far as I'm concerned. I'm more concerned about the natives and what they'll do to us."

Acton suppressed a frown. Unlike Tommy, he was equally concerned about being found by either group. The local gang wouldn't be satisfied with just the gold. They would want revenge for their current predicament. They'd likely beat then shoot the men. It was the women he was concerned about. If these gangs were looking at days, weeks, or months of being stranded here, and they were thinking ahead, they wouldn't kill the women. They would keep them.

And he shuddered at what they might do to them.

Repeatedly.

The natives were another matter. He didn't worry about them raping the women—everyone would die. The question was, would the deaths be swift and merciful, or would there be some ritual of pain and punishment. If he had to choose a fate for them, he would rather they all take the pain and death, rather than a swift execution for the men and days on end of brutalization for the women they left behind.

Everyone was staring at him now, and he had to tell them something.

"If we're confronted by the gang with guns, we surrender. I'll try to negotiate with them. Professor Palmer and I will offer them a ransom so high, they won't be able to refuse. If they're as greedy as we know they are, they just might take it."

"And the natives?" asked Mai, her voice quaking.

He sighed. "If it's the natives, we fall back to the boat and try to defend ourselves. We'll retreat into the water if we have to, and if it comes down to it, we fight them hand to hand. At that point, we're fighting to survive. There will be no negotiation. The moment they attack, it's us or them. I'm sorry, I can't sugarcoat this in any way to make you feel better. You need to understand that they will kill us, so it'll be a choice between them killing us, or us killing them." He pointed at the ground. "Everybody keep your eye out for a sharp rock that you can use. If you see one, take it, if you already have one and see another, pass it on to someone who hasn't found one yet. I want everyone armed with something in the next five minutes."

Everyone was terrified now, including himself, and part of him regretted his bluntness. But it had to be said. If they were attacked by the natives, there would be no negotiation. Several years ago, an American had come onto the island in an attempt to bring them to Jesus. They had killed him, and when a team had come in to try and recover his body, they too were attacked.

It would be kill or be killed.

He just prayed it didn't come to that.

Milton knew what had happened, and they had friends that could trace where their satphone was last used. The wreck should be easy to spot by satellite, and if there had been any coverage for the past hour, they would know there were survivors. Depending on how devastated the region was from the eruption and the resulting tsunami, rescuers could already be on the way, and they might only have a few hours to survive.

But he couldn't count on that. They could be here for days or worse. If the devastation from the tsunami were anything like 2004, the world would be busy trying to save millions, and there'd be little concern for a dozen students and their professors stranded on an island with plenty of resources.

But for now, he had to focus on protecting these people made his responsibility by Jannarkar being overwhelmed over the fate of his wife.

"Is everyone ready?"

Uncertain nods.

He forced a reassuring smile. "Okay, remember, keep your eyes and ears open and watch the ground for anything that can be used as a weapon. And keep quiet." He pressed forward, deeper into the devastated forest. Twigs snapped, people muttered, some sobbed as the group moved deeper into the trees. He didn't bother admonishing them for the noise, but suddenly it all stopped.

He glanced over his shoulder to see everyone on a knee, Tommy's fist raised high in the air, a lone finger pointed to their right. Acton turned. He didn't see anything, but he could hear somebody crashing through the trees. He raised the speargun and positioned himself between the group and the incoming hostiles. Laura took up position at his side, several good-sized stones in her left hand, one raised over her shoulder in her right. Tommy and Mai joined him on his other side and a surge of pride threatened to overwhelm him as everyone else spread out in a wedge, armed with nothing but rocks, heavy branches, and empty fists.

If they were about to die, they would do so together as one.

There were no cowards here.

Fear wasn't cowardice. Lying down and doing nothing in fear perhaps was, but that was nowhere to be seen here today. The crashes continued to near and were almost on top of them. He peered into the trees and spotted something moving. He aimed his speargun, hoping that if he could take the first out by surprise, it might scare the others off.

But what emerged from the forest wasn't at all what he expected.

The Blessed Land

Jara split between two trees then skidded to a halt, his heart leaping into his throat at the sight of a dozen Outsiders, most with skin almost as dark as his, others with skin as pale as the sand on the beaches. His jaw dropped in shock at the sight, uncertain of what to make of these sandy things. He had heard tell of one from several seasons ago that had landed on their shores. Men from another tribe had killed him and told the story, but he hadn't really believed them.

The sandy skin just wasn't something you could even imagine.

Though there was no denying what his eyes told him. These sand-colored people were real and standing before him. And every one of them had something gripped in their hands, ready to kill him. He held his knife in front of him. "Stay away from me, Outsiders!"

One of the sand-faces lowered a strange-looking stick then handed it to a female with even paler skin, and hair the color of which he had never imagined, though the fading light could be failing his eyes. The man raised his empty hands and said something unintelligible. The voice was calm, reassuring, and if he didn't know how evil the Outsiders were, he might believe the sand-face meant him no harm.

Shouts behind him, from the men he had just escaped, had him spinning on his heel, peering into the darkness. The sand-face said something. Jara glanced at him over his shoulder. He was beckoning him, as if he wanted him to join the group. His eyes darted across all the faces, and none were looking at him. They were all staring into the forest at the approaching sounds, and they were scared, just as he was. Could those men that had captured him be their enemy as well? He had always been taught that cooperation was the key to success, that the lone individual was the one most likely to fail or die.

The man beckoned him once again, yet he remained frozen in place, uncertain of what to do. The smartest thing would be to strike out on his own, leave his pursuers to discover these people. And in fact, he was about to do precisely that when the woman with the strange hair stepped forward, extending her hand toward him. She said something, her voice so gentle, her smile so friendly, it put him at ease.

And against every instinct, he reached out and took her hand. She squeezed it gently, and the man who appeared to be in charge said something, his attention no longer on him, and led the group deeper into the forest.

Jara followed, still gripping the woman's hand, uncertain if what he was doing was wise. Outsiders were the enemy, each and every one of them. They were to be repelled or killed the moment they set foot on the sacred land. The story, told by the elders, handed down from generation to generation, spoke of how these Outsiders would invade the homes of other tribes. Once they settled, there was no getting rid of them. The only hope to survive was to make sure they never got that foothold, for once they did, it would be the end of everything. It would be the end of their very way of life. And if the shaman who communed with the gods were to be believed, once their homeland was cursed by the Outsiders, his people would be abandoned, their women left barren, and within a generation, his people would be no more.

A pit formed in his stomach over what he was doing. By going with these people, was he helping give them, the Outsiders, the very foothold the elders warned against? Would it be better to just die?

No, he had to survive long enough to warn his people. The wave that had hit had devastated everything while he was gathering crab. He had to get back home and help his people. And besides, once he found them, they were far greater in number than these people who he believed might be trying to help him. It would then be up to the elders whether to force them off the island, or kill them where they stood.

Either way, it wasn't his decision to make.

But for now, he would travel with these people for protection, and if it became necessary, abandon them to the others. For only one thing mattered.

The preservation of the world the gods had blessed his people with.

Heading West from the Yacht Wreck

North Sentinel Island

Andaman Islands, India

Laura held the native's hand, the young man trembling despite his outward appearance. He was dark-skinned, almost central African, and impossibly fit. He wore nothing but a leather belt with several loops, all empty, that might have once held knives or other implements. He had similar leather bands around his upper arms and a simple round headdress that sat atop his head, woven into his curly hair. He had no piercings or tattoos, no deliberate decorative cuts.

He was like anyone else on this wonderfully broken planet save his lack of clothing. He reminded her of the natives they had met in the Amazon a couple of years ago, and wished there was some way to communicate with him and learn his ways.

Yet there was no time for that. The sounds of people crashing through the trees were loud now. James led them deeper into the forest, and the light was fading fast as they continued forward. More of the trees stood tall, having survived the onslaught of the tsunami, providing them with more cover, but they needed some place to hide other than the trees.

She turned to the young man, releasing his hand. She made a circle with her thumb and forefinger and held it up in front of them. Then with her other hand, walked her forefinger and middle finger toward the hole, mimicking a person, then stuck both fingers inside as if that person were taking cover. "Do you know where we can hide?" He wouldn't understand a word of what she was saying, but she hoped from her tone and her visualizations, he might comprehend what she was asking. She pointed at herself, then at the others, then walked her fingers again toward the shelter made by her other hand.

He stared at her puzzled, then his eyes widened as his jaw dropped. He wobbled his head from side to side, and he repeated her motions, then stabbed a finger into the darkness. Still wobbling his head, he grabbed her hand and pulled her toward James at the head of the group, determined to lead them somewhere.

Hopefully to safety, and not death.

Acton's head spun toward the call from his wife. His eyebrows shot up at the sight of the young native holding Laura by the hand, leading her. He stopped, raising a fist. Everyone dropped to a knee as the young man's pursuers still crashed through the forest behind them. "What?"

"I think he knows a place for us to hide."

Acton eyed the young man who appeared as scared as everyone else, but he was also fully aware of what the native's beliefs were when it came to outsiders. He could just as easily be leading them into a trap. Yet what choice did they have? He had no idea where they were going, and for the moment, the native had as much to lose as they did if they were caught.

Acton held out his hand to the forest that lay ahead. "Please, lead the way."

The young man's head shook oddly then he rushed ahead silently, as if his feet had eyes of their own and knew exactly where to step. He glanced over his shoulder and beckoned for them to follow. Acton turned to the others. "Let's follow him, but remember, if he's leading us into a trap, everybody falls back to the beach."

Terrified stares were the only response. Somebody shouted behind them and Acton rose, immediately heading after the native, the others following suit. They were led deeper into the forest, and the burning in his shins was the first clue he had to the fact they were slowly going uphill. Through an opening in the trees, he caught a glimpse of the skyline ahead and a black mass blocking out many of the stars. As his eyes adjusted, the mass coalesced into a rocky hill ahead, and if they were being led there, it might mean a cave.

From what he had read about this island, these people didn't live in caves. They lived in villages consisting of huts and communal structures, so if the young man were indeed leading them to a cavern of some sort, then it wasn't an ambush.

They broke through the trees into a rock-strewn clearing. The young man didn't slow. He continued directly toward the rock face that lay before them then disappeared. Acton peered into the dark as he slowed, then spotted a hand beckoning him, as if the rest of the young man's body were embedded in the stone itself. He continued forward, squinting, and then found the sliver of an entrance, invisible to the naked eye at any other angle than the one he now had.

The young man urged him inside, but Acton instead turned to the others and waved them forward. Laura took up position on the other side of the entrance as Tommy and Mai went through first, Acton giving them both pats on the back. Jannarkar was helped through by a couple of his students, then the rest followed.

"Is that everyone?"

Laura nodded. "Yes."

The shouts from the forest were close now. He urged Laura inside with a hand to the small of her back then followed. They made their way deeper inside, the opening barely shoulder-width, and he wondered if their friend Reading, with his broad frame and barrel chest, would have fit. They continued to make their way until it widened into a large chamber.

One of the students had their cellphone out with the flashlight mode enabled. Everyone huddled around it, and the young native stared at it, his eyes wide, his mouth agape, this probably the first artificial light he had ever seen. Acton put himself in the center of the group, holding up a finger to his mouth. "Everybody remain absolutely quiet. They're outside now." He pointed at Amit, holding the phone. "Watch me. If I signal you, turn that off."

Amit gave him a thumbs-up. Acton readied his speargun and headed to the opening that led to the entrance. He could hear the shouts from outside, and they threatened to be drowned out by the pounding of his pulse in his ears. Laura stepped up beside him, a rock in both hands. A foot scraped behind him and he glanced over his shoulder to see Tommy and Mai, both similarly armed, standing with them. If their pursuers and their automatic weapons made it inside, there would be no surviving this, despite the bravery and determination on display.

A voice, particularly loud, sounded close to the entrance. Acton turned and pointed at the phone. It went dark. A hint of light was at the far end of the entrance tunnel. Angry shouts continued, but none grew louder. He remembered his tactical breathing and slowly drew in breaths through his nose and out his mouth. His heart calmed, the adrenaline fueling his panic ebbing slightly.

Laura placed a hand on his shoulder. "I think they're leaving."

He cocked an ear and smiled slightly as the voices faded, soon replaced by nothing but the breathing of those around him. He turned toward the others, and in a whisper, gave them the good news. "They're gone. You can turn the light back on."

The chamber was soon filled with light from several cellphones.

Acton pointed to Tommy. "You stay here. If you hear anything, let us know, quietly."

"Yes, sir."

He could see the fear in Tommy's eyes. He patted him reassuringly on the shoulder. "Don't worry, I think we're safe for now. It's dark. They'll probably want to return to the beach and their boats. They won't start searching until morning."

"I hope you're right," said Mai.

Acton flashed her a grin. "I'm always right. You should know that by now."

She giggled and slapped a hand over her mouth, her eyes wide at the sound that echoed through the cave. Acton and Laura returned to the group. He pointed at the cellphones. "Everybody turn their cellphone off to preserve the batteries. Just leave one on for now. Break out the supplies. There should be some candles in there. Let's get a few of those lit, but not near the entrance."

The bundles and bags were opened, the supplies searched, and within minutes, three candles were lit and placed on rocks toward the rear of the cavern they found themselves in. The young native huddled near one of them, away from the group.

Laura turned to Acton. "I'm going to see if I can get his name. Try to establish some sort of communication. We need him to trust us."

Acton agreed. "He'll have been raised to fear outsiders. We can't trust him at all, but right now, we need him more than he needs us. If we can keep him here with us voluntarily, then it should buy us a night. But if he runs out of here, he could go and get others, and we're sitting ducks in here."

Laura squared her shoulders. "Then it looks like I have a friend to make."

The Refuge

The Blessed Land

Jara scurried a little bit deeper into the corner. He wasn't a fan of caves, and since a child, had been raised to be wary of them, for just as they provided shelter to these people now, they often were the den to something that would happily tear you apart and make a meal of you. Fortunately, this cave had proven empty, as it usually did, and no animal would return with these numbers inside.

Though for him, it wasn't the possible inhabitants of the cave that made him leery, it was the confined space and the complete and total darkness. The elders told of tools and other indicators found in the past that suggested his ancestors had once dwelled in caves just like this, but now they lived in huts, in structures made of wood and mud and stone. He stared at these strange Outsiders and the magical things they carried, the most fascinating of which was a slim shard of stone that could glow on command. Were these the demons told of in the stories, with magical powers granted to them from the masters of the underworld? Or was it that they had merely learned how to coax the light from the stone just as his forebearers had learned to build homes rather than live in caves?

He wasn't sure what to believe, but one thing he was certain of was that these people didn't appear to mean him any harm. They were just as scared as he was of those outside, and appeared content to share this hiding space with him. Some food and water in an oddly shaped container had been given to him a short while ago, and he had eagerly devoured it, experiencing flavors unlike anything he had ever tasted before.

The woman he was certain was the mate of the man in charge, approached him with a smile, her teeth not bared. Yes, when his people laughed and smiled, their teeth would show, but only with those you were familiar and at ease with. Someone new that you were meeting for the first time, you always kept your lips pressed together rather than display that which could tear flesh from the body. It was simply considered polite. Once a rapport was established and friendship or kinship granted or proven, then the teeth could be displayed freely.

The fact this woman appeared to understand that had him wondering if their ways were as his. The elders told stories of outside invaders arriving, always openly hostile, and as he glanced at the others, some terrified, some quietly sobbing, others with smiles on their faces, teeth fully bared, he wondered if the open hostility was merely new arrivals smiling in sincere friendship, and his people had merely misunderstood. Though if that were the case, why did this woman know not to show her teeth? If he survived this ordeal, he would talk to the elders for their thoughts.

She pointed at the stone beside him and said something. It sounded like a question, and he wondered what question she might be asking. He stared where her finger was pointed, then concluded she was asking if she could sit beside him. He pointed. "Yes."

She sat, then pointed at her chest, saying a single word, then pointed at his. And, again, he wondered what he might do if he were in her situation.

She wants to know my name.

He tapped his chest. "Jara."

Her smile broadened, a slight hint of her teeth revealed. She repeated his name, though it wasn't quite right, the actual word she said meaning 'breeze' in his language.

He repeated his name. "Jara."

"Jara."

He smiled, then pointed at her. She repeated her name.

"Laura," he said.

Her smile broadened, her teeth fully revealed, but he forgave her for it. Perhaps in her culture, an exchange of names was all it took to establish the rapport necessary for open-mouthed smiles. He returned the smile, repeating her name, and she repeated his. She extended her right hand toward him and he stared at it, his eyes narrowing. She reached out with her other hand and took his right hand, placing it in hers, then closed her grip gently and pumped it twice, smiling the entire time before letting go.

She said something, probably an explanation as to why she had done it. It was similar to the wrist clasp that his people did when greeting others. He extended his right hand and took hers, then clasped her wrist. She smiled and returned the gesture. Perhaps this woman and the others could indeed be trusted, at least for the night. In the morning, he'd decide what to do. There was strength in numbers, but if these people were as scared of the others as they appeared to be, it suggested they had no way to defend themselves against the loud sticks that the others carried.

In this case, strength in numbers might merely mean a greater chance of escape if he could outrun them should they be discovered in the morning. But these people had taken him in and shared what they had with him. The only safe place he could think of to go tomorrow would be his village. At a minimum, he had to return there alone to warn them of the enemy that had arrived on their shores. If he told them about these people, he wasn't sure what they would do. Everyone had been raised from birth to fear the Outsiders, to repel them before they reached the shore, and to kill them the moment their feet hit the sand.

Last night, if he had stumbled upon just one of them, he would have killed them, but because there were so many, he had decided it was more important to warn his people than to exact a toll for the trespasses of these Outsiders. He yawned, and she did a moment later, smiling at him. He smiled back, for he knew what that meant.

She was a caring person.

Only a caring person would yawn after another did. These weren't bad people, but he had to figure out how to make certain their intention was to leave the island rather than stay and attempt to replace his people as its primary inhabitants. If he could be assured their intentions were pure, that they were here merely by accident of the wave, then they didn't deserve to die, either by the hands of their mutual enemy, or those of his people.

Laura yawned again and said something, placing both her palms flat together then to the side of her head, tilting it. He smiled.

She's telling me it's time to sleep.

He agreed and lay down. She rose and patted him on the shoulder, saying something before returning to her mate. He reached out and pulled the candle a little closer, then closed his eyes as he attempted to figure out a way to communicate with these people, her hand gesture indicating sleep having given him an idea. Attempting to communicate using words would take forever, but hand gestures might not. He opened his eyes a sliver, regarding those gathered, wondering if they were smart enough to understand drawings. His mother had always said a drawing was worth a mouthful of words, and she was right. Hunters would always draw out plans in the sand, silently conveying instructions rather than verbalizing them and potentially scaring off their prey. Children drew them for fun, and some adults even drew them purely for pleasure.

He closed his eyes, wondering what he should draw to make certain they were leaving the island when everything was over, and as he attempted to scrawl an image on the back of his eyelids, he drifted off to sleep.

Jara's Cavern

North Sentinel Island

Andaman Islands, India

Acton stood with Jannarkar as Laura joined them. "Did you get anywhere with him?"

"His name is Jara. He now knows my name."

"Anything else?"

She tilted her head slightly. "I don't think verbal communication is going to work beyond names. However, I was able to suggest he try to get some sleep with some hand gestures, and he definitely got the gist of what I was telling him. I think non-verbal communication is going to be the best way to work with him. The question is, what are we going to try to communicate?"

Acton glanced over at the young man lying by himself, his eyes closed. Others were spreading out the blankets used to carry their supplies on the cold rock floor, and settling in for the night, huddling together in groups to share body heat. Acton beckoned Tommy and Mai over and handed them a blanket he had reserved earlier. "You two take this and try to get some sleep. Laura and I are going to take the first watch. We'll wake you in a few hours and then you two can take over. Is that okay?"

They both nodded. "Yes, sir," said Tommy. They headed to an unoccupied area and laid the blanket down then got on top, spooning.

Jannarkar frowned. "What can I do to help? I'm so ashamed of how I behaved earlier."

Acton smiled at their old friend. "You've got nothing to be ashamed of. Laura and I have been through this a lot, and even Tommy and Mai have had some misadventures, which is why I chose them to be the second watch. Your job is to care for your students. They'll draw strength from you. Just get some sleep, as much as you can, and in the morning, we'll figure this out."

Jannarkar sighed heavily. "You're right, of course." He looked about the cave. The two girls were huddled on a blanket, and the four boys were together with one on the ground and the other covering them. One of the girls waved at him.

"You could join us, sir. There's room."

Jannarkar gave her a look. "That wouldn't be appropriate, now would it, Jivi?"

Jivi giggled. "You're married, sir, don't worry."

Acton reached out for his friend, squeezing his shoulder as all the muscles slackened in the man's face at the mention of his wife. Jivi slapped a hand over her mouth, her eyes wide in horror as they teared up.

"Oh God, I'm so sorry, Professor," she finally managed.

Jannarkar waved a hand, sucking in a deep breath. "No, it's not your fault."

One of the boys sat up. "Sir, we'll split into two groups." The two larger boys stood, taking one of the blankets, and found a new place to set up, and the two smaller boys shuffled over to one side. Jannarkar joined them, lying down on the sliver of blanket, his back to his students.

"God, I hope Sushma is alive," murmured Laura as they both turned their backs on the others.

"I can't see how she is, unless they left long before the eruption." He stepped over to the opening leading to the outside and listened for a moment, but heard nothing.

Laura joined him. "What are we going to do?"

He chewed his cheek for a moment. "I think we're safe until morning, and then, well, I think our choices are limited. We have two assumptions we can work under. One is that Greg was able to reach out, and our friends know where we are and they'll come looking for us. Or, nobody knows we're here, and nobody will ever come looking."

"I don't think I much like that assumption."

"Neither do I. If we have to stay here long-term and save ourselves, the only way is to build a raft and head east and hope to be either picked up by a ship or to reach land."

"We have eleven people we're responsible for. We'll probably have to build two rafts, if not three."

Acton agreed. "That's not a problem. There are plenty of resources here that we could build something with. The bigger problem is time. It might take us days or even a week, perhaps even longer since we don't have the proper tools. The real problem is, how can we possibly build anything without being discovered? We've got armed gang members that if they don't know we're on the island yet, will tomorrow, I'm sure. And we've got hostile natives who for as long as encounters with them have been recorded, have killed or attempted to kill everyone that's ever set foot on the island."

"Then what do we do?"

He glanced at the others behind them. "If we assume nobody knows we're here, then the only thing I can think to do would be to put some distance between ourselves and the gang, and try to build those rafts."

Laura gripped his arm. "What about this? Rather than trying to save everyone all at once, we build a raft big enough for two people. They go and get us help. We could probably build that in a day, maybe two, and it'd be small enough that we could build it in the forest, out of sight. We keep most of our people in here. In fact, we could do a lot of work in here. We could make all the rope, we could strip down the logs, craft the paddles—"

Acton's eyes widened and he held up a hand, cutting her off. "Wait a minute, we're forgetting something."

Laura stared at him. "What?"

"Our boat has an emergency raft."

Her eyes widened. "The inflatable!"

"Exactly. It's stored in one of the compartments above deck. If we could get that, we could inflate it, probably send at least four people, maybe even six, for help. It would already have paddles in the kit. They probably just need to be screwed together."

Her grip on his arm tightened. "But how do we get it? Those gang members are still out there."

"If we wait until daylight, they're going to be exploring up and down the beach for sure, and they'll find the wreck. That's where they'll set up camp because of the gold. But right now, I'm willing to bet they're back at whatever wrecks they arrived on, probably with as big a fire as they can build, thinking it'll scare away the natives."

"That's just going to tell them where they are."

"Exactly." He stared her in the eyes. "I have to go get it. Now."

"I'll go with you."

He firmly shook his head. "No, I need somebody with a cool head here in charge, and that's you. Ritesh is too upset."

Laura glanced over her shoulder at the young native. "Maybe you should take him with you."

Another firm head shake. "No, I don't trust him. If it's just the two of us, he's liable to run off and bring his people directly to us. Right now, if I go and get that emergency raft, we could have people in the water before daylight."

She hugged him hard. "I hate it when you're right."

"Well, then you must hate me all the time."

She chuckled. "You and your jokes."

He handed her the speargun and she pushed it back toward him. "No, you take it."

"No, it's the only weapon we've got, and there are more of you."

She gave him a look. "You know as well as I do that if they come for us, this is just going to piss them off. But if you're out there and you run into one of them on patrol, you could take him out and buy yourself the time to get away and back in hiding."

She was right. If the group were discovered by either natives or gang members, the confrontation wouldn't be won with a single speargun and a few arrows. But if he ran into somebody one-on-one out in the forest, it just might save them all. He took the speargun and gave her a kiss. "I love you."

"I love you, too."

He grinned at her. "Don't wait up."

With his heart hammering, he squeezed through the narrow opening, emerging into the darkness, lit only by the stars and the moon above.

And he prayed he would see the woman he loved again.

Viper Chain Gang Wreck

North Sentinel Island

Andaman Islands, India

Pritam sat near the fire roaring into the night sky, his men keeping it constantly fed. Rhythmic drumming in the distance had his heart pounding, though he hid his fear from his men. Weakness was never tolerated, and it would only invite someone to challenge his leadership. Right now, he had to keep a firm hand, for everyone was scared. They were on the Forbidden Island. No one had dared say its name yet, at least not within his earshot, but there was no doubt.

The one they had captured earlier wasn't from anywhere civilized. There was only one place outside of the Amazon you would ever find someone like that, and it was on North Sentinel Island. He had grown up with the stories of the ferocious warriors that lived here and shunned everything from the outside world, that wouldn't hesitate to slaughter anyone unfortunate enough to step on its shores. Now, here they were, their boats wrecked, on an island where no one was allowed to come near. No rescuers would ever be searching for survivors here, even if they were looking to help the natives, for they knew the natives would attack anyone the moment they arrived. Whoever was on this island would be left alone to fend for themselves.

He stared back at their boats washed ashore, only a few hundred feet apart, their hulls crushed. There was no way to repair them. They were flimsy when they had left the harbor. These were meant for traveling the coastline, not for heading out on the open sea.

A thought occurred to him that had him chewing his cheek. If they had survived and been swept here, what had become of the Americans and their gold? The boat they were on was a seafaring vessel, modern, well-built. If he and his men survived, then those they were pursuing may have as well, and their boat could be washed up nearby.

His heart raced in excitement instead of fear. There might be a way off the island, and they might have the gold as well. He stood and his men turned toward him as the drums continued to beat in the distance, meant no doubt to instill fear in the enemy. Yet they also gave away their position, and they were deep in the forest, posing no threat to him or his men.

"We need to get off this island." He pointed at their wrecked boats. "If we made it here, then those Americans with the gold might have as well. There could be a boat nearby that we can push back into the water and sail home with our prize." He pointed at two of his men, then to his left. "You two go that way. Walk for fifteen minutes, then come back."

He pointed at another two then in the opposite direction. "You two do the same. If there's a boat here, we could be gone before morning."

The four men he had tasked rose, though hesitated.

He glared at them. "Is there a problem?"

One of them finally had the balls to speak up. "Shouldn't we, umm, go in a group? We won't stand a chance against those natives."

Pritam slapped his hand against his AK-47, the rattle comforting. "You have these. They have sticks and stones. Take some extra ammo, and if we hear gunfire, we'll come. Now go. The sooner you're gone, the sooner you'll be back."

The men grabbed some extra magazines from the others then headed out, both pairs setting a slow pace.

He cursed. "Get a move on! You'll cover more distance!"

The slow walk turned into a jog, and they were soon out of sight. He sat back down and closed his eyes. He desperately needed sleep, though if his hunch were right, they might be out of here in less than half an hour, incredibly rich. His smile spread as he lay back on the sand, both of his hands clasped behind his head, enjoying the beat of the drums, taking comfort in the distance between him and them it conveyed.

Approaching the Yacht Wreck

North Sentinel Island

Andaman Islands, India

Acton rushed through the trees as quietly as the dead of night would allow, praying he would find his way back. The sounds of the forest were all around him, and in the distance, he could hear drumming that could only be from the natives. He recognized it as an intimidation tactic and a call to arms. The sound would carry for miles, and anyone within the vicinity would know to come back home to help the tribe.

Though it was also meant as a diversion. Those who didn't know better would think their enemy was cloistered around the drums, but they would be wrong. The drums were merely a rallying point where hunting parties and other villagers would convene before being dispatched. It was more likely the natives on this island were only feet away from whomever they were targeting, instead of the several miles the drums would suggest.

The question was, how many natives were there? The tsunami had been devastating and could have wiped out large numbers of the small population in this area. And the other question was, who were they targeting? He had to assume it was their pursuers, though it could be both sets of survivors.

He heard something and paused, a smile spreading as he realized it was water crashing onto the shore. He was near the beach. He continued forward, and moments later, his feet hit the sand. He scanned left then right, spotting the boat several hundred yards away. He listened but could hear nothing beyond the waves and the drums. He raced along the tree line toward what he hoped would be their eventual salvation.

It was more difficult going than the open beach, but the moonlight was too bright and he would stand out like a sore thumb. It was also too exposed. With the trees so close, he could at least dart back into the forest if he were spotted, then hopefully lose his pursuers. The boat was tantalizingly close now, and as it lay on its side, it appeared remarkably intact from this angle. The idea of repairing it jumped to mind until he remembered the gash in her hull on the opposite side.

No, their best bet, for now, was the emergency raft. They could send four to six people on it, but it was a 25-mile trip by paddle—not sail or engine. That would mean they would need to send all of their water and most of their resources. They could potentially replenish those supplies on the island, but at sea, they'd have nothing. He frowned. With the supply limited, it would be better to send only two. They would require fewer resources, and with the raft lighter, might make better time.

But who would those two be?

He was now parallel to the boat. It was only a hundred feet away. He knelt, peering down the beach in both directions, seeing nothing but the glow of a fire perhaps a mile away. That would be the gang members. He sprinted toward the boat, then once under the cover of its listing hull, paused, catching his breath as he listened, still hearing nothing but the waves and the pounding of the drums in the distance. He scrambled up the ladder and onto the deck, then opened the compartment with the emergency raft, almost crying out in relief. He hauled it out and grunted as the small bundle was far heavier than it appeared. The raft should inflate itself, though he grabbed the back-up hand pump just in case. He double-checked to make sure both oars were still strapped to the side as the rental agent had explained during their orientation when picking up the boat for the first time.

He tore some cargo netting from one of the bulkheads and used it to wrap up the supplies, and was about to toss the bundle onto the sand when someone shouted. His heart leaped into his throat and he cursed as he dropped flat onto the deck. He peered toward where he had heard the sound and spotted two men silhouetted, running toward him, excited chatter exchanged between them. He didn't understand the language, but recognized enough of it to know these weren't locals. One held an automatic weapon over his head in triumph, confirming his suspicions.

And also confirming they hadn't spotted him yet.

He scrambled to the other side of the deck and tossed the bundle over the higher side of the listing vessel. A loud splash had his eyes closing and his shoulders sagging at his stupidity. The boat was at an angle to the shore and what was beach on the starboard side that he had climbed up, was evidently water on the port side. The chatter halted and then something was snapped out in a questioning tone.

They had heard it, and they knew they weren't alone.

He eyed the hold where the gold was. He could reach it from here and lock himself inside, but they could just riddle the deck with bullets, and with the weapons they had, would make quick work of the thin skin that would be protecting him. He eyed the wheelhouse, but there was no place he could hide where they wouldn't eventually find him then force him to lead them to the others.

There was no doubt he would be captured if he remained here.

This was a fight to the end, and he only had seconds if he hoped to do anything about it. He grabbed some rope that lay on the deck then pushed off from the gunwale on the listing side, darting up the deck. Gunfire erupted behind him as he swung over the starboard side and dropped into the water. Instinct would be to head inland, but he resisted that urge and instead headed deeper into the water as he unfurled the rope then tied a thick knot in the middle of it. He wrapped both ends around the palms of his hands as he crouched behind the bow of the boat while the hostiles shouted excitedly between each other, revealing their locations. One was on the deck now, and the other was at the front of the boat, no doubt expecting him to have run into the forest.

Acton rounded back to the starboard side, hugging the listing hull that hid him from the one on deck. The other one was about halfway between the boat and the forest, his back facing him as his head swiveled from side to side, searching for him. This might be the only time the two of them would be separated. He stared at his feet and found a palm-sized rock. He rose and hurled it as hard as he could toward the forest. It reached the tree line and cracked against a trunk, the distinct sound drawing everyone's attention.

The one closest to the trees shouted, sprinting toward the sound. His partner responded and footfalls on the deck had Acton rewrapping the rope in his hands. The man jumped, landing on the sand, his back to him. Acton reached forward, his hands held high, and dropped the rope in front of the man's face then yanked back. The knot hit the man's windpipe. Acton spun around, positioning his back against the man's as he pulled with all of his might with both hands, leaning forward and lifting his enemy's feet from the ground. The struggle behind him was furious, and as the life gurgled from the man's mouth, bile filled Acton's own at the thought of what he was doing. Yet he had no choice. This was survival, and these people would kill him and the others without hesitation.

And what they might do to the women sickened him.

He both felt and heard the snap of his opponent's neck. He let go then quickly unwrapped his hands. A questioning shout from the partner had Acton reassessing the situation. The other one had obviously heard the struggle. Gunfire interrupted his debate, and Acton dove for the cover of the hull, but not before grabbing the AK-47 lying on the ground beside his victim. He slammed against the boat, checked the weapon, then raised it. The gunfire continued for several seconds then stopped. He heard the magazine eject, his opponent reloading.

This might be his only chance.

He leaned out, took a bead on the man, and fired two shots, center mass. The man cried out then dropped in a heap. Acton slung the weapon then searched the first man for anything of use. He discovered three magazines and a hunting knife. He rounded the boat, grabbed his bundle that still sat in the water, and added his find. He slung it over his shoulder and hurried over to the second man lying silent in the sand. He dropped the bundle then his boot onto the man's hand, still gripping his weapon. He groaned. Acton leaned in and punched him several times in the face, knocking him out. He liberated him of his gun and discovered another good-size hunting knife and two mags. He added them to the bundle then checked the man's wounds, finding one to the stomach and one just right of the heart. He was bleeding badly and would die if left untended.

Acton had little sympathy for the man, and he debated what he should do. He could try to save this man's life, but that would put all the others at risk. Shouts to his right settled any debate as he spotted a group of men running toward the scene, torches and automatic weapons clasped tight.

The rest of the gang was arriving.

He grabbed the bundle and scrambled toward the tree line. The shouts behind him would cover his escape, so he didn't bother being careful picking where he placed his feet. Instead, he sprinted as deep into the forest as he could before they arrived. His heart pounded and his muscles screamed from the heavy load as he struggled to hear what was happening behind him, but he couldn't make out any sounds over his own heavy breathing. He skidded to a halt and froze, breathing in through his nose, slowly holding his breath before exhaling, struggling to calm his nerves. He could still hear the shouts behind him, but there were no signs of pursuit. He breathed a sigh of relief and continued back toward the cave with his prize.

And that was when he noticed something had changed that had his heart racing harder.

The drumming had stopped.

Jara's Cavern

North Sentinel Island

Andaman Islands, India

Laura stood just in the mouth of the cave entrance, an ear cocked to the night. She had heard gunfire in the distance from the direction the boat lay. She desperately wanted to go and help her husband, but she had nothing but her training. While she might disarm and take out one of the hostiles, perhaps even two, unless she could get control of one of their weapons in time, she would be mowed down by the others. Her eyes narrowed as she noticed that the rhythmic drumming of the natives had stopped, leaving her to wonder what it meant. Had the gunfire scared them away? Was the gunfire in response to a native attack that began the moment the drums ceased and she just hadn't noticed?

None of that mattered. All that mattered was whether James was okay. Even at a cautious pace, he should have reached the beach within fifteen minutes, perhaps even ten. If her estimates were correct, the gunfire had begun around the time he would have arrived. Retrieving the life raft should have taken only a minute at most, which suggested he had never had a chance and was attacked when he arrived, was surprised while he was on board, or intercepted making his escape.

None of the possibilities brought her any comfort. She hated not knowing, their history together suggesting too many horrifying possibilities as to what had or what was happening to him. She loved that man harder than she had ever loved anyone, and wanted to grow old with him, her dream to sit-side-by side in their old age, hand-in-hand, reliving the life they had led with their friends and family surrounding them. Her finger absentmindedly traced the scar on her stomach, the scar she barely noticed anymore except in these moments when it reminded her she could no longer have children, and they would never have a family of their own.

A sound behind her had her spinning.

"It's just us, Professor."

She sighed at Tommy and Mai.

"Is everything okay?"

"James went to get the life raft off the boat. I heard gunfire."

"I'm sure he's okay," said Mai in an attempt to be comforting. "Is he overdue yet?"

Laura shook her head. "No, the gunfire was about five minutes ago. If he headed straight back, then he should be here in another five or ten, depending on how carefully he's moving."

Tommy grunted. "If someone's shooting at me, I'm not going to be too concerned about making any noise. I'd be at full tilt."

Laura agreed. She heard something in the trees and held a finger to her lips. She waved them back, deeper into the cave as she peered into the dark, her grip on the rocks she held tightening.

A shadow emerged carrying something large. It might be James, but she couldn't be sure. She held her position and waited. The shape came to a stop, and whoever it was, scanned the cliffside. It had to be him. More sounds from the trees sent her pulse racing. Whoever it was obviously couldn't find the opening, though knew it was there. It had to be him.

She stepped out. "James," she hissed. The head spun toward her then whoever it was rushed forward. As they closed the last few feet, she sighed in relief as she recognized him.

"Inside, quickly," he whispered, and any reunion she had planned was cut off as the sounds of pursuers neared.

She stepped inside the cave and he followed. They made their way through the tunnel, then he placed the gear gently on the ground. Her eyes widened as he handed her an AK-47 and two magazines. He grabbed a second one and stuffed two mags in his pockets, then headed back to the cave entrance. Everyone was stirring now and she turned to Tommy and Mai. "Keep everybody quiet. Lights out." They both rushed deeper into the cave, extinguishing the candles and whispering for everyone to remain quiet.

She joined James at the entrance. He held a finger to his lips then pointed at his eyes then outside. He held up four fingers. She steadied her breathing, listening. His pursuers were close, and she had a sense they wouldn't be so quick to give up the search a second time. If he had two of their weapons, it suggested two of the enemy were down or dead. She ran her eyes over him in the dark, barely making out anything, but he appeared unscathed.

There was a sound mere feet from their position and James raised his weapon. There was a shout that sounded as if it were only inches away from the entrance. He held his position, not giving into panic. Anyone else might have stepped out and opened fire, but right now, at this very moment, there was no proof their location had been compromised. Her heart crawled into her throat as the drums of the natives resumed, and she couldn't be certain, but to her, they sounded closer, louder. It could be her panic or her position nearer to the cave entrance.

It didn't matter. It triggered a panic response she immediately recognized and took action to control, taking slow, deep breaths through her nose and out her mouth. There was another shout, this one sounding like a snapped order, and whoever was just outside the cave entrance called an acknowledgment, and her shoulders relaxed as his footfalls faded, sounds of a hasty retreat being beaten by the others, no doubt wishing to return to whatever defensive position they thought they had against the natives.

James stepped forward, poking his head outside. She stayed back, silent until he rejoined her. They remained quiet as they returned to the cavern. He whispered to the blackness. "It's okay. They're gone. Relight the candles."

Several cellphone screens lit the area, then moments later, every candle in the place was lit, revealing the terrified faces of those he was responsible for. He smiled, holding up his hands in an attempt to calm them. "I've got good news." Several eyes brightened, but the rest weren't buying it. He pointed out the raft. "That's an inflatable raft. It can hold six people." Concerned looks were exchanged and he held up a hand cutting off any debate that might be about to begin. "But it's too far back to the main islands for six people. We don't have the supplies, so we're going to send two people with all the food and water we can spare. Those two people and I are going to head to the shore. We're going to inflate the raft, and then those two will head directly east. It could take you several days. We're going to give you our flare gun, so if you see a boat, you launch a flare and they'll hopefully come and get you, then you can call for help. But if you don't, just keep heading east and you'll hit the main island. As long as you head east, it'll be absolutely impossible for you to not reach land."

Jannarkar stood. "And who will these two people be?"

Acton turned to Tommy. "I think you should be one of them. You said you knew how to work a boat."

"Well, there's not much to work when just paddling, but my entire youth wasn't misspent. I spent a lot of time on the water with my parents."

"Good. I want you to go because you've worked with our friends in the past. They'll listen to you before they listen to one of Professor Jannarkar's students." Acton turned to Jannarkar. "I'd like you to choose one of your students, somebody fit who can paddle that boat, someone who can keep a cool head."

Jannarkar's eyes widened as he regarded his six students, all wanting to be picked to escape their hellish circumstances. And it was clear no decision would be forthcoming from the man, not in the timeframe they had.

Acton stepped forward, peering into the eyes of each of the six students. "Ask yourselves, who among you can do this? Remember, everyone here is counting on you. If you know you're not strong enough to paddle for perhaps days to find us the help we need, please excuse yourself by sitting down. Perhaps you've got an injury, asthma, perhaps you're afraid of the water. Whatever it is, if you don't feel you can do it, please don't remain in the running. There is no shame in withdrawing."

The two girls looked at each other, exchanged a few whispered words, then Nandini turned to him. "While I feel I'm just as capable as any man, I barely weigh forty kilos. There's no way I can row a boat."

Jivi, just as slight, stepped forward. "While I may weigh a few kilos more than her, I've never rowed a boat in my life." They both sat, as did another boy.

"I'm so sorry, but the very idea terrifies me," he explained.

That left three boys who stood facing him, their chests thrust out. All appeared fit, but he didn't know these people. "Who has the most experience on the water?" A quick huddle was held, then broke moments later. Two of the boys sat, leaving Amit standing.

"I will go, Professor Acton. I grew up on the water. I've been rowing since I was a kid."

Acton extended a hand and the young man shook it. "Excellent. Okay, Amit, you and Tommy are our guys. The three of us are going to head for the shore, inflate the raft, and get you out of here while the sun is still down. Say your goodbyes. We're leaving in five minutes."

Operations Center 2, CIA Headquarters
Langley, Virginia

Leroux couldn't tear himself away from the displays curving across the front of the operations center. Down the left and right edges, feeds from all the major news networks worldwide reported the aftermath of the massive eruption, the scenes coming in heartbreaking. Entire coastal villages were wiped off the map, not a single structure standing. From what he could see of the main end of the island, where the professors had originally been, the wave had been so high, it had washed over the island's twelve-mile width then continued, broadsiding North Sentinel Island and its forbidden native population.

But for the past twenty minutes, he hadn't paid attention to any of those feeds. His entire time had been spent watching the satellite images of the three factions now battling for survival on an island no one was allowed to go to.

Tong sighed in relief behind him as the hostiles pursuing one of the survivors retreated into the woods for some unknown reason. As far as they could determine, the professors and those with them had found shelter in a cave. And until one of them had emerged and returned to the boat for some reason, they hadn't confirmed that. He was certain it was Acton, for only he would have the balls to do something so foolish, but he had retrieved something before being attacked by two of the pursuers from the Andaman Islands.

"It's a life raft," said Child, spinning in his chair before flicking his finger on his screen toward the displays at the front, a schematic of the boat appearing. One of the cargo hatches that matched the one opened by Acton was highlighted along with the standard manifest. "That's where the life raft is held."

Leroux spun toward Child. "A life raft?"

"Yup. That's what the specs say. It assumes, of course, that the rental agency made sure it was fully equipped."

Leroux scratched his chin. "We're not talking you or me renting the cheapest boat we can find. These people are rich, and all their travel arrangements are made through their agent. Past experience suggests that agent would make certain she was renting them the safest boat possible." He turned back toward the displays. "And besides, we know he took something from there, and now with some context, it certainly looks like it could be an emergency life raft. How many does it hold?"

"Just a second." Child scanned his screen then frowned. "Six."

Tong spun toward him. "Six, that's it?"

Child threw up his hands and shrugged. "Hey, I didn't design the damn thing."

"Is there a second one on board?"

Child shook his head. "It doesn't look like it."

"Why would they only have a life raft for six?" asked Tong. "There are eleven of them from what we counted."

"You're forgetting one thing," said Leroux as he returned to his station. "There were only four of them when they rented the boat. The other seven were never supposed to be there. We have to assume something happened that put them all on that boat. Until we saw those other hostiles, I was inclined to believe it was the eruption. But these other survivors are armed and clearly have hostile intent, which suggests they were pursuing the Actons and perhaps the others. They were on an archaeological dig and might have found something that attracted unwanted attention. What it was doesn't matter. We have eleven innocent people pursued by what was a group of twenty armed hostiles, and now eighteen, thanks to the handy work of whom we're assuming was Professor Acton."

"Not to mention the natives," muttered Child.

Leroux returned his attention to the display, the latest satellite footage shown. The computer had detected, mapped, then classified anything moving or giving off a heat signature big enough to be a human. The natives on the eastern part of the displayed area appeared to have split into three groups. One, farther inland, several miles from the shoreline, appeared stationary. The location contained several structures suggesting this was their permanent home. There was another smaller group less than a mile from the shore of half a dozen, then a larger group of nearly fifty just on the edge of the tree line spread between the wrecked boats.

He had read the briefing notes on North Sentinel Island, and the intent of the natives was clear to him. They would do what they always did—repel any invaders with brutal force. And while he didn't care what happened to the hostile survivors, he feared for the innocent natives who were about to go up against automatic weapons for the first time in their history.

They didn't stand a chance.

A thought occurred to him and he headed for the door. "I have to see the Chief. I'll be back in a few minutes. Text me if anything happens."

"Yes, sir," said Tong.

The door hissed then unlocked, and as he stepped through, his mind raced as he pieced together a cogent argument for immediately sending help to rescue eleven people in the middle of a regional humanitarian crisis affecting millions.

Jara's Cavern

North Sentinel Island

Andaman Islands, India

Acton gave Laura a hug then held up a finger, cutting off what he knew she was about to say. "I need you to stay here." He tapped her rifle. "You're the only one who knows how to use this. They obviously don't know where the entrance is, and they don't even know if we're actually here." He cocked an ear for a second. "The drums are still going, so they'll be more concerned with the natives than us."

"What if they left a lookout?"

He shook his head. "I can't see anyone being willing to do that, though it's definitely a possibility. One lookout we can deal with. They found our boat, so my guess is they're busy trying to figure out how to get that gold and themselves off the island without getting killed by the locals. It's still dark, and the sooner we're out of here, the sooner I'm back, and the sooner help is on the way."

She gave him a lingering kiss then sighed as she pulled away. "Be careful."

"I'm always careful."

She gave him a look.

He shrugged. "Okay, I always intend to be careful."

"Mm-hmm."

He gave her a quick peck on the forehead then took point. As he headed through the tunnel, he came out the other end and listened, hearing only the forest and the drums. Tommy was right behind him with Amit taking up the rear. Everyone had supplies slung over their shoulders, much of it water, its weight certain to make the journey to the shore difficult.

He stepped out farther, his weapon raised, and scanned the tree line about ten yards from his position, but could see nothing moving. If there were a lookout, they either hadn't spotted him yet, or intended to return to the main group to get reinforcements. He held out a hand indicating for Tommy and Amit to wait. He stepped out a little more, hugging the cliff face, and slowly walked ten paces from the opening.

Still nothing.

If there were a lookout, they were holding their position, otherwise he would hear them in the forest as they left to report. He stepped away from the rock wall and hurried to the tree line, then listened one last time.

Nothing.

He beckoned toward the cliff face for Tommy and Amit to join him. They emerged with the raft and scurried over to his position. They all took a knee. "I think we're clear. Now, here's what we're going to do."

He indicated a bearing. "We're heading in this direction. That should take us far enough away from any of the boats that survived, so we shouldn't be discovered by our friends. And it sounds like the natives are in the opposite direction. It's essential that at least one of you gets in the raft and gets away. When you pull that cord, that raft will inflate almost instantly. If we're being pursued, whoever gets to the water first with the raft inflates it, gets in, and starts paddling. The other one, throw in whatever supplies you can and get in yourself, but don't wait for each other. If we're under attack, one of you has to get away. Understood?"

They both nodded, exchanging fearful glances.

"Good. Now, let's pray that none of that's going to happen." Acton rose. "You two head that way. I'll be right behind you. Just keep going no matter what you hear."

Tommy stared at him. "Shouldn't we stick together?"

Acton squeezed the young man's shoulder. "Trust me, just go. We don't have time to waste debating this."

Tommy frowned but ended his protest. He and Amit scurried off as Acton slunk into the tree line then waited.

And a minute hadn't passed when his worst fears were confirmed and a shadow moved by only yards away.

There had been a lookout after all.

Director Morrison's Office, CIA Headquarters

Langley, Virginia

The CIA's National Clandestine Service Chief, Leif Morrison, indicated for Leroux to take a seat as he finished up a call. The Chief appeared as tired as he felt. It was all hands on deck as the country scrambled to determine the extent of the damage around the region, what American military, government, and Agency assets were affected, and then what those same assets could do to assist in the humanitarian crisis.

And then there were the operations that were actively underway. The last he had heard from Kane, he was heading back into the region, though only in general—he shouldn't be anywhere near the coastline.

Morrison ended his call and leaned back, squeezing the bridge of his nose as he shut his eyes. "You'll be happy to know your friend, Agent Kane, is safe, though not for lack of trying."

Leroux's eyebrows shot up. "Sir?"

Morrison waved a hand. "Nothing. Things go wrong on ops all the time. This one got a little hairy, but he made it out with only a couple of new holes that didn't do any permanent damage. What have you got for me?"

Leroux suppressed the urge to ask more, and instead took the Chief's word for it that Kane was fine. "It's about the professors."

Morrison sighed. "Those two are constant headaches."

Leroux chuckled. "They do seem to get themselves into more trouble than the average citizen, though I can hardly think they can be blamed for getting caught up in a tsunami."

"No, I suppose not, though they're the only ones on the entire planet that I'm aware of that got caught up in a tsunami while being pursued by armed hostiles. So, what's the status?"

"It looks like they found shelter inside a cave, but there's been an encounter between them and their pursuers. We believe Professor Acton has killed two of them while retrieving a life raft from the shipwreck."

Morrison steepled his fingers in front of him, resting his chin on top. "A life raft? So, they might be able to save themselves?

"No, sir, there are eleven of them, and it's only designed to fit six." His phone vibrated with a message and he quickly read it. He wagged the phone at Morrison. "According to Sonya, three of them just left the cave with what we believe is the raft."

"So, they're sending three for help."

Leroux chewed his cheek for a moment. "I'm guessing two. One of the three is almost definitely Professor Acton, and there's no way he'd leave the group alone. I'm guessing they've chosen two of the others, and he's escorting them to the water to make sure they get away safely." The phone vibrated again in his hand and he muttered a curse as he read it.

"What?"

Leroux sighed. "It looks like someone was watching their hiding place and is now following them."

Morrison frowned. "So, they might not be saving themselves."

"Maybe. But there's another problem."

"What's that?"

"The natives look like they might be getting prepared to attack the professors' pursuers."

"Didn't your briefing suggest we should expect a hostile reaction from them?"

"Yes, sir. All indications from the dossier on this island suggests they will absolutely attack and kill anyone that steps foot on their land."

Morrison leaned back and scratched his nose. "Then doesn't that sort of take care of one of our problems? If the natives take out the pursuers, and the professors and the other survivors are hidden away, then they can wait for local authorities to come and rescue them."

Leroux shook his head. "No, you're forgetting one thing."

"What's that?"

"The natives have never encountered automatic weapons before. There are almost twenty armed men with modern weaponry who won't hesitate to slaughter them. The population estimate for that island is anywhere from two-hundred to five-hundred people, and we're showing dozens at that location. We're assuming they're all healthy men. If that number is wiped out in a battle, those casualties combined with whatever happened with the tsunami, could decimate the population. Combine that with the fact that those same hostiles will be looking for shelter and resources, they could move inland to the villages and kill anyone who opposes them. Though the scale is small, relative to their population, we're looking at genocide."

"Genocide?"

"Yes, sir. If that significant a portion of their male population is wiped out in a single incident, their population might never recover."

Morrison regarded Leroux before finally speaking. "What exactly are you asking of me?"

"We have three American citizens, one British National who's a Lawful Permanent Resident, plus seven other innocents, presumed Indian, in immediate danger from an armed group who may violate international law by committing genocide against a protected indigenous tribe. We have an obligation under international law to assist."

Morrison eyed him. "I'm not exactly sure I agree with your interpretation of the law, however, Washington certainly needs to be made aware of what's going on. I'll make some calls. You find out what assets we have in the area that we might be able to spare."

Leroux rose. "I'm on it."

Morrison reached for his phone and Leroux hurried from the office, eager to return to the operations center to check on the status of the three that had left the safety of the cave. He just prayed they didn't lose their lives in an effort that might no longer be necessary.

Outside Jara's Cavern

North Sentinel Island

Andaman Islands, India

Acton's heart hammered as the lurker carefully made his way through the trees after an apparently unaware Tommy and Amit. He flexed his fingers on his weapon, relieving the tension. He could fire, but it would reveal their position. For the moment, to their lookout's buddies, he was merely someone still doing his job and alive, having seen nothing. But the moment a gunshot rang out, his opponent became someone in distress, whose buddies would come to check on him, and with him dead from a gunshot, they would know who had killed him and that they were in the area. In the light of day, they would find the cave entrance and all would be lost.

He slung his weapon and drew the hunting knife, his task now much more difficult and far too personal. Shooting someone from a distance was one thing, but close up, in hand-to-hand combat, was an entirely different beast. When he could feel the heat of their body, smell their sweat, hear their breath, what was merely a distant target became a flesh and blood human being.

He rose and crept forward, for this human being meant to harm those he loved and cared for, those who had become his responsibility to protect. He advanced as quickly as he could while his pulse pounded in his ears, all the while praying he didn't step on some stray twig or branch that would give him away. He could hear Tommy and Amit ahead, struggling with the raft and supplies, and he paused at his own foolishness. He removed the bundle slung over his shoulders and gently lowered it to the ground. There was no way he could fight encumbered with such a heavy load.

He gingerly removed his hand then turned to resume the pursuit when the bundle fell to its side, plastic water bottles crinkling. The figure ahead of him spun toward the sound, his weapon raised. Acton leaped to the right, rolling behind a tree as gunfire tore through the space where he had stood. As he came to his knees, he unslung his weapon, stealth no longer an option. All he could do now was deal with the immediate threat, then worry about what was coming mere minutes from now.

He leaned out from behind the tree providing his cover and took aim. His opponent spotted him, readjusted, and opened fire, muzzle flashes lighting up the forest. Acton ducked back behind the tree, the shots of a weapon on full auto never very accurate when delivered by the untrained, though enough of them hit the tree trunk he was hiding behind to cure him of any thought that he was protected by incompetence.

He readied his weapon, waiting for the man to have to reload, when a roar erupted as his opponent charged his position, firing single shots as he neared. He only had seconds to decide what to do, the shots more accurate now. He inhaled deeply through his nose as he struggled to control the panic that threatened to settle in. He crouched down then leaned out on one knee, squeezing off several rounds, but his opponent dodged to the side, using the tree Acton was hiding behind to narrow the field of fire. He was almost upon him now, and would be coming at him from behind. Acton rolled onto his back and took aim. His opponent emerged, rapidly spinning toward him to finish him off.

Acton squeezed the trigger and the man cried out, his left shoulder jerking back. Acton fired again, but the weapon remained silent. He was out of ammo. The man stopped pointing his rifle at Acton, the pale moonlight revealing a toothless grin. Acton raised his hands, still lying on the ground as the man said a few pointless words in Hindi.

Then they both turned as something large crashed through the forest toward them.

Tommy hadn't been sure why Acton hadn't stayed with them, but when the first shot fired, he knew exactly what was going on. Acton had suspected someone might be following them, and had obviously been right. Tommy had dropped the raft and pointed toward the water. "Remember what he said. You go, no matter what."

Amit nodded then repositioned the load, sprinting into the darkness. Tommy raced toward the gunfire, the fact it hadn't stopped indicating the professor was still alive, though for how long was what worried him.

He used the noise to cover his approach, sprinting full tilt, unconcerned with any sounds he might make. He had to reach the professor. He could see muzzle flashes just ahead. As he ran toward the scene, he reached down and grabbed a good-sized branch lying on the ground and tested its heft as he continued forward.

And then the gunfire stopped, and a lump formed in his throat as it could only mean one of two things.

Either the professor had won, or the professor was dead.

A roar escaped his throat as he spotted Acton's adversary just ahead, raising his weapon and pointing it toward the ground, only one squeeze of the trigger away from finishing off the man who had done so much for him and the woman he loved. He raised the branch over his shoulder as he charged forward, oblivious to the futility of the situation and the risk to his own life.

All he cared about was stopping what was about to happen to his mentor.

"Hey!" he screamed as loud as he could in an attempt to halt the inevitable shot.

The man turned, his weapon swinging with him, and Tommy's eyes bulged at the realization he was about to die. He dove to his left, rolling on the ground as gunfire erupted. He regained his feet, sprinting toward the nearest tree, the muzzle flashes tracking him. He hurled himself toward the only cover within reach and hit the ground hard as two single shots rang out and the gunfire from his enemy fell silent.

An eerie calm swept over the forest, and all he could hear was the drumbeat in his chest echoed in his ears.

"James?"

Tommy nearly cried out in relief at Laura's voice, calling tentatively into the night.

"Over here," called Acton.

The tension in Tommy's muscles eased with the knowledge two of the most important people in his life were still alive.

"Tommy, was that you being an idiot?" asked Acton.

He grinned, then his shoulders shook uncontrollably as he sobbed, the stress of the situation finally coming into focus. Footsteps neared, his sobs having masked their approach. His heart leaped into his throat in a panic as his immediate thought was of a second hostile about to overwhelm him.

"What's this now?" asked the gentle voice of Laura as she knelt beside him. She put her hand on his shoulder and he thrust his arms out, grabbing on to her and hugging hard. She returned the embrace and his entire body shook as this woman who was like an older sister, perhaps even a mother, held him, gently stroking his hair.

"It's all right. It's over," she repeated.

More footsteps, and moments later Acton joined them. He knelt beside them and squeezed Tommy's shoulder. "Thank you."

Tommy let go of Laura and wiped his eyes clear. "Thank you for what?"

"You saved my life. He was squeezing that trigger when you charged him. If you hadn't explicitly ignored my instructions, I'd be dead now, and he would have reported back to his buddies where we were hiding.

You saved all of our lives." Acton patted him on the shoulder. "You're a hero."

Tommy wiped his eyes clear again. "Some hero. I'm just a blubbering coward."

Acton laughed then stood, extending a hand. "You wouldn't believe how many heroes cry like babies when it's all over, especially that first time when it's only after the fact they discover they have what's needed buried deep inside them. You did what was necessary, you put your own life at risk to save another, and in my books, that meets every definition of hero."

Tommy took the hand and Acton hauled him to his feet. Acton gave him a thumping hug, then grabbed him by the back of the head, staring him directly in the eyes. "You did good." He gave Laura a hug and a kiss. "About time you showed up."

She shrugged. "I figured it would be more dramatic if I waited."

"Ha-ha. Where's Amit?" he asked, turning to Tommy.

"I told him to keep going for the water."

"Okay. Let's hope he did that, but I'm going to go double-check."

"I'm coming with you," echoed Tommy and Laura.

Acton shook his head. "No, I'll go alone."

"Bullshit," said Tommy. "If we catch him in time, I'll go with him. There's a better chance of the two of us surviving."

Acton regarded him for a moment. "Your balls are clanging today, son. Fine. Laura, go back to the cave. Get everybody ready to move. I don't think we can count on them ignoring this place anymore. They could be here any minute examining that cliff face, up close and personal."

"Okay, I'll take care of it."

Acton gave her another kiss and she raced toward their hiding place. He gathered up the supplies he had dropped, then pointed ahead. "You lead the way. We need to get your supplies."

Tommy nodded and they rushed through the forest, no longer concerned about anyone hearing them. Even if the dead man's friends were on their way, it would take them time. He found where he had dropped his supplies and gathered them up, and within moments they were sprinting toward the beach. They broke through the tree line, the moonlit coast ahead, and spotted Amit, the raft inflated and in the water.

"Amit!" hissed Acton.

The young man spun, his oar held high in fear. It dropped as he recognized them. "Professor Acton! Tommy! When I heard the gunfire..." He shook his head. "I thought you were dead."

"I almost was," said Acton, slapping Tommy on the back. "But my friend here saved me."

Amit's eyes bulged with respect. He was about to say something when Acton cut him off.

"No time. This whole area could be flooded with hostiles at any moment." Tommy tossed his supplies into the raft, as did Acton. Acton shook both their hands. "Good luck. Remember, head east."

"How will we know?" asked Tommy.

Acton pointed at the glowing horizon. "Keep heading toward the volcano. You can't get to it without running into the main island." He patted the raft. "Check the pouches. There should be a compass built into this thing. For now, just get away from the shore and out of range of their guns. Head straight out to sea then take a bearing. Once you're out of range, you'll have time to relax a bit, then work in shifts. You need one eye scanning the horizon at all times in case a ship is nearby. Fire a flare if you see one."

"Yes, sir," said Tommy as he climbed inside.

"Good, now go get us help."

"Good luck, Professor." Tommy wanted to say something in case this was the last time he ever saw the man, but a lump formed in his throat, silencing him. He drew a deep breath as he grabbed his oar.

Acton regarded him and smiled. "I know, son. No need to say anything."

Tommy's lip trembled, now more than ever certain tonight was the last night he would ever see the professors or his beloved Mai again. This was the end of his new life, a life he never dreamed of having, a life so fulfilling and complete, it could never be replaced. This wonderful life was about to end, never to be reclaimed, and it was devastating. "Tell Mai I love her."

"I will," said Acton, as he pushed on the raft, sending them deeper into the water. "But you're going to tell her that yourself when you save us all again. Now go, and don't look back."

Tommy dipped his oar in the water as he and Amit paddled furiously away from shore, and he once again violated Acton's orders and looked back, but the man was gone. He refocused his attention to the waters ahead and paddled in silence with Amit toward safety and hopefully help.

He was convinced the only way to save everyone was if they came across a ship, for there was no way the others would survive for the days it might take to reach the main island.

And again, his shoulders shook at the thought of what they might discover when they returned, only the worst-case scenarios playing through his mind.

He squeezed his eyes shut as they burned. He attempted to bury his fears yet he couldn't, Hollywood having provided him with too many examples of the brutality those he loved might face in the coming hours or days. He inhaled deeply and held the breath, then opened his eyes as he paddled harder, scanning the horizon, determined to get the help that would save those he loved.

Operations Center 2, CIA Headquarters
Langley, Virginia

Leroux entered the operations center as a round of cheers erupted. He smiled, holding up his hands. "Thank you, people. I expect that kind of welcome every time I return to the room from now on."

Everyone laughed and Tong pointed toward the displays, filling him in. "The life raft just left the island with two people on board."

Leroux wagged his phone. "You said there was a hostile following them?"

"Yes, but they took him out. My theory is it was Laura Palmer."

Leroux returned to his station. "Did anybody bet against you?"

Child jerked a thumb over his shoulder. "Only the new guy."

Leroux glanced toward the newest member of the team sitting in the far corner, appearing sheepish.

Joyce Bachelor shrugged. "Hey, how the hell was I supposed to know she's some highly trained civilian super-soldier?"

Laughter filled the room, most having dealt with the professors for years.

"You'll quickly learn never to bet against the professors. While they may lose a lot of battles, they always come out okay in the end. I recommend you read both their files. Not only is it entertaining, but you'll be able to better anticipate what might happen in the future."

She eyed him. "So, I should expect to deal with them again?"

"If they survive this, then, yes."

"Good to know."

Leroux turned to Tong as he sat. "The Chief's talking to Washington now to see if we can launch a humanitarian mission under the guise of preventing a genocide."

Her eyebrows shot up. "Genocide?" She stared at the screen showing all the identified targets, including the natives. She grunted. "Yeah, I suppose it could be considered a genocide considering the numbers. Do you think he'll get approval?"

"I don't know, but let's assume he does. He wants us to identify any assets in the area that might be able to help."

"Well, we've got a lot of assets there, obviously, but we can't exactly send in people expecting a normal rescue mission. This has to be armed."

Leroux agreed. "Armed and disciplined. We have to expect that any rescue mission will be attacked, but we don't want our people inadvertently causing the same genocide we're trying to prevent." He pursed his lips. "Check on Bravo Team's status."

Tong checked her computer. "They're not involved with anything that we know of, but that doesn't always mean they're not actually out on a mission."

"Get me Colonel Clancy."

"Yes, sir."

Dawson/Harris Residence, Lake in the Pines Apartments

Fayetteville, North Carolina

Command Sergeant Major Burt "Big Dog" Dawson lay in a hammock on the balcony of the apartment he shared with his fiancée, Maggie Harris. It took up almost the entire slice of heaven, and it meant if Maggie wanted to be out here with him, she would have to be in the same hammock. And that wasn't necessarily a bad thing. He had just been cleared for active duty, his leg all healed up now, and today was his last day off. He was itching to get back into the mix. He hated having his team off on missions without him—it always made him feel guilty.

They had all been through it, though. Everyone was injured from time to time, though he was certain this was the first time anybody had been caught by a fishing net. There had been fishing accidents where the unskilled had hooked themselves or a brother-in-arms with the barb, but that was never combat.

A literal net had been cast, and his enemy had snagged their prey, though it ultimately failed. But now he felt 100%, life was good, things were back on track with Maggie and the marriage, and he was missing the camaraderie with the boys. Someone was always dropping by, so he was still in the loop, but it wasn't the same.

The door to the balcony slid open and Maggie stepped onto the few square feet not taken by his massive hammock, a gift the team had bought him when they heard he'd be laid up for a few weeks. He was certain none of them realized just how big it was, though that little shit Niner was snickering the entire time.

"Can I show you something?" she asked.

His eyebrows bobbed suggestively. "The neighbors might see."

She gave him a look. "Get your mind out of the gutter, Sergeant Major."

He shrugged. "It seems comfortable there."

"Uh-huh. What do you think of this hairstyle?" She held out a magazine folded over about halfway through. She had been obsessed with her hair ever since she had been shot in the head, and had only recently finally come to terms with the fact her concerns over its appearance were entirely psychological, and that her hairline had fully recovered some time ago. That realization had restarted the wedding plans. At first, they were thinking a quick city hall wedding just to get it over with, but cooler heads had prevailed, and he was determined to give her the wedding of her dreams, though he had no idea how he'd afford it. Fortunately for him, she realized that, and wasn't the type of girl who needed fancy. She just wanted their friends to share in their happiness.

He eyed the hairstyle then looked at the one she was currently sporting. "Hon, you know this isn't my thing. You could have a buzz cut and you'd be gorgeous."

She snatched back the magazine. "A lot of help you are."

He shrugged then grabbed her caboose, hauling her in closer. "Want to give the neighbors a show?"

She swatted him. "What's gotten into you today?"

He shrugged. "I don't know. Excited about going back to work, maybe?"

She grunted. "Sometimes I think you'd rather spend your time with your buddies than with me."

He grinned. "You could always join up."

She gave him a look. "You wouldn't be able to handle it."

"What do you mean?"

"I mean, the first time I kicked your ass, this relationship would be over."

He laughed and pulled her in even closer. "That sounds kind of hot."

She eyed him and he squeezed a little harder. She inhaled sharply and her eyes flared, running over his body as if sizing up a piece of meat. It excited him, and he reached up with his free hand and pulled her face toward his.

And as their lips met, the doorbell rang.

They both groaned, their foreheads pressing against each other, their lips denied.

"Who the hell could that be?" she cried. "If it's Niner, I'm kicking him in the balls."

"If it's Niner, he might just like that."

She sighed and rose as the doorbell rang a second time. "I'll get it." She stormed back into the apartment, yelling at whoever it was. "This better be important! I was just about to get it on with my man!"

He chuckled.

She better pray it's one of the guys.

The door opened and there was a gasp of concern. He immediately rolled out of the hammock, rushing into the apartment, unable to make out the murmured conversation at the door until he neared the front hallway.

"I'm so embarrassed, Colonel."

Colonel Thomas Clancy's laugh set Dawson at ease. He scrambled for his shirt as he realized he had nothing but shorts and wood on. He yanked his Hawaiian shirt off the back of the couch and slipped it on quickly, buttoning it up before stepping into sight.

"Sergeant Major, sorry to interrupt you on your last day off."

Dawson smiled at his commanding officer, a man that he implicitly trusted to always have his back, a soldier's soldier. They were Delta Force, officially 1st Special Forces Operational Detachment—Delta. They were America's elite. When their country needed to reach out with a scalpel, it was men like him and his team that were called into action, the vast majority of what they did remaining unknown to the public they served.

And if Clancy were here, in person, something out of the ordinary was happening.

"Colonel, you never need to apologize for paying us a visit. I just wish I was more appropriately dressed."

Clancy smirked. "I have a funny feeling I could have walked in on far worse."

"Sir!" exclaimed Maggie, her cheeks flushed.

Both Dawson and Clancy roared with laughter and Dawson showed him inside, gesturing at his usual seat, offering it to the Colonel instead.

Clancy sat.

"Can I get you anything, Colonel?" asked Maggie.

"Just a glass of ice water, please."

She looked at Dawson and he held up two fingers. She left for the kitchen to get the waters and then returned with them. "I'll go make myself busy so you two can talk."

Clancy waved a hand. "No need, this isn't classified."

Now Dawson was extremely curious. "What's this all about, sir? What's going on?"

"It would appear our professor friends are in another situation."

Dawson was about to groan when Maggie beat him to it. "Are you kidding me? What is it with those two?"

Clancy raised a hand in their defense. "Now, this one is not their fault. They can't be blamed."

"Are you sure?" Maggie sighed as she dropped on the couch beside Dawson. "I'm convinced that those two are magnets for trouble. Even if it's not their fault, it somehow is. It's like they did something so horrible, that karma's trying to balance things out by making them miserable."

Dawson suppressed a frown, for her assessment was entirely correct. The professors were always getting into trouble. Quite often, it was their own fault for sticking their noses where they shouldn't be, for traveling to areas of the world that weren't safe, but they were always trying to do the right thing, and more often than not, lives were saved.

And on more than one occasion, they had stepped up and saved his or one of his team member's lives.

And when the team had been disavowed, it was Laura Palmer and her tremendous wealth that financed the operation that cleared their names and brought the guilty to justice. He owed them his life, and so did most of the team. And to a man, they would do anything for them, not only to repay them for past favors, but to redeem themselves for past sins.

Karma could never be rebalanced for what had happened in Peru.

"What have they got themselves into this time, Colonel?" asked Dawson.

"You heard about the eruption in the Indian Ocean?"

Dawson gestured at the television on mute in the corner, images of the disaster playing on the screen. "Yes, sir." He rolled his eyes. "Let me guess. They're caught up in it?"

"In ways only they could manage."

He leaned forward. "Go on."

"From what we can gather, they were on the Andaman Islands for some archaeological dig, a last-minute invite. They arrived in the morning, and the volcano erupted several hours later, less than one-hundred miles from where we believe they were. We know they were on a boat at the time the tsunami hit, because Dean Milton had phoned

Acton to see if he was okay. The phone remained active, but we weren't able to establish communication. Our friend Mr. Kane was contacted through unofficial channels, and that got the CIA involved. They were able to find the Actons' boat with eleven survivors, plus they found three more shipwrecks with about twenty armed hostiles that, at this point in time, and the professors' history, we have to assume were in pursuit of them."

"Well, if you know where they are, what's the problem?"

"The problem is that they're on North Sentinel Island."

Both he and Maggie shrugged. "So?" she asked.

"It's a forbidden island."

Maggie's eyebrows shot up. "Forbidden island? What does that mean? Some guy named Tattoo shouts every time he sees a plane?"

Dawson chuckled. "That's Fantasy Island, dear."

"Oh, right."

Clancy continued. "It means there's an uncontacted tribe there, and it's illegal to travel to the island. They're extremely hostile and attack anybody who tries to set foot."

Dawson chewed his cheek. "Can't they go in with a heavily armed rescue party, get everybody off the island, and leave the natives alone?"

"If the natural disaster hadn't just hit the entire region, then that would be a possibility. Unfortunately, there won't be any rescue parties available to go to a forbidden island where they might be attacked. And what we're seeing with satellite footage is that this is heading to a conflict that could result in genocide."

"Genocide?" exclaimed Maggie. "What do you mean by that?"

"It's estimated there are only several hundred natives alive, and our satellite imagery indicates about sixty of them have congregated in the area where the survivors are. The concern is that the natives have never encountered automatic weapons, nor intruders that are willing to fight back. Should they engage the armed hostiles, it's feared all of these men could be wiped out, seriously affecting the viability of the remaining population."

Maggie shook her head in disbelief. "I never would have thought something like that would be described as genocide, but I guess you're right." She took Dawson's hand. "You want to send Bravo Team in?"

"Yes. Six-man team. Voluntary. Apparently, Kane somehow called in a favor with the Indian government. I've already been contacted by my counterpart at Indian Special Forces, Para SF, and he's working on getting a small team with choppers in to help, but there are no guarantees. They're stretched thin with what's happening, and they're going to have to ship-hop a couple of times to refuel. The Indian government, however, has given us permission to mount our own rescue. Washington is classifying this as a humanitarian relief mission to prevent a genocide and rescue American citizens and foreign nationals stranded in Indian territory due to the natural disaster. Strings were pulled to get permission, but no assets in the region are on offer as they're all committed to the humanitarian crisis. Unofficially, Washington doesn't want us involved, but with who the professors are, and their track record, strings were pulled from multiple directions. Bottom line is, you're on your own. You could be going in there with no way out. Are you interested?"

Dawson didn't hesitate. "Absolutely."

"Then pick your team and report to the Unit ASAP. The sooner we get you on the other side of the planet, the sooner we can save the professors and the others, as well as this defenseless uncontacted tribe."

Clancy rose and Dawson and Maggie followed. The colonel extended a hand and Dawson took it. "Thank you, Sergeant Major. I knew I could count on you."

"Always, Colonel." Dawson closed the door after Clancy and Maggie hugged him.

"You be careful."

He winked at her. "Aren't I always?"

She glanced down at his now healed leg. "You and I both have different definitions of being careful."

He gave her a kiss and pulled out his phone. "Let me get the team together. You go to the bedroom."

"Why?"

He ripped his shirt off and dropped his shorts. "Somebody wants to say goodbye."

Yacht Wreck

North Sentinel Island

Andaman Islands, India

Pritam cocked an ear and tossed the gold bar onto the sand with a thud. "Silence!"

His excited men, all holding gold bars found in a flooded hold, fell silent, the gunfire he thought he had heard in the distance now distinct. "Shasi's in trouble!" He pointed toward the forest. "Let's go!"

Gold bars dropped all around him and they raced into the forest and the darkness to save their comrade. He wasn't worried about the gold— it would be there when they got back. There was no one to take it. All he cared about right now was finding the bastards responsible for their current situation. If those Americans hadn't stolen the gold and put it on their boat, none of them would be here now. They would be safely back home, counting their riches.

Though deep down, he knew that wasn't true. The tsunami they were hit by definitely also hit the island he called home, and if that were the case, they might have died if they had been outside and exposed. He frowned as he charged through the trees toward the cliff face he was convinced was hiding those he sought. His home might be gone, his friends dead, and when this was all over, they might have nothing to go back to. But that gold could change things. If he wanted to be worshiped, then rebuilding his neighborhood was one way to guarantee it.

The drums in the distance continued their pounding, reminding him of what that meant. If home were gone, there would be no one to search for them. They could be here for days, weeks, or months. He had checked the gash in the hull of the Americans' boat, and it might be possible to repair it, but it would take time, and would be a risk to put out to sea.

A risk he wasn't willing to take.

The safer bet was to build a boat or a raft of some sort to save themselves, but he was quite certain none of them had the knowledge. He smiled slightly, the drums suggesting a solution. The natives would know how. Surely, they had the expertise to build at least rafts, and would have the tools. When he was finished with the Americans, they would seek out the natives in the morning and force them to do their bidding.

As he sprinted through the trees, his mind raced with the possibilities. They could be here for some time. Once they subdued the natives then put them to work and exploited their resources, life here could perhaps be quite comfortable. A smile spread. In a place like this, he could be king. With the natives enslaved to do his bidding, he would be all-powerful. His heart slammed a little harder with the thought of it. Power, control, both men and women doing his bidding. The smile spread even further.

The women.

Perhaps escaping this place wasn't the urgent necessity he had thought.

Jara's Cavern

North Sentinel Island

Andaman Islands, India

Acton reached the cliff face and spotted someone waving to him from the hidden opening. He sprinted toward them and plunged into the darkness.

"I'm glad you made it, Professor." It was Mai. He gave her a one-armed hug.

"You're not the only one. Is everybody ready?" he asked as they continued through the narrow pathway.

"Yes, sir. But everybody's wondering where we're going to go."

"I don't know. All I know is we have to get out of here." He emerged into the cavern, lit by several candles. Everything that hadn't been consumed in their brief stay was bundled up. Laura rushed forward and gave him a hug.

"We're ready."

He glanced over at their native guide. "Does he have any idea what's going on?"

"I haven't had much time to communicate with him, though through context, I think he understands. He heard the gunfire and has seen our reaction to it."

Acton smiled at Jara, careful not to bare his teeth. Jara smiled back then scurried closer to them, sitting on his haunches as if to show subservience. Acton extended a hand and the young man took it. Acton gently pulled him to his feet, wanting him to know he was an equal here. Jara smiled, revealing some teeth, then pointed at the entrance and waved his finger at everyone, then walked them across his opposite palm.

Acton nodded. "Yes, we're all leaving."

Jara darted for the exit, beckoning them to follow.

Acton looked at Laura and Jannarkar. "What do you think?"

"He seems earnest," said Laura. "And it's not like we have much choice."

"He could be leading us to our deaths, but we'll certainly be dead if we remain here," agreed Jannarkar.

"Then it's settled." Acton clapped his hands together. "Okay, people, let's follow our friend and hope he knows somewhere else we can hide. Everybody keep quiet and remember, if we have to, we retreat to the water."

Laura followed Jara with her weapon ready, and the others lined up to follow. Acton took up the rear with Jannarkar, who gave him a weak smile.

"Thank you, Jim. No matter what happens, thank you."

Acton slapped him on the back. "I'm not doing anything you wouldn't do if the roles were reversed. Now, let's get the hell out of here."

Jannarkar said nothing, instead plunging into the narrow passageway. Acton soon emerged into the night and followed the long line of survivors across the cliff face, Jara and Laura already out of sight around a bend. He could hear the approaching enemy's footfalls in the forest, the armed hostiles making no attempt at a stealthy approach. It had him thinking that whatever their intentions were, they would be extremely violent, and he feared for those he was responsible for, especially the women.

He gripped his weapon tighter, wondering what his responsibility was to these people. Should he fight to the last bullet then hand to hand, hopelessly outgunned and outnumbered, or should he preserve the ammo to prevent the inevitable. He shook his head as he followed Jannarkar. He had no right to play God, he had no right to kill those he was responsible for. He had to remember there was always hope. Tommy was out there on the water. They could come across another ship at any moment, a ship that would have communications capabilities to call for help.

Milton knew where they were, or at least had been. There was no way he hadn't already reached out for help, help that could already be on the way, help perhaps only minutes or hours away. Who was he to be the executioner of these innocent people, when even if they endured hell for a few hours, might be saved to live long, fulfilling lives?

He sighed as he rounded a bend, the cliff face abruptly tapering into the ground. His eyes burned at the thought of Laura and Mai and what might be done to them should they be captured, and it made him all the more determined to protect them. He came to a stop and fell back toward the cliff face, peering around the edge of the stone. Half a dozen men emerged from the forest, then another dozen, all armed, heading directly for the cliff face. It was clear they had no idea where the cavern was, but they were spreading out and would eventually find it, an always inevitable outcome, though he had hoped it would be the light of day that would have disclosed their position after they were long gone.

He retreated carefully, making certain to not reveal their escape route. The others were out of sight now, but he knew the general direction. He kept moving forward, continually picking up speed, peering into the dark as he struggled to hear the telltale signs of the others.

"Jim." A voice quietly called out at him that he recognized as Jannarkar. He slowed up and saw a hint of a silhouette ahead. Jannarkar reached out for him, taking him by the arm. "I thought we'd lost you."

"No, I was just checking to make sure we weren't being followed."

"And?"

"We're not, for the moment, but they've arrived at the cliff face. We left just in time. Where are the others?"

"They've been following the edge of this hill, so they should be just ahead."

"Then let's go. Last thing we need is to lose them."

Jannarkar led the way and Acton followed, continually checking over his shoulder for any signs of pursuit.

"Professors, over here." The accent was thick and Acton presumed it was one of Jannarkar's students. They followed the voice and the young man opened his mouth to explain when Acton cut him off.

"We'll talk when we're safe."

The young man nodded then led the way. A few hundred feet later, another voice whispered at them and they made a beeline for it, the process repeated several more times. Apparently, the group had noticed they were missing and had wisely left the trail of human breadcrumbs.

That sounds like Laura's doing.

Finally, Laura's distinct voice whispered to their right. "Over here."

The now large group joined her, and she pointed just to her left. "On your hands and knees and crawl through the hole. It goes for about twenty feet, then it opens up. The others are already inside." The students headed in first, then Jannarkar. Acton gave her a hug and a kiss, then she scrambled into the narrow opening. He followed, immediately feeling claustrophobic.

This was an opening Jara and his people might be comfortable in with their slight frames, but for the Caucasian male physique, it was a bit too tight for his liking. Instead, he focused on the literal light at the end of the tunnel. He could see the flickering of candles rapidly approaching as everyone wiggled their way through on their bellies. He emerged into another cavern, not as large as the previous, but large enough and hopefully impossible to find.

Acton turned to Mai. "Headcount?"

"Now that you're here, nine people. Everyone's accounted for." She paused, her eyes wide. "Tommy?"

"He and Amit got away safely. They'll be fine." He gave her another one-armed hug. "You might be interested to know that he saved my life."

Her eyes glistened as she beamed with pride. "He did?"

"Yes, but I'll let him tell you the story when you see him." He grinned. "It will probably be much more spectacular by the time he does."

She giggled. "I have no doubt a zombie or two will make it into the story."

Acton chuckled. "You're probably right." He let her go and turned to find Jara huddled in the farthest recesses once again. He walked over to the young man that had once again found them shelter. He knelt in front of him and placed his hands against his chest. "Thank you very much for helping us."

Jara stared at him, saying nothing. Acton gave him a smile then rose and returned to the others.

"It's cramped in here and a little low, but our friends outside shouldn't be able to track us," said Laura.

He agreed. "And I can't see them possibly finding that entrance, so we should be safe here."

Mai put a damper on the optimism. "But what about Tommy and Amit? They don't know where we are."

Laura put a hand on Mai's shoulder, giving it a gentle squeeze. "No, they don't. In the morning, we're going to have to start a watch at the coast. For now, I suggest we all try to get some rest."

Acton turned to the group. "I want everybody to hydrate and get some food into them."

"What about bathroom breaks?" asked Nandini.

Acton chewed his cheek for a moment. "Anybody need to go number two?"

Head shakes around the room had him relieved, but these were tight quarters and the air was already stagnant. Urinating in here would quickly turn the place into a college bar bathroom.

"What about the water bottles?" asked Mai. "When they're empty, perhaps we could use those?"

Acton shook his head. "No, we're going to need to refill those with fresh water, perhaps for days or weeks." He sighed as he looked at Laura. "Who knew it would be our bladders that would be our undoing?"

She smirked. "I'm just glad you didn't eat Mexican last night."

He grinned. "Let's agree now that nobody gets to be banished because of their bodily functions."

Laura turned to the others. "Being familiar with my husband's bodily functions, I highly suggest none of you agree to those terms." Snickers filled the cave, the first universal relief expressed since they arrived on the shores of this forbidden island.

"Professor, what about this?"

Acton turned to see Daivik near the rear of the cave, pointing at the floor. Everyone walked over to see what he had found. A small stream, if it could even be called that, was running across the ground and draining through a hole in the wall. It appeared to be a natural spring. He took a knee and filled his palm then took a sip, swishing it in his mouth, detecting no salt. "This is fresh water." He gave Daivik a fist bump. "Good job. You just solved two problems. Okay, people." He pointed toward the source. "We refill our water bottles from this end, we do our

182

number ones at that end. Everyone try to have as good an aim as possible. I realize that might be more of a challenge for the ladies."

Laura grunted. "I've seen our bathroom floor, and it's never been my pee that's been on it."

Acton grinned sheepishly. "Unless there were witnesses, I deny everything."

"Uh-huh."

More snickers.

Acton swiftly changed the subject. "One problem solved. Now, everybody try to get some sleep. Laura and I will take first watch and try to solve the number two problem."

Blankets were laid out then the students paired off as the professors huddled near the entrance.

"What are we going to do?" asked Jannarkar. "There's no way we can survive in here for any great length of time."

Acton blew air out through his lips, causing them to vibrate. "We've got fresh water, shelter, but you're right, as soon as someone needs to go to the bathroom for real, we're going to have to start rotating people outside to do their business, and that means we can be discovered. And eventually, we're going to run out of food. Now, we can go a couple of weeks without eating. It would be brutal, but we'd survive as long as we stayed hydrated. But it's pretty damn cold in here, and that's going to weaken our systems. We need to be able to build a fire for warmth or at least be outside during the day to soak up some sun." He turned back to the chamber. "Put out all the candles except one." His instructions were immediately followed.

"We need to keep those candles going as long as we can if we're going to be stuck in here. It's one thing to be in here like this, it's a totally other thing to be in the pitch dark for a week or two."

"What about trying to establish contact with one of the local tribes?" suggested Laura.

Jannarkar shook his head vehemently. "They'd kill us without hesitation."

She nodded toward Jara, already asleep. "He would seem to suggest otherwise."

Jannarkar regarded him. "While I have to admit I'm surprised at his willingness to help for the moment, I have to assume it's merely out of self-preservation. He realized he stood no chance alone against those men. Put him with ten or twenty of his brethren, and his attitude could rapidly change."

Acton had to agree. "You're right. We can't risk it. We have to try and stay as isolated as we can until we're rescued."

"Days or weeks," sighed Jannarkar.

"Or months," added Acton. "There's just no way to know. That tsunami that hit was large, but we have no idea how far it went. If it were just local, then we can expect plenty of help in the area, but if it was a repeat of the Boxing Day Tsunami, the entire region could be devastated and we'll be way down the priority list even if Tommy manages to get us help. At the moment, our best hope might be some friends of ours that I have no doubt have been contacted by now."

"Who are these friends?" asked Jannarkar. "You mentioned them before."

Acton shook his head. "Well-connected friends that I can't talk about."

"And they can help?"

"They can if they get permission or are resourceful enough. We just don't know what's happening on the shores of the Indian Ocean. All the assets they might be able to use on a normal day could be tied up. And depending on where they are and what they're doing, they might not be able to come for days or weeks regardless. We have to be prepared to settle in for the long run."

Laura looked around. "I just can't see it, James."

He had to agree. He had little doubt he and Laura could tough it out with Mai, but he didn't know these other students, and he didn't know Jannarkar well enough either. Were they mentally tough enough to hold out? He wasn't sure, and he didn't want to bet all their lives on whether one or more of the students would panic or go mad in the dark, revealing their position to those seeking them. He glanced at the three automatic weapons they now possessed and the limited ammo sitting against the wall. "We know they found our boat, which means they found the gold. Other than revenge, they have no reason to seek us out anymore."

"Revenge can be a strong motivator," said Laura.

"Agreed. But are they willing to leave the gold?"

"What do you mean?"

"Right now, we're too close to them. If we were to move, say, south, just a few miles, would they be willing to risk leaving the gold behind just for revenge? I'm thinking they would just stay put and let us go."

Laura's head slowly bobbed. "I think that's a fairly reasonable assumption, but what about the natives?"

Acton frowned, glancing at the weapons. "With those guns, we could defend ourselves, but it might mean killing natives who are completely innocent in all of this. I don't know about you, but I think I'd rather die than kill innocent people."

Jannarkar sighed. "It's quite the moral dilemma we've found ourselves in. Stay here and perhaps go mad, venture outside and either die at the hands of people who know no better, or protect ourselves by killing those ignorant souls." He frowned. "And in the end, we might die regardless, because we may run out of bullets before they run out of people."

Acton shook his head. "It's an impossible choice. If we knew there were another shelter away from here, then I would say let's move there so that at least we're farther away from our pursuers. But without a destination, it's too risky." He chewed his cheek then held up a hand. "Here's my proposal. We stay in here. Tomorrow morning, we'll scout out the area a little bit better to see if we can find a location for a latrine that's out of sight, start searching for foodstuffs, and see if we can make this place a little more comfortable. We'll have to find a blind or set up one to watch for a rescue team. I think we're going to have to try to tough it out here for as long as possible, and pray that Tommy and Amit are successful in finding help, or our friends are in bringing it. Agreed?"

Laura and Jannarkar both nodded. "It's as good a plan as any," said Jannarkar.

"And it can always be revised," added Laura.

"Good," said Acton. "Now, I'll take the first watch. You guys go to sleep."

Jannarkar waved a hand, dismissing the idea. "No, you two have done enough. It's my turn. You get some sleep. You're clearly the brains of this operation, and there's a lot to do in the morning. I'll take the first watch. Like you said, the likelihood of them finding us is slim to none."

Acton patted his friend on the shoulder, giving him a smile. "Thank you, my friend. I'm too tired to protest, but if you find yourself getting sleepy or you hear anything, don't hesitate to wake us."

"You can count on it."

Acton found a spot with Laura and the two of them huddled on the last blanket. He wasn't even certain if he could have counted to ten before he was out like a light.

Bay of Bengal

Tommy stared out at the horizon, searching for signs of anything on the water beside themselves. Acton had said land should be 25 miles due east, but without a motor, it would take a long time. He glanced over his shoulder to check how far they had managed to go, and if it were more than a couple of miles in the past several hours, he'd be stunned. He spotted something and his eyes narrowed as his paddling slowed.

Amit glanced over at him. "What's wrong?"

"Look."

They both stopped and turned to face the shore. Two large bonfires were visible on the beach, the larger of the two near where he would guess their shipwreck was.

"Do you think they're burning the boats?" asked Amit.

"I can't see the guys who are chasing us burning a boat loaded with gold that they might be able to repair in time."

"Maybe the natives did it."

"That would be more likely, but look." He pointed to their right. "What do you think that is?"

Amit leaned forward, squinting at the sight of at least a dozen moving small fires. "Torches?"

Tommy's jaw dropped in recognition. "Ahh, that must be it."

"But would the natives use torches? Wouldn't it give away their position?"

Tommy shrugged. "I don't know. They might be thinking that with those large fires, their enemies can't see them."

"What do you know about these natives?"

Tommy's eyebrows rose as he smirked at Amit. "I would have thought you'd be telling me."

Amit grunted. "I'm only first year. I don't really know much. When I was chosen to come, I just read up on the Andaman Islands, and when I saw that this island was forbidden, I figured there was no way we'd end up here, so I skipped that chapter."

Tommy grinned at him. "I bet you're regretting that now, hey?"

Amit chuckled. "Yeah, a little bit." He turned back around and dipped his oar in the water. "So, do you know anything about the natives?"

Tommy resumed paddling. "As a matter of fact, the professors filled us in on the whole area during the two-day boat ride here."

"Well, two days sounds about right. How about you fill me in? It might help pass the time."

"Fine, but it's pretty dry."

Amit grunted. "With everything that's been happening, dry sounds good."

"Well, first things first. They're not exactly an uncontacted tribe. Apparently, a couple of hundred years ago—"

A brilliant flash on the horizon ahead silenced Tommy. It was obviously the volcano, and now that he had a bearing on it, he could see the thick black smoke blotting out the stars ahead. It had him doubting the task at hand. "Should we really be going toward that?"

Amit jerked a thumb over his shoulder. "If we go that way, we're looking at over a thousand kilometers."

"There's nothing else in between?"

Amit shook his head. "No. The only hope we would have would be to find another vessel." He gestured toward the erupting volcano. "We don't have a choice. We either return to the island we just left, or we continue forward."

"And if there's another tsunami?"

"If it's powerful enough to make it across the entire island, then it probably would have killed us anyway. We got lucky because we were in a good boat with a skilled pilot, far enough away from the coast that most of the power had been taken away." Amit sighed. "But I don't really know what I'm talking about now, do I?" His shoulders sagged and he stopped paddling. "I just wish I had never agreed to come on this trip." His shoulders heaved as he turned to Tommy. "Am I ever going to see my family again?"

Tommy's chest tightened as he pictured Mai. Until her, his heart had only ever experienced crushes, but never love. She had changed his life, and he couldn't imagine her not in it, and he hoped she felt the same. He reached out and squeezed Amit's shoulder. "You will." He pointed toward the horrors ahead. "We just need to get to that island and call for help."

Amit clasped a hand over Tommy's. "Then let's do this."

They both put their oars back in the water and struck a steady rhythm, the flickering of the sky ahead giving them a bearing.

"Now, you were saying that something happened a couple hundred years ago?"

Tommy smiled then laid out the history as he remembered it, related to him over the past two days crossing the Bay of Bengal, and why the inhabitants of North Sentinel island so distrusted outsiders.

Over the Atlantic Ocean

Dawson, Niner, Atlas, Spock, Jimmy, and Jagger sat across from each other in the specially modified Gulfstream G650 business jet as it reached cruising altitude, their thirteen-hour journey to the other side of the world only just beginning. The gentle gong indicated it was safe to move around the cabin, and an Air Force flight attendant appeared.

"If you gentlemen need anything, just let me know," he said.

Dawson looked at the others. "Round of waters?" Heads bobbed in agreement.

"I'll get right on it." The Airman disappeared in the back and Sergeant Carl "Niner" Sung put a foot up on the table.

"So, what the hell did I volunteer for? If our destination is the Indian Ocean, then I have to guess that somehow the professors triggered that volcanic eruption."

Sergeant Leon "Atlas" James grunted. "Knowing them, if they did, they'd just ride that tsunami to safety."

192

Everyone chuckled, the exploits of their academic friends well known among Bravo Team. Dawson cocked an eyebrow and Sergeant Will "Spock" Lightman threw one up even higher, reclaiming the podium. "You'd be surprised that some of what you just said is somewhat accurate."

Niner eyed him. "Huh, which part?"

"They were in the area on a yacht."

"Must be nice to be rich." Niner shook his head. "One of these days, Acton's luck is going to run out."

"You just won't stop holding out hope that he buys it one of these days so you can move in on his old lady," rumbled Atlas with his impossibly deep voice.

Niner shrugged. "She deserves to be happy."

"And you think that lovely lady will be willing to settle for a pathetic amoeba like you?"

"Amoeba?"

"Yeah, it's a single-celled—"

"I know what an amoeba is. I'm just wondering if you're calling me that because you think I have the mental capacity of a single-celled organism, or that it's the smallest thing you could think of."

Atlas shrugged. "A little from Column A, a little from Column B, I would think."

Niner slapped the impossibly muscled man on the arm. "That was one of your better ones. Usually, you just go for the lowbrow, but I think you upped your game by incorporating a little bit of science."

Atlas grinned. "Vanessa's big on the Discovery Channel."

Dawson cleared his throat. "If you two ladies are done, I'd like to continue."

Both men bowed with a flourish in their seats. "You may continue, my good sergeant major," said Niner.

"Thank you. So, as I was saying, they were on their yacht when the volcano erupted. From what we've been able to piece together, mostly from information from Dean Gregory Milton, they had been at a fundraiser in India and received a last-minute invite to go to a dig site on the Andaman Islands, where an old shipwreck had been found. They arrived the morning of the eruption and several hours later were on the boat. We're estimating they were only on land for several hours, which doesn't make sense. You know how the professors are. Even if the shipwreck proved to be unimportant, they would still stick around."

Niner chuckled. "If they found a nail on the beach, they'd be setting up a major operation to determine whether it was from Home Depot or a Spanish galleon."

Snickers.

Dawson continued. "Thomas Granger and Mai Trinh were on this vacation with them, and we presume were on the boat, but there was also a group of other survivors, we believe at least seven in total."

Spock's eyebrow shot up again. "Eleven people? How big is this yacht?"

"Not that big. That suggests they were on there for some special reason. And if it were only a few hours after arriving, it suggests something went wrong on the island and they were fleeing. Just before they were hit by the tidal wave, or I guess tsunami—"

194

Niner's hand shot up. "What's the difference?"

Dawson tilted his head at him. "When we get back home, you can call your daddy and have him pull Volume T from his Encyclopedia Britannica set and ask him."

Niner shrunk back in his chair and leaned closer to Atlas. "How'd he know my dad has a set of Britannica?"

Atlas' eyebrows shot up. "Your father still has a set of encyclopedia? Why doesn't he just use Wikipedia?"

"Umm, because it took him twenty-six months to get that set, and there's no way in hell he's throwing it out, even if they stopped doing the annual updates years ago." Niner noticed Dawson staring at him. "Umm, you weren't done?"

"Nice try. As I was saying, Professor Acton was on the phone with Dean Milton when the wave hit, so we know from tracing the call exactly where they were. Langley managed to track the phone and still has a location on it, but it's not being answered, so we think the phone was thrown clear. They used the new position of the phone, and now have satellite footage of the professor's yacht on the eastern coast of North Sentinel Island, just to the west of their original location, with eleven survivors."

"So, this is a rescue op?" asked Spock.

"It is in part."

"In part?"

"The professors and whoever is with them aren't the only survivors. We found three other boats wrecked with about twenty armed hostiles, and there have already been multiple engagements between them and the professors."

Everyone leaned forward, Atlas voicing their concern. "And the result?"

"At this point, as far as we can tell, Professor Acton has removed two hostiles from the equation, and Professor Palmer, one."

Niner grinned at Atlas. "I would have thought my girl would be ahead." Fist bumps were exchanged.

Sergeant Eugene "Jagger" Thomas raised a finger. "I still don't see why we're going in. Why can't the Indians handle this themselves?"

"They've got their hands full. Their entire eastern coast has been devastated, and it's complicated because of where they shipwrecked. They're trying to send us a couple of choppers and some crew, but there are no guarantees they'll get there in time to be of any help."

Niner eyed him. "There's something you're not telling us. This doesn't make sense."

Dawson frowned at him. "Perhaps if you stopped interrupting, I'd have been able to tell you."

Niner wagged a finger. "It's a poor chef that blames his ingredients."

Spock's eyebrow shot up. "What the hell does that have to do with this?"

Niner shrugged. "Hey, I couldn't think of the right metaphor."

"So, you thought you should just throw any old one out there?"

Niner shrugged. "I had to say something."

"And here we go again," groaned Dawson.

Atlas slapped a meaty hand over Niner's mouth. "Go ahead, BD. If he says anything, I'll just squeeze."

Niner's eyes bulged.

Dawson leaned forward. "Here's the bottom line. The professors and this group are alive on the island. There were twenty armed hostiles, now apparently seventeen, but their luck is going to run out. But that's not the problem. North Sentinel Island is a forbidden island."

"Forbidden island?" mumbled Niner.

Atlas squeezed and Niner held up his hands in surrender.

"Yes, forbidden island. There's an uncontacted tribe there, and it's actually a crime to come within five miles of the coastline. Anyone who arrives is usually viciously attacked. One of our more idiotic countrymen attempted to visit them several years back. He was warned away twice, came back a third time, and they killed him."

Niner raised a finger and Dawson waved his hand, giving him permission to speak. Atlas removed his paw. "Did they cook him?" The hand was slapped back over Niner's mouth.

"No. From the briefing notes I have received from Langley, they apparently buried him, which would suggest they respect their enemies, but don't want anyone interfering with their lives. From what I've read in the file, their encounters with outsiders have usually not gone well for them throughout history, so they appear to have adopted a policy of shoot first, ask questions later."

"So, we're concerned they might attack the survivors?" asked Spock.

"Yes, that's a concern, but that's not why we're going in. With the natural disaster, most resources in the area are being tasked to help where there are the most victims. Eleven survivors on a remote island is extremely low on the priority list when they've got millions upon millions of people affected. And that includes our own resources. All of our assets in the region are devoted to humanitarian relief, and even Washington wasn't willing to send people in, despite the fact at least three of those eleven people are American citizens."

"What changed their mind?"

"Genocide."

Five eyebrows cocked.

"Genocide?" mumbled Niner. Atlas removed his hand.

"Yes. Apparently, there are only a few hundred of these natives left on the island. The concern is that they're going to attempt to engage the armed hostiles, and they've never encountered automatic weapons before, nor an enemy that is willing to fight back. It appears as if at least fifty natives are gathering in the vicinity. If they engage the armed hostiles, they could be wiped out. Washington's concern is that if there are only a couple hundred left on the island, and fifty or sixty males are slaughtered in the prime of their life, it could devastate the population and it might never recover. It could eliminate them completely."

Niner blasted air through his lips. "Man, when you hear the word genocide, you never think in such low numbers."

"No, but it was enough to convince Washington that something needed to be done about it. The Colonel offered us up, and Kane somehow pulled some strings with his contacts in India to get the limited amount of help on offer."

Sergeant Gerry "Jimmy Olsen" Hudson finally chimed in. "So, let me get this straight. There are six of us, twenty armed hostiles, and fifty-plus natives hellbent on killing us."

"Yes."

"I'm not sure I like those odds."

"It gets worse. Rules of engagement for the armed hostiles are that we can take them out without hesitation the moment they fire on us. It's the natives that are the problem. They'll probably see us as hostiles as well, and could engage. Under no circumstances are we to kill them, even if they're about to kill us. It's the mission. If we end up killing them, we'll be the ones committing genocide. We need to get in, eliminate the hostiles, rescue the professors, and then get out."

Spock leaned back and folded his arms. "Is this some sort of Prime Directive thing, like we're not supposed to let them see us or any of that sort of thing because we could impact their culture?"

Niner snorted. "Leave it to you to come up with the Star Trek reference."

Spock gave him a look. "Hey, I didn't give myself this damn name."

"Then you shouldn't have been cocking your eyebrow so damn much."

"Okay, Beaver." Niner flipped Spock the bird at the mention of his previous callsign.

"No, it isn't," continued Dawson. "The natives are well aware that we exist and have seen our technology before. They just don't want us there, so our mission is to get in and get out. It doesn't matter if we're seen. It doesn't matter if we scare them with some well-placed weapons fire. All that matters is that we prevent any of them from getting killed, and that includes by us."

"So then, what's the plan?" asked Atlas.

"You saw the HALO gear we loaded?"

Atlas smiled. "Don't tell me."

"Yup. We're heading in first. Our Indian friends couldn't promise when they'd be there, so it was decided the six of us on the ground would be the best way to at least protect our people."

Spock shook his head. "They might know we're out there, but if they see six demons dropping from the sky, breathing hellfire upon the land, it could affect their culture for generations."

Dawson shrugged. "One man's demon is another man's angel. Hopefully, by our deeds, they'll know which one."

Atlas jerked a thumb at Niner. "We could always stick him in the wedding dress he's already got picked out for himself."

Everyone roared with laughter as Niner batted a hand. "You be careful now. I also packed those bridesmaids' dresses I picked out for you."

Atlas eyed him. "Sometimes, I just don't know when you're joking."

On board the Norham Castle

Northwest of Krakatoa

August 31, 1883

Sampson stared at what the lookout had spotted in the distance, and he wasn't certain if he could believe his eyes. They had seen nothing but death and destruction since this calamity began, and he had been so convinced the world was ending and that he would never see his family again, he had given up all hope. Yet in the distance, if his eyes were to be believed, a light shone brightly on the horizon, stretching for as far as the eye could see.

He glanced over his shoulder and spotted Smithers. "Doctor, come here and look at this!"

Smithers hurried over and took a sip from his flask, too many of the crew having embraced their vices with the end so near. "What?"

Sampson pointed into the distance. "Tell me what you see?"

Smithers steadied himself on the railing and peered ahead then squinted harder. "What am I looking at?"

"You tell me."

Smithers pursed his lips. "I see a light."

"What do you make of it?"

"We're all going to die, so I would suggest we head for the light so we can be done with this entire horrid affair. The sooner the better, I say!" Smithers stumbled off below decks, leaving Sampson to shake his head. He turned to the lookout in the crow's nest above.

"What do you make of it?"

"I think it's sunlight, sir! Like at the outer edge of a storm!"

Sampson smiled. For that was exactly how he interpreted what he was seeing. If there were sunlight ahead, then it meant either the calamity hadn't spread across the entire world, or this indeed was just something natural rather than biblical, and his wife and children were still out there, waiting for him.

He headed for the bridge and gave the order. "Make your course north-by-northwest." He pointed ahead. "Straight toward the sun!"

Cave of the Great Mother

The Blessed Land

Present Day

Jara woke with a start then noticed the water at his feet. He sat up, his eyes surveying the cavern as he remembered where he was and why. The intruders were all asleep, including the man at the entrance whom he presumed was supposed to be standing watch. Despite the fact these people had helped him, he still didn't trust them. They were the Outsiders, the invaders. His people told stories, some from only years ago, others from generations ago, and they rarely ended well for his people. Outsiders arriving on their shores and taking, killing, bringing disease. He had seen the ruins of empty villages that had once housed many of his people, but they were few now. The Island had once teemed with life, swarming with his proud people, masters of every corner.

But now, there were only a few scattered villages.

What if these people brought another sickness, despite their good intentions? What if others heard they had been treated with kindness? Others could follow in greater numbers. He had no idea what lay beyond the reef that surrounded his home. Legend had it that in the time of his great-great-grandfathers, invaders had come and taken several elders and children that hadn't escaped in time. The children were returned sometime later, diseased. Soon after the children succumbed to whatever illness the invaders had given them, untold numbers died.

According to the oral history he had been told, those two children were the only members of his people to have ever left the island and returned. The gods had meant them to stay here, to make this their home. And his people had learned the hard way that the Outsiders weren't to be trusted, even those that had pretended to come in peace, leaving offerings of strange fruit and other trinkets.

They were always betrayed.

Why couldn't the Outsiders simply understand that they wanted to be left alone? Unless their intentions weren't pure. If the animal bites you when you try to pet it and then bites you again when you try once more, even a child knows the creature doesn't want to be pet and moves on. Yet the Outsiders kept returning. Despite being attacked, despite being killed, they never learned the lesson. It had to mean they wanted something if they were so foolish to keep coming back.

He had seen the shipwreck, so he knew these people he was with now weren't here by choice, and might indeed have pure intentions. It was who might follow that he feared. He faced an impossible choice. He could warn them of what was about to happen, but then they would leave the cave, and if his people found them, they would be merciless. And every instinct he had, every lesson taught since he was a child, had him certain he would join with his tribesmen and slaughter those who slept peacefully only an arm's length away.

Yet if they stayed here, they would surely die as well. Not by his hand, but by the hand of the Great Mother herself. This was her domain, not the domain of his tribe who merely borrowed it from time to time with her blessing.

He rose, casting his eyes over the others.

Let the gods decide their fate. I want no part of it.

He stepped past the sleeping guard then scrambled out the tunnel, breathing in the fresh air and letting the sun bake on his skin for a few moments, a smile spreading as he listened to the waves crashing nearby, high tide on its way in.

Let the gods decide their fate.

Yacht Wreck

North Sentinel Island

Andaman Islands, India

Pritam stared at the pile of gold stacked neatly on the beach. It was more money than he could have ever imagined. He had no idea how much each bar was worth, but it had to be in the millions of rupees. However much it was, would change the balance of power on the streets. And it was his. Yet for the moment, it might as well be a pile of worthless rocks, since there was nowhere to spend the money on this forsaken island. No one was coming to rescue them, and even if they were, they would never let them keep the gold. They would have to kill the rescuers and take whatever vessel they came in to save themselves.

But that was merely a fantasy scenario. No rescuers were coming because no one knew they were here, and no one would think to even look. They had to save themselves. He wasn't sure where they were on the island, though the volcanic eruption visible on the horizon from the beach suggested they were on the eastern coast. Home was barely a stone's throw away. If the boat they had been chasing were functional, they could be there in about an hour with their winnings.

He sighed.

So close, yet so far.

The yacht's engine roared to life, startling them all, and he spun toward the boat to see the shallow water churning, one propeller out of the water, spinning freely. The engine fell silent and one of his men, Nair, poked his head out from the wheelhouse. "The engine still works, boss. If the tide keeps coming in, we can push her over on her good side, then see if we can patch the hole. We just might be able to get the hell out of here."

Pritam suppressed his relief. He couldn't show any sign of weakness despite his desperate fear. The drums continued to pound in the distance. He wasn't certain if it were his imagination playing tricks on him, but he could swear they sounded closer than they had during the night. These natives could attack at any moment, and the longer they were here, the weaker they would become. He was already desperately thirsty, as were the others. It would soon become a problem, yet it clearly wasn't for those who lived here. There was water here, they just had to know where it was. By tomorrow, they would be so thirsty, they wouldn't be able to concentrate. And in a couple of days, their lives would be at risk and they'd be in no state to repel any attack.

He muttered a curse. It was exactly what the natives wanted—keep them on the beach until they were overcome with thirst and hunger. He couldn't let that happen. He eyed the gold. The key to unlocking all of his dreams was sitting here on this beach, and only an hour away was where he could fulfill those dreams. But only if he were alive.

He pointed to Nair, the closest thing they had to a handyman, standing on the deck of what could be their salvation. "Do whatever it takes. I want that thing seaworthy today."

"Yes, sir."

Pritam turned to the others, stabbing a finger toward the forest. "Who's tired of hearing those damn drums?"

A chorus of "I am!" replied.

"So am I. We need water, we need food, and those primitive bastards have both. They sit hiding in the trees thinking they're intimidating us, but they're not, are they?"

This time, a chorus of "no."

"I say we take the fight to them. We remove the threat they pose, then take their water, take their food, then just for fun, take their women."

Hoots and hollers replied as the one incentive that always worked with his men was mentioned. And again, the thought of becoming king of this primitive land crossed his mind. He patted his weapon. "Everybody distribute the ammo evenly. We'll leave in five minutes."

He turned and stared out at the ocean and the violently erupting volcano on the horizon. So far, the wind hadn't carried the ash here, and he was forced to wonder whether he truly would be better off staying here and ruling this island relatively unscathed, rather than return to a home that might no longer exist. He eyed the boat. If they could make it seaworthy, they could return home, and if nothing were left, come back here.

Either way, he would be king, either of this island, or the streets where he grew up, no matter what the cost.

Jara's Second Cavern

North Sentinel Island

Andaman Islands, India

"James, wake up!"

Acton groaned then bolted upright. They were in the pitch dark and something was wrong. His entire side was wet. He scrambled to his feet as sounds of panic filled the cave, water sloshing around his ankles.

"Everybody wake up!" he ordered.

Laura turned on her cellphone, activating the flashlight function. She played it around the cavern and they both cursed at what they saw. There were at least six inches of water on the floor, and the cave entrance was even worse. More phones turned on, casting a dull glow around the entire cavern.

"What's going on?" asked Mai, her panic clear.

Acton ignored her and turned to Jannarkar. "When did this start?"

Jannarkar stared at the ground sheepishly. "I don't know. I'm sorry, Jim, but I fell asleep."

"Why didn't you wake us?"

"I thought you needed your rest. I thought I could stay awake."

Acton suppressed his frustration. There was no point in assigning blame. All that mattered now was saving themselves. They needed to get out of here fast. He knelt and scooped some of the water up and tasted it, spitting it out. "Salt water."

Laura's eyes narrowed. "Salt? You mean this is the tide coming in?"

"Yes. But why would..." He spun, finally realizing something he had missed—their native savior was gone. "The little shit set us up!"

Laura gasped as she, too, noticed Jara was missing. "You don't think he did this on purpose, do you?"

"If he didn't, where is he? He left while it was safe to go, leaving us here." Acton sliced the air with his hand. "There's no time to assign blame. We have to save ourselves." He pointed to the floor, now covered in murky water. "Somebody find the rope. I'm sure there was some in our supplies."

Daivik held it up. "Right here, Professor."

Acton grabbed one of the water bottles and downed the contents. "I'm going through to the other side to make sure it's still passable. It should be, but we don't know what our so-called friend did. He might have blocked the other end."

Laura pointed at the water bottle. "What's that for?"

"In case I can't hold my breath, I can at least exhale into this and then breathe it back in. It'll be mostly carbon dioxide, but it won't be water.

It should buy me a few more seconds." He quickly wrapped the rope between his hand and elbow, counting out the number of loops in his head, making sure it was long enough, then tied one end around his ankle and tossed the rest near the entrance. "If this stops playing out, then you pull on this rope and haul me back in. If you feel three tugs, then that means stop pulling, I'm okay. If I fail, someone else is going to have to try and get through. Tie it off at the other end, then everyone else uses the rope and the water bottles to pull yourself through."

"Why can't we just stay here?" asked Nandini. "Surely the water doesn't reach the top."

Acton shook his head. "The entrance is already blocked off. That means there's no fresh air getting in here. There are nine of us in here now. We'll use up all this air in no time. That's why it was so stale in here when we first arrived. We have to get out of here now."

"What about the supplies?" asked Mai.

"Forget them. Everybody drink a bottle of water to use it for your escape. Stuff your pockets with whatever you can, but don't be dragging anything behind you or bulking up too much, because if you get stuck, you'll kill everyone behind you." His eyes drifted around the room, making contact with every one of them. "Understood? If you try to take too much, you *will* kill everyone behind you." He gave Mai a hug and Laura a kiss, then dropped to his knees. "See you on the other side."

He took a deep breath, placed the water bottle in his mouth, gripping it with his teeth, then crawled into the flooded hole. If he felt claustrophobic the first time, it was nothing compared to this. He focused on the goal ahead, a light literally at the end of the tunnel. It was obviously daytime outside, and it gave him hope that the native who had betrayed them hadn't blocked the way.

As he thought about it, he couldn't blame the young man. He hadn't killed them in their sleep, he had merely abandoned them. He would have been raised to fear outsiders. He had probably been terrified the entire time, and as soon as Jannarkar had fallen asleep, had taken advantage of the first opportunity he had to escape and rejoin his people. But none of that mattered now. He just prayed that Jara didn't bring back his friends, because that would be the end of them all.

He scrambled forward, mostly using his elbows to get ahead, his fingers clawing at the sides as he struggled to calm himself, yet his heart insisted on pounding far faster than it needed to. And as panic set in, the light impossibly far ahead, his lungs were ready to explode. He kept moving forward, he kept making progress. He could sense the rope on his ankle that would save the others. It would be an easy passage from the cavern to the outside if he could just secure the rope, yet he had to make it first.

His lungs were about to give out, his pulse overwhelming in his ears, and finally, he could take it no more. He exhaled with a cry, then his lips instinctively wrapped around the end of the bottle, and he sucked in as much air as he could. He could hear the plastic collapse, providing him with little to none of the oxygen he needed. He exhaled again and gasped in again, forcing himself forward. He weakened, yet the light filled his vision, the end was almost there. The plastic bottle saving his life expanded and contracted repeatedly, faster and faster as his panic threatened to take over.

Then something changed. His hand was out of the water. He cried out in one final gasp, pulling with all of his might, pushing with his elbows, his knees, his toes, wriggling his entire body. His other hand, then his forearms, then his elbows felt the freedom. The top of his head broke through the surface and he spat out the bottle as he tilted his head to the side, the water running along his face, marking the distinct separation between life and death. And finally, his nose and lips made it clear as he spun over onto his back. He gasped in lungful after lungful of air, calming his hammering heart, his burning lungs settling, the stars he had begun to see fading away.

The rope tugged on his foot. He raised his knee toward his chest three times. Three gentle tugs replied, his message received. He took a moment then climbed out of the hole. A small tree was near the entrance. He tied the rope off, then gave three more tugs. Three tugs replied. He kept his hand on the rope as it became tauter, and he could tell someone was pulling themselves through. He watched, ready to grab their hand and pull them those last few feet. It seemed impossibly long, but he finally saw a hand on the rope. He reached forward and grabbed it, then hauled Nandini to safety.

She gasped for breath, though appeared in better shape than he had been, the rope doing its trick in cutting down the time it took to clear the short distance. He gave three tugs and three more replied.

"How are you doing?" he asked.

She coughed. "I'll be fine."

"Good." He pointed to a large tree nearby. "Get behind that and stay low. Keep your eyes out for any movement."

She nodded and scurried away. As the tugs on the rope continued, indicating the next person was making their way through, he secretly prayed it would be Laura, but he knew her. She would be the last. He grabbed the hand the moment it became visible and gasped in relief as Mai's face appeared. She grabbed on to him and hugged him hard, sobbing. As he held her with one arm and reached down and gave three tugs, waiting for the three in response before fully embracing her.

"You're safe now."

She pushed away and gave him a look as she wiped her eyes. "I'd hardly say we're safe, Professor."

He chuckled and patted her cheek. "You're right, of course. You're safe from that." He tilted his head toward the tunnel. He pointed to another tree nearby. "Get over there, stay low, keep an eye out for anything that moves or any sounds."

She gave him one last hug, then scampered over to her assigned lookout.

The process was repeated multiple times, and he was slightly miffed when Jannarkar appeared ahead of Laura, though the man likely had little choice. Laura finally appeared, gave him a hug, then turned around and pulled the rope through. One of the blankets appeared, cinched at one end, and they both reached in and yanked it clear.

"I thought I said no supplies," he admonished her with a smirk.

She shrugged. "I figured I was the last one, so let's take a chance." She untied the bundle, revealing their three weapons and all their ammo.

Jannarkar eyed what she had saved. "Why did you bring weapons? Why not food and water?"

Acton rolled his eyes, his frustration nearing the surface. "Because we don't need food to survive the next few days, and water we'll find. The most likely thing that's going to kill us are those armed men. We need to be able to defend ourselves if we're to survive this."

Jannarkar sighed heavily, apparently not pleased with the explanation.

Acton finally snapped. "What the hell is it this time, Ritesh? This is life and death. You need to start thinking logically. You haven't been since this started. I realize the loss of your wife is distracting you, but this has to stop. There'll be plenty of time to mourn later. You have five students here that are your responsibility, not mine, and you've done nothing to help them. I'm sorry for being so blunt, but you need to get it together. You put us in charge. If you're not happy with the way we're doing things, and you want to take back that responsibility, then so be it. What would you have us do next, Professor?"

Jannarkar stared at him, wide-eyed, shocked at the tongue-lashing. Everyone was staring at him, including his students. His shoulders collapsed in defeat as his chin sagged into his chest, his eyes closed. "No, Jim, you and Laura are doing an excellent job. This isn't what I do. I'm out of my element. I can't stop thinking about my wife, I can't stop thinking about what might be happening to my country." He looked up at Acton, his eyes red, swimming with tears. "I'm so ashamed. I'm so useless. I wish I were more like you, but I'm not. It's just not in my nature. I'm a teacher, a scientist. I'm not supposed to be running around with guns, hiding from blood-thirsty natives, trying to save students from a natural disaster that could be killing thousands." He gripped his forehead, squeezing at his temples. "I don't know what to do!"

The moment the words had escaped Acton's mouth, he had regretted them. He rarely lost control, especially with someone he knew. He should have bit his tongue, he should have kept his frustrations to himself, but he hadn't. He reached out and squeezed Jannarkar's shoulder. "I'm sorry, my friend. I'm as scared as you are, and I mourn along with you for your wife, and I fear for Tommy out on that ocean as I would fear for my own son. We're all going through something we never should have to, and we'll all react in our own unique ways. You have nothing to be ashamed of. Laura and I have been through things like this too many times to count, so we know what to do. It doesn't mean we're any braver than anyone else here. It's just that we have more experience. I shouldn't have snapped at you."

Jannarkar smiled. "It's okay, Jim. If the roles were reversed, I probably would have done the same thing." He sighed heavily. "I'll do whatever you say."

Acton chuckled. "Debate is fine, my friend, and even questioning my decisions is fine." He clenched a fist and held it up to Jannarkar's face with a smile. "But question Laura, and you get the knuckles."

Jannarkar laughed, then turned to his students. "I'm sorry for the way I've behaved. It's inexcusable."

The students nearest him rushed forward, denying his need to apologize and expressing their understanding.

Acton turned his attention to the weapons. He grabbed one then a third of the ammo. He turned to the group. "Has anybody ever handled an AK-47?"

Jivi held up a hand. "I have, Professor. I spent four years in America and my father became a bit of a gun nut. I've fired pretty much everything you can think of."

"Do you think you can kill a man?"

Jivi's confidence slipped. "I don't know. I hope so." She drew a loud breath. "I think so, if it's the choice between him or me, or him and one of us." She nodded firmly. "Yes, I think I can."

"I have no doubt." He held out the third AK-47 and two mags. She took them, then ably checked her weapon. She flicked the safety off.

Acton shook his head. "Keep the safety on and the weapon pointed at the ground at all times. If we're about to see action, turn the safety off but keep the weapon aimed at the ground unless we're in a firefight. And if we get in one, don't use full auto, just take single shots. We don't have any spare ammo." As he delivered the instructions, he could see she was getting tense. He smiled, patting her arm. "Don't worry, the whole point of this is to get away from the bad guys, not go toward them. Take a deep breath. You'll do fine."

Her chest swelled then she exhaled. "I'll be fine, Professor. You can count on me."

"Good." He rose, then pointed away from where the boats were wrecked. "Okay, everyone, we're going to head in this direction, away from those armed men. Everybody keep the chit-chat to a minimum. If you see anything that's edible, collect it but don't eat it. We need to check to make sure that whatever it is, it's safe. If you see any sign of fresh water, raise your hand." He pointed at the ground. "Everybody collect the empty water bottles that you used. Hopefully, we'll have them refilled before the end of the day."

Bottles were collected off the ground and Acton headed forward to take the lead, Laura remaining to cover the rear. He pointed at Jivi. "You stick with Laura."

Laura flashed her a smile.

They started forward, leaving their initial hiding place even farther behind, and Acton wondered how any rescuers that Tommy and Amit might bring would find them. He could see the devastation of the volcano on the horizon, and stared up at the heavens, saying a silent prayer of deliverance for those suffering from the effects of the massive natural disaster, for Tommy and Amit on the water, for those with them here now, and for the innocent natives of this forbidden land who faced their very own end of times, their own biblical Armageddon brought by the hell-spewing volcano that had deposited demons upon their shores in the form of the armed gang whom they now shared this small island paradise with, against their will.

God, please help us all.

Near the Cave of the Great Mother

The Blessed Land

Jara flipped over a rock and smiled, grabbing some tubers and tossing them in his mouth, chewing them with zeal. He was starving, and these were one of his favorite treats. He dipped his hand in the water of a small natural spring and quenched his thirst. He could have been back at his village by now, but he had to know the decision of the gods. A smile had spread the moment Laura's mate appeared, and then his teeth were fully revealed when Laura herself emerged, the last of the group.

The gods had decided that their lives were worthy of saving, and it had him wondering about the teachings. The gods were there to protect them from the Outsiders, and these people were clearly Outsiders. Why they had allowed them to live had him curious. Perhaps the gods had decided that his people didn't need protection from these particular ones. Perhaps it meant not all were to be feared.

He popped one final tuber in his mouth then rose, setting a direction for his village, for these were questions too large for someone of his station to ponder. That was for the elders. Perhaps they could make sense of what he had witnessed.

It was an interesting thing to think about. In his entire short life, the past day had been the most exciting of it. Life here was always hard and fairly routine. You would wake up, the women of the village would feed everyone, and then depending upon your particular skill set, you went off to do whatever you did every single day—hunting, fishing, gathering, mending, building. By the end of the day, if you weren't exhausted, you hadn't done your job well. The communal meal as the sun set, where stories were told, was always the most enjoyable. He loved sitting with his family, listening to a tale of an exciting hunt, of something spotted on the water or in the air from the Outsiders, or a tale passed down by their ancestors.

The gods provided for them as long as they put in the work. And though bellies were rarely stuffed, they were equally rarely empty. It was a good life, a peaceful life, as long as the Outsiders stayed away. As he made his way deeper inland, the trees felled by the wave that had hit yesterday were fewer, and he became hopeful his home might have been untouched. He glanced over his shoulder at the sky behind him and the thick billowing smoke that continued to fill it, strange flashes of varying colors racing along the underbelly of the unleashed beast. He had seen nothing like it before. The thick cloud of darkness was growing closer, and he had to wonder if surviving yesterday's calamity were merely a reprieve with the worst yet to come.

The elders told of the end of times when the evil of the outside world would finally overwhelm their shores. It would be the end of everything, the end of their home, the end of their way of life, the end of their existence on this world. However, as long as they kept their faith in the gods, they would be rewarded, and in the end, join their ancestors that now dwelled in the night sky, their weapons buried, their bellies full, and nothing but laughter to fill their days.

It was a wonderful thought, though he enjoyed his time here, and had no desire to leave this place any time soon.

A low rumble echoed over the land, the very ground he stood upon shaking for a moment, and he shivered as it occurred to him the choice might not be his to make.

Bay of Bengal

"I'm awake, I'm awake," protested Tommy as he opened his eyes. He immediately squeezed them shut, blinking several times, his eyeballs desperately dry, as was his mouth. He pushed up on his elbows and squinted at Amit. "What is it?"

Amit pointed and Tommy rolled over onto his knees and stared ahead. He muttered a curse at the sight. The wind had shifted and the dark clouds that had filled the horizon heading east, were now nearly directly overhead. "How far do you think we've traveled?"

Amit shrugged. "I haven't a clue." He jerked a thumb over his shoulder. "We can still see the island."

Tommy cursed again at how close it still appeared, though at least it was filling only a part of the horizon instead of the entirety. Without anything to reference, he figured they were anywhere from five to ten miles from shore, though he really couldn't say. All he could say with confidence was that it wasn't far enough. He redirected his eyes forward. "I figure we've gone about a quarter of the way at best."

Amit shrugged. "I have no idea." He stabbed a finger at the clouds ahead. "That has me more concerned. It looks like it's raining to me."

Tommy peered ahead and had to agree. "So, it's raining. A little rain never hurt anyone."

"Have you not read about Krakatoa?"

Tommy's eyes narrowed. "Krakatoa? Is that like the Indian Godzilla?"

Amit's eyes shot wide, staring at him in disbelief. "Are you truly that ignorant?"

Tommy glared at him. "No need to get insulting. I've heard of Krakatoa, but I have no idea what it is."

"It's the biggest volcanic eruption in recorded history. When it exploded, the sound was heard for thousands of miles. The shockwave from it encircled the globe multiple times."

Tommy cursed. "That's incredible."

"It's the loudest sound ever to have been experienced by man."

Tommy gestured at the inferno ahead. "Certainly this isn't that, is it?"

"I don't know. That explosion that we initially heard was certainly louder than anything I've ever experienced, but it doesn't matter. This is a massive eruption, which means ash is being thrown into the air. That rain is going to be no ordinary rain. It's going to come down as mud."

Tommy still wasn't making the connection. He stared at their raft. If it rained, they could put up the canopy and the water should just roll off into the ocean, keeping them relatively dry underneath. His eyes widened as he realized what Amit was getting at.

Mud, not rain.

The mud might not run off. It might just stick and weigh them down, then eventually sink them. "What are we going to do?"

Amit frowned. "I don't know. If we go forward, we might die."

Tommy's shoulders slumped. "But if we go back, we'll all die for sure." He thought of Mai and the professors. They were counting on them. If he and Amit failed, everyone he cared about would be dead. He shook his head as he drew in a long breath. "We have to go forward. We're their only chance."

Amit stared at him, the fear in his eyes matching Tommy's, but then gave a curt nod. "Then let's do this."

Tommy grabbed his paddle and took up position, as did Amit, and the two of them paddled as fast as they could, hoping to close as much of the gap between them and help before they were inundated by what was to come.

Heading Inland

North Sentinel Island

Andaman Islands, India

Pritam slowly made his way through the thickening trees, his men spread out in a semi-circle ahead of him. The drums were loud now, no more than half a mile away. They hadn't encountered anyone yet, though there had been a few shouts that were dismissed as overactive imaginations. Yet he had to wonder. These natives would know this forest as well as he knew the streets of his home. Whenever he was forced to avoid the police or some rival gang, he always managed to escape because he knew his domain. And the natives here would be the same. They might have hunting blinds set up that his men would never spot. They might be up in the trees, they could be disguised, lying on the ground. They could be anywhere or they could be nowhere. Were they brave warriors who wouldn't hesitate to engage when the time was right, or were they cowards terrified of what he and his men represented?

He was torn between which he preferred. With their weapons, they would win any direct engagement, but men would be lost, and that could potentially include himself. But no engagement meant the threat would always be out there, and would eventually have to be faced.

If they could find where these natives lived and capture their women and children, he had no doubt the men would engage. Kill enough of the defenseless, and they might just surrender and become their slaves. A smirk crawled up his cheek as something stirred down below at the thought of all the women he would have at his disposal. He paused, a frown forming as he wondered what it would be like to be with a woman who didn't want him. He wasn't naïve enough to think those back home slept with him because they liked him. Most did it because of what he could provide, yet they willingly did so. He had never raped a woman before, and he wasn't sure he wanted to start now.

But with that gold back home, he could have any woman he wanted, and he'd pay them to make him believe they wanted to be there. He sighed. He had to get off this island. He had more money than he could have ever dreamed of, sitting in a pile on the shore behind them, and he needed to enjoy it.

They had only two options. One was to repair the boat that had contained the gold now sitting on the beach, and the other was to have the natives build them a boat with the skills he hoped they possessed, though couldn't be sure they did.

His nostrils flared as doubt set in. How would these natives know how to build a boat that could survive the ocean, when they never left the confines of their island? He scratched behind his ear and winced, something having bitten him in the night. They could take the engines from their boats and mount them on a raft. They didn't have far to go, so it should be possible. He drew a deep breath, some confidence restored. They would have the natives build them a raft, then they would mount an engine on it and send a couple of the men back home to get a real boat. They couldn't risk putting the gold on some makeshift contraption. Should they capsize, get hit by a wave, anything, the fortune would be lost.

No, he had to be patient, he had to play this out right. But for any of this to happen, they had to survive, and to survive, it meant eliminating the threat. The row of men in front of him stopped and he could feel the tension in the air. He crept forward, joining the others. "What is it?"

"There's movement ahead, and I can see smoke from fires."

And that's when he noticed the drumming had stopped. "Prepare for attack!" he shouted as he fell back. Somebody cried out to his left and his head swiveled to find Baiju, a friend of many years, gripping a spear embedded in his stomach as he collapsed to the ground.

This was it. His entire future would come down to the next few minutes. He raised his weapon. "Open fire!"

Jara's Village

The Blessed Land

Jara froze in the center of his abandoned village. Smoke still rose from the fires in front of each hut, and the communal fire still burned, though it was clear it hadn't been stoked for hours. There was no doubt as to what was happening. His people knew that the Outsiders were here. The men had gone to repel them, and the women and children had retreated deeper into the forest to hide. This was confirmed by the loud sounds he had heard only twice before, once when he was captured, and once when he was hiding in the cave. The oddly shaped sticks that the Outsiders carried that could damage things from a distance were being used, which could mean only one thing.

His family and friends were in trouble.

He should be with them, and he would have been if he hadn't been out collecting crabs when the wave hit yesterday. He rushed into the hut that he called home and grabbed his stone knife, his bow, some arrows, and several long spears before sprinting toward the battle. He feared his tribe couldn't win, certain more than ever this was the end of times foretold by the elders. Today could be their last day in their home, and tonight they would be feasting around the campfire of the ancestors.

And despite knowing he would die, he felt strangely comforted in the knowledge that though his life would end today, along with all of those he knew and loved, it wasn't the end, it was merely the beginning of something far greater. His chest ached with the thought, and he took one last look at the village he had called home his entire life, then raced toward the terrifying sound of the Outsiders and their powerful weapons.

South of the Yacht Wreck

North Sentinel Island

Andaman Islands, India

Acton raised a fist and dropped to his knee, everyone following suit as the rattle of gunfire erupted behind them. It had started as a single weapon, then was joined by perhaps a dozen more, a sustained burst lasting at least ten or fifteen seconds, then more sporadic ones after that. This was a large engagement. His thoughts turned to Jara, and he wondered if the poor kid had run into their pursuers. He doubted it, as he couldn't believe the gang members would waste so much ammo on a single target. No, this was the engagement he had feared. The drums had stopped, the battle had begun, and the innocent natives of this island were for the first time encountering automatic weapons and hostiles with no concerns over preserving this ancient culture.

They were being slaughtered.

Laura joined him. "What should we do?"

Acton looked at Mai and the others. "If they weren't here, you know what I'd do."

"And you know I'd be right there by your side."

Jannarkar joined them. "What do you think?"

Acton shook his head. "We have a responsibility to the students."

Jannarkar agreed. "But doesn't our responsibility go beyond that?"

Acton regarded him. "What do you mean?"

"I mean, if it weren't for us"—he pointed at the forest, toward the gunfire—"that wouldn't be happening."

"How do you figure?" asked Laura.

"We found the gold, we decided to take it, we were pursued. If we hadn't have done even just one of those things, those people would never be here, and the natives would never be in danger."

It was the first courageous thing he had heard Jannarkar say since the moment this fiasco began, and the man was right. To a point. It wasn't anyone's fault that the volcano had erupted and the resulting tsunami had carried them here, though he was correct that if they had left the gold where they found it, they never would have been pursued, and those gang members would have never been on the water to be brought here.

He turned to Laura. "What do you think?"

"I think the link between this being our fault and merely bad luck is tenuous at best, though as a human being, regardless of how I got here and why those people are here, I feel compelled to help."

Acton sighed. "So do I." He gave her a look. "You do realize this is why we're constantly in trouble."

She shrugged. "Maybe this is what happens when two do-gooders with weapons training get married."

Acton turned to Jannarkar. "If we're going to help, only Laura and I can. Nobody else knows how to use a gun except for Jivi, and she needs to stay here to protect the group."

Jannarkar ran his hand through his hair. "Forget what I said. I can't ask you to do that. It's too dangerous. There are only two of you against God only knows how many."

Acton shook his head. "We're not going to directly engage them. That would be a suicide mission. Let's just go see if we can find out what's happening and determine if there's any way we can help."

Jannarkar gripped Acton's shoulder. "Are you sure? No one would think any less of you if you stayed here and protected us."

Acton placed his hand over Jannarkar's. "Don't worry about us, but promise me one thing."

"Anything."

"If we don't come back, I want Chris Pratt to play me in the movie they make about this. Or Nathan Fillion if it doesn't prevent a reboot of Firefly."

Jannarkar's eyes shot wide.

Laura leaned in, raising a finger. "Angelina Jolie, please."

Acton turned toward her, eying her like a piece of meat and growling like a tiger. "I like how you think."

She vogued.

"Any last words, my dear?"

She smacked her AK-47. "Today is a good day to die?"

He laughed and readied his own weapon. "Yippee ki yay, mother—"

Heading Inland
North Sentinel Island
Andaman Islands, India

Pritam ejected his spent magazine and slapped a fresh one into his weapon. "Cease fire!" he shouted, and the guns fell silent. He wiped his hand across his cheek, just under his left eye, then examined his fingers. Blood. It had been a ferocious, brief encounter. Arrows, spears, and rocks had been hurled back at their bullets, and though he was certain they had inflicted more damage, he couldn't help but think there was no way they could win in a war of attrition. Crashing in the trees grew fainter, indicating their enemy was fleeing. They could be facing hundreds, perhaps thousands. He had no idea. He knew nothing of the numbers that lived here, and nothing of this island beyond the fact that these natives existed and it was forbidden to travel here.

Someone groaned to his left and his head spun toward the sound. "Baiju!" He rushed over to find his old friend lying on the ground, gripping a spear that had impaled him through the stomach. He gently rolled him over, revealing the tip had gone all the way through.

"I'm sorry, boss. I screwed up."

Pritam grabbed him by the shoulder. "No, you didn't. There were just too many of them. If it's anyone's fault, it's mine."

Baiju reached up and grabbed him by the shirt. "Tell my kids I died fighting a dozen of them singlehandedly."

Pritam clasped his friend's hand. "A hundred."

Baiju smiled, his eyes fluttering. "A hundred. I like the sound of that."

Then his face went slack, his final breath shallow.

Pritam clasped his friend's hand to his chest and closed his burning eyes, grieving for a brief moment before letting go and standing. Weakness couldn't be shown. He turned to the others. "Report."

Shabbir, the second most senior man, stepped forward, the one who would challenge him should things continue to go bad. "We lost four, and three are wounded."

"How badly?"

"They'll live as long as they don't get infected."

He jerked a thumb over his shoulder toward the shore. "If you're wounded, get back to the boat. There's probably some medical gear there. Clean your wounds, patch yourselves up, and then get back here." He stepped toward where the enemy had engaged them. Trees showed the scars of their bullets, and there was blood on the ground, but not a single body.

"Where the hell did they go?" asked Shabbir. "Surely we killed some of them."

Pritam shook his head in disbelief. How could they kill four and wound three of his men, and every one of them walked out of here? It made no sense. He gripped his weapon tighter as anger filled him. He had lost good men today, and there was no way that was going unpunished.

These people had to pay.

Approaching the Scene of the Battle

The Blessed Land

Jara rushed toward where his people battled the Outsiders. The strange sounds had fallen silent, and he feared the worst. He had seen the power of these weapons and his people didn't stand a chance unless the gods directly intervened and joined the fight in person.

He heard something ahead and he froze, ducking behind a large tree. People were approaching in numbers. He peered out from the thick trunk and spotted several of the men from his village. He stepped out so they could see him, and gasped as more came into view, most helping a wounded man or carrying one of their dead.

His heart ached at the sight of his best friend, Tolk, being helped, blood oozing from his shoulder. He rushed forward. "I'll take him."

Tolk was handed over and the other man fell back to cover the retreat.

"What happened?"

"It was Outsiders. They attacked us with these strange weapons that fire invisible arrows. We didn't stand a chance. The gods have abandoned us."

"How many of them?"

"Ten or fifteen, I'm not sure."

"Did you kill any of them?"

"I'm not sure. We definitely wounded some, but it wasn't enough. We need more men. We need some of those weapons they have so that we can fight back."

"You know it's forbidden to use anything from the Outsiders. The gods would punish us if we did."

Tolk shook his head. "Surely there must be exceptions made, surely they'd forgive us if we use the Outsiders' weapons to repel them and save those who worship them. Surely the gods would forgive us."

Jara followed the others, noting they weren't heading back to the village. Instead, they were heading toward where the women and children were hiding. The Chief was just ahead, issuing orders as messengers were sent to let the others know they were coming, and to get help from other villages. Everyone would be needed to defeat these Outsiders, and the very notion terrified him.

Without a means to fight back, they would lose this battle, and every warrior here would fight to the death to protect these lands from those who would intrude upon it. And in the end, no one would be left but the women and children, and they would be defenseless against whatever the Outsiders had planned for them.

Yet the gods had shown their power just yesterday with the massive wave that had brought the Outsiders. Why they would have done so made no sense to him. It had to be some sort of punishment. His people must have sinned somehow, and to further sin by using the tools and the weapons of the Outsiders would surely bring a greater wrath.

He froze in his tracks as a thought occurred to him.

Tolk stared at him. "What?"

"I might have an idea."

His friend eyed him. "Your ideas sometimes lead to trouble."

Jara smiled at his friend. He had known him all of his life. They had been born in the same season, so had played together for as long as he could remember. He couldn't imagine being closer to anyone, even his own brothers if they had survived the last wave. He grinned at his friend. "That almost never happens."

Tolk's eyes narrowed. "What's going on? Where were you last night? I haven't seen you since the wave hit."

"It's too long a story, but I'll tell you when this is all done." He flagged one of the others. "You take him. I have somewhere I need to go. I'll be back as soon as I can."

And with one last flash of his teeth, he sprinted into the forest and away from his people, praying that what he was about to do didn't displease the gods and bring further suffering to those he loved.

Operations Center 2, CIA Headquarters

Langley, Virginia

Leroux cursed as everyone stared at the display. Because of the dense foliage, it was difficult to tell exactly what was going on, what the computer was tracking. They still had three main groups, with more entering the fray, but too many of the original players were doing questionable things. The initial group of armed hostiles appeared to have taken heavy casualties. Four targets hadn't moved in several minutes, and they were either wounded or dead—the more the better, as far as he was concerned. The natives they had engaged were retreating rapidly and had left no one behind. He found it impossible to believe they had suffered no casualties, and he wasn't the only one in the room.

"Maybe they took their dead with them," suggested Therrien.

Leroux shook his head in disbelief. "That has to be it. The briefing report did say they bury their dead. So, maybe they don't leave their dead behind, if at all possible."

Tong turned in her chair to face him. "Why should that surprise us? We do the same. We only leave our dead behind if we have no choice, and then we always try to go back and get them. Is it so strange for them to do the same?"

Leroux's head bobbed. "You're right, of course. I made the false assumption that because they're primitive with their technology, they're also primitive in their humanity."

"You weren't the only one." Child tapped at his keyboard and several photos appeared, taken of the natives decades before when a rare expedition had been allowed on the shores. "I had assumed they'd look like you see in the movies, all kinds of bone piercings and tattoos and whatnot, but other than the fact they're buck naked, they look perfectly normal."

Leroux stared at the photos. These were proud people who deserved to live out their lives undisturbed in the Eden they had yet to be ejected from, where they hadn't yet learned shame. He just prayed they'd save them before it was too late.

He eyed the enhanced satellite image of the two dots that had broken free of the survivors, and he had little doubt they represented the professors, and they were heading directly toward the fight. He shook his head at their foolishness, yet admired them at the same time. He doubted he would ever have the courage to run toward the gunfire, especially when the odds were impossibly against him. Yet here were these two foolishly brave souls, charging into the fray like the knights of old without a thought for themselves, instead willing to lay down their lives for people they had never met, people who would just as soon kill them where they stood. His chest ached for them as he checked the countdown timer indicating when Delta would be in the area.

And it was far too long to do anyone any good.

"Uh-oh," said Child behind him.

Leroux's head spun toward Child's station. "What?"

Child pointed at the screen as he tapped at his keyboard. The image zoomed out, showing dozens of new targets converging on the area. "It looks like more of them are coming to the party."

Leroux frowned. "I'd hardly call this a party."

"They're moving again, sir," said Tong.

Leroux adjusted his focus then cursed as the armed hostiles again advanced, and his heart sank at the thought they were witnessing from above the genocide they had feared. He turned to Tong, his voice subdued. "Make sure all of this is being recorded. We may be witnessing the end of a civilization."

A silence swept through the room as the gravity of the situation was finally recognized by everyone, and eyes glistened and heads bowed as silent prayers were said.

To their God, and to those these innocent people worshipped.

Approaching the Scene of the Battle

North Sentinel Island

Andaman Islands, India

Acton continued forward, Laura just behind him, covering their rear. The gunfire had stopped, and that meant one of two things. Either the gunmen had lost, or the natives had, and he was willing to bet it was the natives. The question was, had they fought to the death, or had they wisely retreated to live and fight another day?

He prayed it was the latter, for he doubted these people could afford to lose so many men in their prime. Their numbers were so low, genetic diversity could become an issue. The gunfight had been brief enough that he was counting on there being significant numbers of survivors and that they might yet save these people, though in reality, how could they? There was just the two of them, and though they had received significant training and had been in too many gunfights to count, they could be facing dozens of armed men.

Add to that the complicating factor of the natives, who would inherently distrust them and might even attack them, and it sounded a bit like Afghanistan to him. We sent in troops to fight the Taliban and free the locals, and rather than embracing the soldiers as liberators, many treated them as hostiles and attacked them merely because they were outsiders. He feared the same would be true here. But they had to take a chance and at least see what was happening.

They continued forward toward where he thought the battle had been fought, his heart hammering at their foolhardiness. With the guns silent, there was no way they could know where the two sides were, and at any moment they could stumble upon a war party that would slaughter them in a heartbeat. With every step he took, he questioned their decision. They should turn around. This wasn't their responsibility. They should return back to the students, to Mai, and protect them.

The logical leap of claiming this was their fault because they had been followed here was tenuous at best, and ridiculous at worst. Once exposed to the reasoning that time allowed, the only way the argument held merit was if they had been intentionally fleeing *to* this island, which they hadn't. They had been carried here by a massive wave and deposited on these shores through no action of their own. This was not their fault. By extending the chain of events back to the decision to take the gold from the dig site, you could extend the fallacious argument back to their invitation to the charity. If they hadn't accepted it, then Jannarkar would have still gone to the dig site, his students would have still found the gold, yet their inexperience in these situations would have had them all slaughtered by the local gang at the dig site, therefore preventing the boat chase that now had these armed hostiles on the island.

Another ridiculous notion.

The situation they found themselves in was no one's fault, it was simply life, and while he wished he could save these people, was it worth the lives of those he loved and those he was responsible for?

He held up a fist and took a knee.

Laura joined him. "What is it? Do you hear something?"

He shook his head. "I think we're being rash."

She grunted. "Since when has that ever stopped us?"

He chuckled. "So, you think we're doing the right thing?"

"I think we're doing the right thing, though not necessarily the smart thing."

He eyed her. "So, you think this *is* our fault?"

She shook her head. "No, I've given it some thought, and I think we got caught up in the moment trying to justify our desire to help innocent people from being murdered."

His head drooped in relief that she agreed with him. "So, what do you want to do?"

"I want to save these people, then save our people, go home, have a long bath, then sleep for two days after eating steak and lobster with garlic mashed potatoes."

His stomach rumbled. "You just had to go there, didn't you?"

She grinned. "You always want me to be honest, don't you?"

He stared at her for a moment. "Wait a minute. Am I in this fantasy anywhere?"

She patted his cheek. "Of course you are, dear. Who do you think drew the bath and cooked the meal?"

He stuck his tongue out at her. "So, do we keep going forward, or do we go back?"

The sound of somebody rushing toward them signaled the decision might already be made. Acton pointed at a nearby tree and Laura scurried over to it, taking cover as he did the same to his left. He raised his weapon, taking aim toward the sound. It wasn't as loud as he would have expected, and it had him thinking it might be a native, expert in traversing the forest ground. He made a clicking sound with his tongue and Laura looked at him. "I think it's a native," he whispered, and she gave him a thumbs-up in agreement.

Suddenly Jara appeared, fear in his eyes. Acton rose and stepped out, indicating for Laura to remain hidden. He didn't hear anyone else approaching, though Jara could be a decoy, and this a trap. He had no way of knowing. He simply couldn't trust this young man, not completely, and certainly not to the point where he was willing to put their lives into this native's hands, a native who had abandoned them to the high tide of their second hiding place, a native who had left them to die.

Jara's eyes widened and he skidded to a halt. Acton aimed his weapon at the man's chest and Jara held his hands out, palms up and empty, equivalent to the outside world's raised hands of surrender. He began talking rapidly, pointing behind him then at Acton's weapon. Laura emerged and the young man smiled.

"Laura!" He reached out for her. She stepped forward and took the young man's hand and squeezed it, then stepped back. Jara stood there for a moment, scratching his arm as if pondering what to do, then his jaw dropped. He wiped his hand across his face, pointed behind him, then took his bow and shook it, again behind him. He then stepped forward and wiped his hand on Laura's cheek, pointed behind him, then tapped her weapon and attempted to make the sound of an AK-47. He then beckoned in an exaggerated manner for them to follow him.

"What do you think he's trying to say?" asked Acton.

"I think he means his people only have bows and arrows, and the people they're fighting, outsiders like us, have weapons like ours, and his people need our help."

Acton chewed his cheek. "You got all that from a few hand gestures?"

She shrugged. "I'm the queen of charades, you know that."

He rolled his eyes. "You *think* you're the queen of charades. You only win because you're playing the British version. I don't have a clue half the time what the hell you're miming. Midsomer Murders? What the hell is that?"

She snorted and Jara eyed her inquisitively. "What do you want to do?"

Acton pursed his lips, regarding the young native for a moment. "If he's inviting us to help, it changes the equation, doesn't it? He can guide us safely through the forest. He should be able to stop his people from killing us on sight, so we'd only have one enemy to face. It doesn't necessarily mean we're getting into a firefight with them, but if we can somehow help these people, they might then just help us when this is all over, because we don't know how long we're going to be here."

"So, we're going to go with him?"

"I'm willing if you are."

Laura reached out and took his hand, giving it three squeezes. "I go where you go."

He frowned. "That's just a copout and you know it. If this goes wrong, you just want to be able to say you were only following me out of morbid curiosity as to what the hell I would do next."

She shrugged. "You know me so well."

"Uh-huh."

She let go of his hand then smiled at Jara, pointing into the forest from where he had come. "We'll come with you."

He flashed his teeth and turned around, heading back into the forest without a word. Ten minutes ago, Acton would have been perfectly content with this new development, but five minutes ago, he had convinced himself they should turn around. And while he had changed his mind once, he wasn't quite yet at the point where he had changed it back.

He just hoped they would live to regret it.

Approaching the Inland Village

The Blessed Land

Jara was elated. With these two Outsiders to help them, these Outsiders who could use their fierce weapons without fear of punishment from the gods, it could turn the tide of this battle. His people had lost and lost badly. They couldn't be expected to win against such weapons despite the numbers overwhelmingly in their favor.

But now there was hope.

He led them directly toward his village's fallback position, where the women and children and the wounded warriors would be staying. He needed to show Laura and her mate what they were fighting for, and to judge the reaction of the others to their being there, for they were still Outsiders. It was still forbidden for them to be on the Blessed Land, and he wasn't wise enough to know how the gods would feel about having them help his people.

The elders would decide.

They traveled in silence the entire way, and they soon approached the small village farther from the shoreline used for rare situations like this, but more often to seek shelter from storms or for hunting parties that didn't make it home in time. He came to a stop and the two Outsiders did the same.

"You need to stay here," he said, pointing at them then the ground. They both nodded, understanding what he meant, then he continued alone toward the village. He emerged from the trees and breathed a sigh of relief at the sight of the huts, the cooking fires, and the sounds of children at play and women at work.

"Jara! Thank the gods!" His mother rushed toward him and embraced him. He returned it, then gently pushed her away as dozens of those he had known all his life came to greet him. He smiled at them all but turned to his mother.

"I need to speak to the elders urgently."

Her eyes narrowed. "Why? What's going on?"

"Mother, please. There's no time."

She pointed to the communal structure. "They're in there."

He gave her another quick hug then marched toward the largest structure in the community. He stepped inside, taking a moment for his eyes to adjust to the dark.

"Young Jara!" exclaimed the shaman. "I thought we had lost you in yesterday's calamity."

Jara stepped forward and knelt in front of the semicircle of elders. He bowed his head. "I nearly was, but the gods spared me. I think to save us."

An eyebrow rose on the shaman's forehead. "A bold thing to say."

"Yes, sir. And I say it with all humility, for I know I'm not worthy to carry any sort of message or gift from the gods, and I can only think I was chosen because I was the only person available."

"What is it you think the gods have asked of you?"

"You, of course, are aware of the battle that has taken place between our brave warriors and the Outsiders."

Heads bobbed around the room. "We are attending to some of the wounded now. These Outsiders are different than the ones we have encountered before. I fear we might not be able to defeat them without the help of the gods, and after the message they delivered us yesterday, I fear their help will not be forthcoming."

Jara smiled slightly. "The gods may not have forsaken us."

"What do you mean?"

"I mean, the great wave brought the Outsiders here, but they also brought another group, a group that saved me yesterday from those we now fight. I believe they are good people, despite not being from this sacred place. I believe they mean us no harm, and will help us fight the evil Outsiders, then leave our shores, never to return."

"Another bold statement. How can you be so sure?"

"Because they have weapons like our enemy does, and when I went to seek their help after we lost the battle, they were already on their way to us."

"Perhaps they were merely coming to help their friends."

Jara shook his head vehemently. "No, they fear those people as much as we do. I saw it in their eyes. But beyond that, I left it up to the gods to decide whether they should survive."

"What do you mean?"

"When we first fled these Outsiders, I took them to the Refuge, near the rock face. We hid in there, but became concerned that we'd be discovered, so I took them to the Cave of the Great Mother."

"The one that floods at high tide?"

"Yes. When they were asleep, I left to come here and seek your guidance on what should be done about them, but I waited to see how the gods would decide their fate, and when the tide rose and the cave flooded, every single one of them made it out alive."

Excited looks were exchanged among the elders, the shaman smiling broadly. "If this is the case, then perhaps the gods have indeed temporarily blessed these people. Do you think they'd be willing to help us?"

"I have two of them with me now with the strange weapons. I believe they're willing to help."

"And what would they ask in return?"

Jara shook his head. "Communication with them is very difficult, for we don't speak each other's language. We've been using hand gestures to communicate, and we seem to be able to cover the basics, but I would suspect that all they would want is when this is over, for us to not repel them as invaders like we normally would, but to instead help them until they can be saved by their own people."

"A fair request, I would say." The others agreed. "Bring these people to us. Let us look into their eyes, let us see if we find the same in their souls as you do."

Jara rose. "Right away." He scurried from the communal building and rushed back into the forest, his heart thumping in excitement that he might be the one to deliver salvation to his village.

Near Jara's Village

North Sentinel Island

Andaman Islands, India

Acton and Laura remained low, hiding behind the largest tree they could find. From what he could tell, the tsunami hadn't reached this far inland. They could hear the sounds of a large number of people, perhaps a hundred yards away, and the fact the children continued to play suggested whatever Jara was doing hadn't yet caused a panic.

A debate raged in his mind over what to do should things not go well. If the tribe treated them as they did any other outsider, they might only have minutes to live, though, with their weapons, they might defend themselves, yet it would mean killing the natives. And even if they got away, they could pursue them then seek out the rest of the survivors.

He glanced over at Laura, keenly watching the tree line for movement, and couldn't take the thought of seeing her in pain before their eventual deaths.

She noticed him staring at her and smiled, a smile that always improved his mood no matter how bleak their situation might be. Her eyes narrowed. "What's wrong?"

"Nothing," he lied. "Just swearing to myself that the next time we're invited to a black-tie affair, we absolutely say no."

She chuckled. "Because you wearing a tie caused all this?"

He shrugged. "Hey, I can't prove it's because of that, but can you prove it isn't?"

She rolled her eyes at him then they both spun toward a voice calling out.

"Laura!"

Acton looked at her. "I think he wants you to go."

She eyed him. "I think he wants both of us to go."

He wagged a finger. "Nope. I didn't hear my name."

"Ha-ha."

"There he is," said Acton, spotting Jara walking toward them unarmed. Acton stepped out from behind the tree and Jara waved at them, beckoning them to come forward.

"What do you think?" he asked Laura.

She shrugged. "Well, this is why we're here. Either we're about to die horrible deaths, or we're about to be embraced. Either way, we'll have an answer shortly."

Acton sighed. "Fine, let's get this over with. But if it looks like they're going to have me for dinner, shoot me."

She stepped out from behind the tree. "To hell with that. You shoot me."

He laughed as they walked toward Jara. "We shoot each other? On the count of three?"

"Agreed."

Acton eyed her. "Wait. One, two, three, then shoot, or one, two, and shoot on three?"

"It doesn't matter."

"What do you mean it doesn't matter?"

"Because I'm shooting on four. There's no way I want to risk you missing me."

Acton laughed. "On three it is."

"Wait, did we actually settle anything?"

He shrugged. "I don't think so, but it doesn't really matter now, does it?"

Jara smiled at them, urging them forward. Acton continued his wary pace, his head on a swivel, but as far as he could tell, they weren't being surrounded. He could make out a clearing ahead, and the smell of burning wood filled his nostrils. They emerged into a large open area cut into the forest, half a dozen huts in a semicircle with a larger structure completing the village.

A woman screamed and everyone turned, gasping at the sight. Children cried out and ran toward their mothers. Jara raised his hands in the air, saying something, his tone reassuring, though his words had no effect. An old man stepped out from the larger structure, his hands raised. He said something and everyone quieted save some of the younger children.

With calm restored, Jara held out his hand, motioning for Acton and Laura to head into what Acton was guessing was a communal building. He slung his weapon. There were no men here, just women and children, and if something were to happen, he wasn't prepared to fight back. The best way to survive this situation unscathed was to present themselves in as friendly a manner as they could. Laura slung her own weapon as they walked toward the old man, who turned and disappeared inside. Jara continued to smile as he led them.

Inside, Acton paused for a moment, letting his eyes adjust, and found half a dozen elders sitting in a semicircle at the far end. Jara urged them forward, then knelt in front of the men, urging Acton and Laura to do the same. They knelt then mimicked Jara's motions.

Words were said, the man at the mid-point of the semicircle addressing them, his voice steady and friendly, Acton sensing no ill will for the moment. He had no idea how they could come to an agreement here, not with the complexity of the situation. They were attempting to negotiate an alliance where two enemies would unite against a common foe, and then should they be successful, agree to remain on friendly terms until they could withdraw from the field of battle to never return.

It was insane.

There was no way hand gestures could accomplish such a complex task.

Jara and the elders spoke, everything friendly. Jara motioned toward them, then reached over and patted the weapon slung across Acton's back, then mimicked firing it, simulating the sound as best he could. More words were exchanged, heads slowly bobbing, some agreement that Acton prayed was mutually beneficial being made. The elders all rose, as did Jara, who indicated for Acton and Laura to stand. They did.

The leader, his ornamentation as simple as the others, though more colorful, stepped forward. He extended a hand and Acton extended his. The man grasped his wrist and Acton did the same, staring directly into the man's eyes. He smiled at him, though kept his lips pressed together. Acton did the same. Still grasping his arm, the elder turned to the others and smiles spread among them all. Apparently, an agreement had been reached, but what that was, he had no idea.

Gunfire cracked the peace and the old man released his grip. Jara excitedly turned to them, pointing at their weapons, but then beckoning them to follow him. Acton unslung his AK-47 and followed, glancing over his shoulder at Laura. "I think we've just been drafted."

She gripped her weapon tight as they ducked through the low entrance and emerged into the village. Half a dozen wounded warriors stood on one edge of the clearing, preparing to defend the women and children, but they would be no match for any enemy. These men had bullet wounds these natives had no experience in how to treat. More gunfire erupted and Jara beckoned them into the forest.

"Are we doing this?" he asked Laura.

She shrugged. "Do we have a choice? If we refuse to fight, they might treat us as the enemy and kill us regardless, and if I'm going to die, I'd rather die in a gunfight protecting the innocent rather than slaughtered out of ignorance."

He reached out and took her hand, giving it three squeezes. "I don't think I've ever loved you more than I do right now."

She flashed him a smile and motioned with a hand over her body. "All this and balls too."

He laughed.

More gunfire, sustained this time, ended their moment.

"We need a plan, one that helps these people and gets us out alive. Any ideas?"

She shrugged. "Not a one."

"Lovely."

South of the Yacht Wreck

North Sentinel Island

Andaman Islands, India

Jannarkar stared deep into the forest as he had since Acton and Laura had left to help the natives. He had known both of them independently for years in a professional capacity, and their frequent meetings at various conferences had allowed a friendship to be established. And when the two of them had become a couple, he and his wife would have dinner with them when their schedules met up, perhaps once a year, with a few emails in between. They were all busy with their careers, allowing little time for much else.

But these were different people from when they had first met. Acton was always the adventurer, an Indiana Jones in real life if there ever was one. Usually casually dressed, spending more time in the field than most, while still taking the time to train the next generation. His students loved him, and he was well respected. Laura had impeccable credentials, was very well respected, though he had never thought of her as one who would foolishly run into the face of danger.

And since she had met Acton, he had heard rumors about some of the things they had been involved with, things so spectacular he couldn't believe they were true. Until today. The two of them had remained calm during this entire situation. Acton had already killed two of their foes and Laura one. And now they were off to help people they didn't even know. It was mindboggling, and if he hadn't seen it with his own eyes, he would simply assume whoever was telling the story was exaggerating or outright lying.

Yet here he stood with half a dozen survivors on a forbidden island, defenseless against what might come. And he had to figure out some way to protect these people who were his responsibility, a responsibility he had shirked by asking Acton to take over. Yet he couldn't think straight. His thoughts were dominated by his wife. Every time he closed his eyes, all he could see was the volcano consuming her.

She was dead. There was no doubt. The only reason he and the others were alive was that the volcano was 100 miles away when it erupted, and all its effects had to cross the main island to reach them. If they had been on the other side, like his wife and her team, they would be dead. And if he didn't think of something soon, some way to protect the others, they too would be dead.

Mai stepped up beside him. "Sir, shouldn't we be finding some place to hide?" Her voice was low, preserving his dignity with his students.

He looked down at her. "Yes, yes, of course. But I'm afraid without knowing this place, I'm not sure where we can go."

"Perhaps all we need to do is stay out of sight and stay quiet. We're far enough from the wreck that those with the weapons shouldn't find us, and if we stay quiet and out of sight long enough, then hopefully the professors can make some sort of arrangement with the natives."

Jannarkar shook his head. "I'm afraid that's wishful thinking, my dear. All attempts to make friendly contact with these people have ultimately failed, usually in bloodshed. I expect we'll see our friends back shortly, and I fear they'll be pursued by those they were trying to help." He sighed. "And then this is over."

Fear swept over Mai's face then she inhaled deeply. "You're forgetting three things, Professor."

He eyed her. "What's that?"

"First, you don't know the professors like I do. If anyone can save us, they can. And if that means negotiating an impossible agreement that everyone before them has failed at, then they'll do it. Two, you're forgetting that Tommy and Amit are out on that water, trying to get us help. And three, the professors have friends, and I know they're on the way. We just need to last a little bit longer. It might be a few hours, it might be a few days, but help is coming, and it's up to us whether they're here to rescue us, or recover our bodies."

Jannarkar regarded her for a moment then placed a hand on her shoulder, staring her in the eyes. "You're absolutely right, but I have one question for you."

"Anything."

"Just who are these friends you all keep referring to?"

She smiled. "If I told you, then I'd have to kill you."

Approaching the Yacht Wreck

North Sentinel Island

Andaman Islands, India

Laura continued through the trees, her husband by her side, Jara leading the way as they raced toward what she feared would be a hopeless battle. Though after what she had seen at the small village, the innocent women and children, the defenseless wise elders willing to trust those they had been raised to fear, and the brave warriors, wounded by weapons they couldn't possibly understand, on their feet with spears in hand ready to die to protect the innocent, there was no way she was walking away from this battle to save herself.

"Well?" she asked.

"I'm thinking."

"We don't have time for you to think."

"It'll take longer if you keep badgering me."

She frowned but shut her mouth. She had proposed a plan, the only thing she could think of, the only thing with any hope of succeeding. It wouldn't win them this war, but it just might win this battle, and victory wasn't always slaughtering your enemy where they stood. Victory sometimes meant forcing your enemy to withdraw from the field of battle, perhaps to fight another day, but not this day. Her plan was the only way she could think of to possibly accomplish that goal.

"I like it," James finally said.

"So, we're doing it?"

"Unless somebody comes up with a better idea."

Jara came to a halt ahead, holding up his fist and taking a knee. Laura smiled as the young man mimicked the move that James had been using. They joined him and both knelt beside him. Jara pointed ahead to several different positions. She squinted, the light dim under the thick canopy of the forest, then spotted several of Jara's people. And once she picked them out, she spotted dozens more, all blending in with the foliage. Jara tapped his ear then pointed ahead. Laura listened. People were approaching, and judging by how loud they were doing so, it had to be the enemy.

James turned to her. "You take the left and I'll take the right."

She nodded. He leaned over and gave her a quick peck, then tapped on Jara's shoulder. He pointed at his chest, then to the right, then at Laura, and to the left. Jara indicated his understanding. James rose and quickly disappeared into the trees. She headed left with Jara, who then broke off. She could hear him whispering to the others, word quickly rippling through the forest, no doubt telling them that she and James were friendly and approved by the elders.

She took up position behind a tree. To her left and right were two natives who both acknowledged her with a closed mouth smile and a bow of the head. She returned the gestures then readied her weapon.

And prayed her plan worked.

Pritam charged through the forest, determined once and for all to put an end to this. He wanted his revenge for what these primitives had done to his men, and then they were out of here. Last night, they had found the cave the others had been hiding in, though he had no idea where they were now. But none of that mattered. He had their gold, which was all he ever really wanted. Yesterday, he needed these natives as labor to get him off the island, though everything had changed. He had just received word from one of the wounded who had returned from the shore that the tide had come in and refloated the boat enough for Nair and the others to tip it over onto its good side, exposing the gash entirely.

Nair was reportedly confident he'd be able to repair the boat and get them off the island and back home. It would just be a matter of time, which gave the rest plenty of it to exact their revenge. There was a thud to his left, then one to his right. His head swiveled in both directions and he cursed as two of his men dropped, arrows in their chests.

"Open fire!" He raised his weapon when a gunshot rang out in front of them, to his right, and then another to his left. One of his men cried out, gripping his shoulder, and his eyes widened as he realized the natives now had real weapons. Where the hell they had gotten them from, he had no idea, but it changed the equation. He jumped behind a tree and opened fire blindly. Another shot rang out, and then another, the muzzle flashes giving him a position to shoot at. He took aim and fired, and two more shots rang out from yet more positions. He had counted six locations so far. If the natives had six weapons, even if they didn't know how to use them, they might still end up taking him out. His men were pouring a steady barrage of lead on the enemy, but they would soon be out of ammo. And once they were, they'd be at the mercy of these natives who now not only had bows and spears, but also had automatic weapons.

Another one of his men cried out, whether it was from an arrow or a bullet, it didn't matter. A battle he was certain they would win only moments ago, was now looking hopeless. "Fall back!" he shouted. "Back to the boat!" He didn't have to tell his men twice, everyone turning and bolting. They raced toward the shore where there wasn't necessarily safety, but if they could reach the water, it would force their enemy to reveal themselves if they wanted to engage, and they might stand a chance at holding them off.

He could hear them in pursuit, scores of them. He burst through the trees and onto the sandy beach, spotting the yacht floating in the water, its engine running. A roar erupted behind him, a chorus so dense it was terrifying. Spears and arrows raced toward them, embedding into the sand, some into his crew. He sprinted toward the boat, afloat, under power, and apparently seaworthy. It was their means of escape, though the pile of gold remained on the beach.

Nair poked his head out from the wheelhouse, his eyes bulging. He disappeared back inside and the engine roared, the boat pulling away from the shore.

"Wait for us, you bastard!"

But he didn't.

Pritam glanced over his shoulder to see at least fifty natives chasing them, then cursed as he spotted a white man and woman, the only two carrying automatic weapons. They had been played. They must have fired single shots then switched positions to make it appear as if there were more guns at play. It was a brilliant move, but now he knew the truth.

"They've only got two guns! Stand and make a fight of it!" He stopped and spun around, some of his men doing the same. He opened fire at their pursuers, the few that had stopped with him joining in. A few of the natives dropped, but the rest broke back into the forest, and within moments the beach fell silent, the only sounds the waves and the engine of the yacht that carried four of his men away from this forbidden island. He stared after them, growling. "I hope you sink."

He turned toward the others and gasped. Only three remained. Several bodies were scattered along the beach, and more had been left behind in the forest. The drums pounded again in the trees as horns sounded, no doubt calling for more warriors.

They had lost. There was no way the four of them could defeat so many, especially when they now had the help of the Americans and their guns, no doubt taken off the bodies of his men last night.

"What are we going to do now, boss?"

Pritam pursed his lips, glaring into the trees, then back at the boat disappearing into the distance. They could have all been saved if that coward had just waited a few more minutes. A decision had to be made, even if it wasn't the right one, but he had to appear to still be in control. He pointed down the beach in the opposite direction of their wrecks. "We go this way."

"Why?"

Pritam glared at the defiant question. "Because I said so! Challenge me again and you'll join them!" He stabbed a finger toward their comrades, dead on the sand. His challenger backed down as they headed uselessly in the opposite direction at the edge of the water. The tree line hiding their enemy was at least 100 yards away, protecting them, he hoped, until he could figure some way out of this. Unfortunately, he wasn't sure how, now that the Americans were helping. He cursed at himself for not having stopped them before they left his home with the gold.

He and his men were going to die here.

And it was all his fault.

Bay of Bengal

Tommy paused, his entire body aching. They could see the island ahead, the volcano still erupting beyond it on the far horizon. A couple of hours ago, a thick wet ash-like mud had begun to rain upon them. The rain canopy was helping, but not completely. The mud was so heavy, they were taking turns scooping out what was getting inside, but his bigger concern was the canopy itself. It was only gently sloped, and the mud was accumulating quickly, making the raft heavy. They were getting lower in the water, and it now threatened to start lapping over the edges.

He had to do something different.

He tossed his paddle inside then extended his arm out and swept it along the canopy, gathering up several pounds' worth of mud in one stroke, then guided it into the water by holding the canopy out over the lip of the raft. His heart hammered in excitement at the successful test. "Amit, get up here! We need to clean off the canopy."

Amit poked his head up and his eyes bulged. "Holy shit, this is far worse than in here."

Tommy swept his arm again, Amit noting the method then disappearing back inside and reemerging at the opposite end. The two of them continued their efforts, and after what felt like hours but was only minutes, they were finished, though the accumulation had already resumed. Tommy collapsed underneath the canopy, gasping for breath, every muscle in his body on fire as Amit did the same beside him. A water bottle crinkled as Amit took a drink then handed it over. Tommy drained what was left.

"I don't know how the hell we're going to keep this up."

Amit sighed. "We don't have a choice. We can't stop or we'll capsize. We have to keep moving forward, keep the weight down, and keep the mud off the raft."

Tommy gripped Amit's arm. "Quiet." They both cocked an ear. He was sure he had heard something. "Do you hear that? Is that a boat?"

They both scrambled out from under the canopy. Tommy rose up on his knees, squinting into the darkness, the sun unable to penetrate the thick cloud overhead, though behind them it shone down on pristine water, indicating the others weren't facing this calamity, at least not yet.

"There!" shouted Amit, pointing just behind them.

Tommy turned and gasped. It was the yacht the professors had rented. They had somehow managed to repair it. He raised both hands in the air, waving at them. "Professors, over here!"

But the boat continued, its heading unchanged.

"They can't see us!" cried Amit.

Tommy cursed and scrambled back inside. He grabbed the flare gun then reemerged, pointing it toward the sky. He squeezed the trigger and the flare shot straight into the air then exploded overhead. The boat adjusted its heading and Tommy and Amit both cried out in relief, hugging each other, giddy with excitement. They were about to be saved by the very people they had been trying to do the same for.

Gunfire erupted, the muzzle flashes unmistakably revealing the source. Amit cried out and tumbled overboard.

"No!" Tommy dove over the side, searching the murky water, unable to see Amit. He heard the engine of the yacht race past, leaving them behind. Whoever it was, obviously wasn't the professors. It had to be the gang members pursuing them. They must have repaired the boat, and he took heart that it meant they were no longer a threat to his friends and Mai.

He spotted a shadow below and kicked toward it. He reached out and grabbed Amit's leg then made for the surface, his lungs begging for air. It was an eternity that left him in excruciating agony, his lungs threatening to burst. He continued to kick, pulling Amit to the surface. He finally broke through and gasped for breath, then continued to pull Amit up. He spotted the raft nearby and kicked toward it. He reached the side and grabbed one of the handholds, then struggled to tip Amit inside. He finally managed to get him back in and under the canopy, then rolled in himself.

He checked and Amit wasn't breathing, though was bleeding profusely from a wound in his left arm. He tilted Amit's head back, checked that his tongue wasn't rolled back in his throat, then began CPR, struggling to remember his Scouts training.

Amit suddenly coughed and Tommy rolled him onto his side, water spewing from Amit's mouth as his lungs cleared. And as soon as he was breathing again, Tommy grabbed a medkit from one of the storage pouches on the life raft and went to work on the wound.

"What happened?" asked Amit.

"You got shot and fell overboard."

"You saved me?"

"Remember, I'm a hero."

Amit chuckled then coughed some more. "Why did they shoot at us?"

"It was obviously the gang. There's no way our people would shoot at us."

Amit's eyes shot wide. "Where are they?"

Tommy shrugged. "Long gone. We're just lucky they didn't hit the raft, otherwise we'd be trying to tread water out here." He finished tying off the dressing and noticed the water lapping inside. "You take it easy. I'm going to go clear the mud off."

Amit reached out and grabbed Tommy by the hand, squeezing it hard. "Thank you. I'm in your debt."

Tommy clasped the hand with his other. "Let's just hope we can survive long enough for me to collect on that."

Scene of the Battle

North Sentinel Island

Andaman Islands, India

Acton rose from behind the tree where he had fired his last bullet. He ejected his magazine, confirming what he already knew. It was empty, and he only had one left. None of the natives they had fought with approached him, but as they shifted along the shoreline, following the few survivors, everyone to a man made eye contact, saying something, then smiling, their teeth exposed. If he understood their culture correctly, it meant they considered him someone they could trust. He returned the smiles, though made sure not to bare too many teeth.

But he spared none of his pearly whites as Laura joined him. He hugged her. "You okay?"

"Yeah, I'm fine. You?"

"I managed to not get shot this time, so I'd say I'm good."

"What now?" she asked.

He frowned as the dozens of natives they had just fought with side by side continued after the four remaining enemy survivors. "They're no longer a threat, and I have no desire to execute anyone, but to maintain this new alliance, I think we should stick with the group just in case something goes wrong."

Laura agreed. "You know they're going to kill them."

Acton shrugged. "I don't really have a problem with that. I just don't want to take part in it unless it's absolutely necessary."

The natives were splitting into two groups, one remaining hidden in the trees, silently following the remaining survivors, the others out on the beach, strolling casually after the four remaining men scurrying down the beach. The drummers led the way, pounding the rhythmic beat, a beat he no longer feared.

"Care for a stroll on the beach?"

Laura smiled. "Don't mind if I do."

He took her hand and they joined the others behind a wall of warriors that had bravely fought what would have been insurmountable odds. He closed his eyes for a moment, enjoying the crashing waves, the smell of the sea, and the rhythm of the drums.

"How long should we stay with them?" asked Laura.

He opened his eyes. "I'm not sure, but we're heading in the direction we left the others, so I think we should continue on, see this through, just in case those four make a stand. They could still do a lot of damage."

She pointed at one of the fallen enemy. "I only have half a mag left. We should collect some ammo, just in case."

Acton agreed. He walked over to the closest body and searched the man, finding one magazine. He took his weapon and slung it over his shoulder.

Laura eyed him. "Planning on pulling a Rambo? One weapon for each hand?"

He chuckled. "If you had a camera, I would absolutely do it, but I'm thinking at a minimum we need to take all the ammo with us off this island, and at best the weapons too. The last thing we need is these people being left with automatic weapons."

Her head bobbed in agreement. "There are a lot of guns here. Perhaps we should collect them later and just get the ammo now in case we have to fight again."

He agreed, though kept the one extra weapon in case one of theirs failed. "Look at this." He nodded toward the tree line. Several natives emerged onto the beach, carrying AK-47s in front of them, a stick used so they didn't make physical contact.

Laura smiled. "Perhaps we don't have a problem after all. It would seem they're afraid to even touch them."

The men approached with the weapons then dropped them on the ground in front of them. One said something, waving his hand dismissively over the growing pile. Acton bowed his head slightly to indicate understanding as more guns were brought forward in the same manner, the pile quickly growing large. These people didn't want their weapons. They wanted nothing to do with their way of life, and it was humbling.

In the West, we thought of ourselves as so superior, not understanding why anyone wouldn't want our way of life, and here these people stood, rejecting that way, rejecting the trappings of a supposedly superior society, desperately struggling to maintain the ways they had lived for hundreds, if not thousands of years, rejecting the outside world entirely and sometimes violently.

And were they any less happy? He'd be willing to bet that any survey taken would show these people were happier than most of the outside world. His brief experience in their village, despite what was going on, showed happy, healthy children, caring mothers, and men prepared to die to protect what little they had. There were no emaciated bodies, no signs of malnutrition. This was a society based on relationships, on community, rather than on the accumulation of things.

It was obvious by the structure of their villages. The huts they had seen were laid out so that they all faced the center. All had fire pits in front of the homes so that as the evening meals were prepared, everyone could talk. There was a communal fire pit in the center, where he had no doubt in the evenings, as the sun set and the work of the day could no longer be performed, everyone in the village would gather and talk of the day, of what needed to be done tomorrow, and then when the plans were set, enjoy the stories told by the elders.

It would be a good life if people from the outside would just leave them alone. Someday, if they decided they wanted to establish contact with the outside world, they could. He had no doubt they were well aware of the islands to the east and the fact that's where the outsiders were.

Acton stared at the large pile and what it represented if their pursuers had succeeded. There was enough firepower here to eliminate every last man, woman, and child on the island several times over. He took Laura's hand. "Thank God your plan worked."

She lay her head on his shoulder. "It's about time you acknowledged I'm responsible for this victory."

He laughed. "I have no doubt these people will be singing songs of your heroics for generations to come."

She patted his chest. "Don't worry dear, I'm sure you'll get a verse or two in their tribute to me."

Somebody screamed down the beach. A woman.

And every muscle in his body tensed. "That sounded like Mai."

"It was!" Laura sprinted forward, reloading her weapon with a fresh magazine. He took off after her, and the urgency wasn't lost on their new friends. Their casual stroll of intimidation and victory ended as he and Laura broke through their line, and their allies charged forward with them, forming a wedge with Laura at the head of it, Acton right behind her. Jara sprinted from the woods to join them, and as Acton ran, he cursed himself for the decision he had made. He could have killed the four that remained earlier, yet he had let them live, not wanting their blood on his hands.

But that decision now could mean the death of the others, and that was blood that would haunt him until the end of time.

Jannarkar cursed at himself. Jivi had spotted the four men first, taking her responsibility with their lone weapon seriously. He and the others

278

had been making their way along the beach, away from the gunfire. It had been his foolish decision to not stay in the trees. He figured they would make better time, and when the gunfire had fallen silent, it suggested to him only one of two possibilities. Either the good guys had won and the threat was eliminated, or the bad guys had, and would be content to stay where they were, secure in their victory and alone with their gold.

Yet how could he have been so stupid to have never considered the third possibility? That the good guys had won, but some of their enemy had escaped. And now, here they approached, four men with guns aimed at them.

"What do I do, Professor?" asked Jivi, her voice quavering.

But there was nothing she could do. If she opened fire now, all of them would be mowed down. It was four guns against one. A sound from farther down the beach gave him hope, the roar of scores of people rushing toward them growing louder. He squinted and he could see a mass of people emerge around a bend they had passed only minutes before, and he spotted his friends at the head of a mass of natives they had feared since they arrived.

He held his hand out to Jivi. "Give me the weapon." She swiftly handed it over, no doubt relieved to no longer hold the responsibility of defending them. "Everybody behind me." They all scurried into a line as the four men continued their approach.

One of them raised his weapon and aimed it directly at Jannarkar. "Drop the weapon, or you die."

Jannarkar gripped his gun tighter, his finger on the trigger, shaking in terror. And it was at that moment he realized just how brave his friends were, what it took to run toward the gunfire rather than away from it. The people behind him were his responsibility, yet he couldn't be sure he'd be able to even fire the weapon. All he knew was that if he did, he would certainly die. The mass of people far braver than him were almost upon them. They would all be saved if he could only buy them a few more seconds.

A calm swept over him as he realized what he had to live for. Nothing. He pictured his precious Sushma and tears filled his eyes. He would never see her again, and she was his life. They had never been able to have children, his students taking their place, and as his opponent squeezed the trigger of his weapon, he could imagine no more honorable way to die than as a teacher saving his students, or as a father protecting his children.

He squeezed the trigger, the report of the weapon terrifying, and the kickback jarring. The gun swung up and to his right, the bullets spraying uselessly until the weapon fell silent.

His opponent laughed at him. "I gave you a chance, old man." The trigger was squeezed, and Jannarkar's body shook as each bullet found its mark. The pain was shocking in that he didn't notice it at first, merely a sensation that built toward a crescendo of agony. He fell backward onto the sand, the weapon still gripped uselessly in his hand as the screams of his students behind him, and those too late to save him, filled his ears.

Jivi rushed to his side as more gunfire tore through the air, her tear-filled eyes staring down at him, but he didn't recognize her anymore. All he saw was his beloved Sushma smiling down at him, her eyes glistening with pride.

He reached up for her. "I'm sorry I failed."

"You didn't fail. You saved us. You saved us all."

But the words fell on deaf ears as the light that was once his soul faded, and he passed on to the next realm, eager for his reunion with the only woman he had ever loved.

"No!" cried out Acton as Jannarkar collapsed, his brave display having bought the few seconds they needed to get in range. The students behind him all dropped to the ground for the onslaught about to happen as Jivi scrambled to Jannarkar's side. A scream of rage erupted from Laura as she raised her weapon and opened fire. He did the same, squeezing the trigger, firing single shots at the four gunmen that remained, the four men he could have killed earlier.

Jannarkar's blood was on his hands, as was the blood of anyone else who died.

The four men moved toward the students, their intent clear. They wanted to use them as human shields. He stopped and took careful aim, Laura doing the same as the natives surged around them, wisely staying out of their field of fire. He took out the leader, the one who had murdered Jannarkar, Laura also getting a couple of rounds in him. Arrows and spears arced through the air from the forest, only those in the trees having a safe angle to let loose so they wouldn't hit the students cowering on the ground. Half a dozen arrows and several spears slammed into those still standing, along with dozens of bullets, and within moments, all four of the enemy were down.

Acton sprinted forward with Laura as the guns were silenced.

"Mai, are you okay?" cried Laura. Out of the tangled mess of cowering students thrust a hand.

"I'm okay!"

Acton gasped in relief and continued forward as Mai scrambled to her feet and sprinted toward them. The three of them hugged each other as a family, all of them sobbing freely. He broke away, leaving Laura and Mai to hold each other, and turned to the remaining students. "Is anyone hurt?"

They shook their heads, but the tears streaking their cheeks and the horror etched on their faces told the truth. They now bore wounds that would scar far deeper than those of the flesh. He took a knee beside his old friend and checked for a pulse, already knowing he'd find none. He took the weapon still gripped in his friend's hand and placed it aside, then gently crossed Jannarkar's arms over his chest as he said a silent prayer for his friend's soul.

"You saved them, my friend. Now be at peace with Sushma."

On board the Norham Castle

Exiting the Strait of Malacca

September 2, 1883

The deck was filled with the entire crew, all huddled as close to the prow as they could manage, and as the first ray of sunlight shone directly onto the prow, a roar went up, a jubilation unlike any Sampson had ever heard, and he joined in, waving his hat in the air in celebration of what they had found.

The world as they had once known it.

He closed his eyes as the sun's rays reached him, their warmth something he had always taken for granted, though never would again from this day forward. He said a silent prayer of thanks to God, then opened his eyes and turned to look behind them at the devastation they had survived, the sky still dark, the eruption still far on the horizon.

Then he sighed as the state of his ship was finally revealed to him, cloaked in darkness all these days.

She was a mess.

But she had carried them through.

And he was determined now, more than ever, to deliver their precious cargo, then return home, never to set sail on these oceans again. His days on the other side of the world were over, and at this very moment, he wasn't certain he ever wanted to taste the salt air again.

First Officer Buckley approached him, one ear bandaged, the other thankfully undamaged. "Captain. A glorious day."

"It is indeed. God has blessed us all."

"He has indeed, sir. Your orders?"

"I think she needs some work, don't you?"

Buckley surveyed the ship from their vantage point. "She definitely does, sir. I'll have the men set about making her shipshape again."

Sampson held up a hand. "Let them enjoy themselves. We've all been through a literal hell these past few days. The world will wait until tomorrow." He turned to face the prow. "I think a change of plans are in order."

"Sir?"

"I think we have pushed our luck too far on this voyage. We've just cleared the Strait of Malacca at great peril. We've seen earthquakes and large waves the entire way. Rather than make our scheduled stop in Burma, I propose we head for the Andaman Islands, resupply there, then go directly across the Bay of Bengal, save ourselves several days, and put some distance between us and the dangers that lay behind us."

"But doesn't that violate our orders?"

"I think Her Majesty will forgive a shortcut after all we've been through, don't you?"

Buckley clearly disagreed, though he held his protest. "I'm sure she would, sir."

"Then make a course for the Andamans. I want to be in India before anything else can tear us asunder."

Bay of Bengal

Present Day

The wind had shifted, now blowing hard to the east. A sliver of sunlight appeared just behind them, and more halos of light broke through the thick cloud cover, the mud-laced rain easing up. Tommy hadn't paddled since they had been fired upon, his entire time spent keeping the mud from accumulating and bailing out the water that managed to get inside.

He sat back on his haunches, his shoulders sagging as he stared up at the heavens and cried in relief as his repeated prayers were answered, God finally showing them mercy. Within minutes, the rain stopped and they were bathed in sunlight, though in the direction they needed to go, it was still a nightmarish mess. He steadied his breathing, then finished his task by unhooking the canopy from all the clasps but two, and letting the heavy muddied material drag in the water behind them, a thick dark streak staining the water.

Amit stared up at him, squinting at the sunlight. "What's happening?"

"The wind shifted and the rain stopped." Tommy resumed bailing out the raft, then scooped up the mud that had made it inside, dumping it overboard. They soon had a shipshape craft once again, though for how long, he didn't know. He hauled in the canopy and Amit held out a finger.

"Wait. Can we make a sail of that?"

Tommy eyed him. "What do you mean?"

"I mean, attach it at the front of the boat. You said the wind has shifted, right?"

"Yes, it's blowing east now."

"In the direction we want to go, right?"

"Yes."

"Use the paddles for supports. Maybe we can create a sail."

Tommy eyed him and then it finally made sense. He unhooked the canopy and repositioned it at the front, hooking it along the bottom. He held it up as high as he could on his knees and the wind caught it, proving the concept. He jammed one of the paddles into a stitched fold, then propped it up in the corner of the raft, repeating the process on the other side. The nylon flapped around then finally billowed out as the wind caught it. They both cheered, exchanging grins and handshakes.

Tommy leaned over to see around their makeshift sail, and as the storm continued to head farther east, clearing their way, he gasped. "I can see the island!" He dipped his finger in the water and there was no doubt they were moving forward, slowly still, though far faster than he could ever manage alone paddling.

And then he spotted something that brought him a surge of hope. Half a dozen boats were racing toward them. "They're coming!" he cried, excitement in his voice as he glanced at his friend. He collapsed into the bottom of the boat, there no need for flares or waving—there was no way they could be missed. They were coming right at them, the rescue party so large they'd be able to continue on to the islands and save the others.

His shoulders shook in relief. They had succeeded, their friends would soon be saved, and as the roar of the engines approached, Amit took his hand and shook it. "You saved us all, my friend."

The boats roared by, the engines at full throttle, and as they passed, coming into view from behind their makeshift sail, Tommy's heart sank and his shoulders slumped as he cried out in terror, for this was no rescue armada. These were the very criminals they had been trying to escape all along. He watched in horror at the sight of the dozens of men in the back of the vessels, armed with machine guns and RPGs.

He was so close to getting help, the island within sight, yet he had still failed, for there was no way his friends could survive the onslaught headed their way.

"What is it?" asked Amit.

Tommy helped him up to a seated position so he could see for himself, for he didn't have the words.

"Oh my God!" gasped Amit. "What are we going to do?"

Tommy shook his head. "There's nothing we can do. They're dead already."

Scene of the Battle

North Sentinel Island

Andaman Islands, India

Acton stood by in silence with Laura and Mai standing on either side of him, holding his hands. Jannarkar's students lined either side of his grave, not a dry eye in sight. As soon as the battle had ended and their enemy had been eliminated, the natives had set to cleaning up the contamination brought to their shores. Graves had been dug for both the innocent and the guilty, though Jannarkar's students had insisted on digging his.

This would be his final resting place. There would be no returning to recover his body. The natives had burned the wrecks that the gang had arrived on, had piled all the weapons and phones and anything from the outside world on the beach, never touching a single thing with their bare hands except the bodies of the fallen. Soon, any evidence that these people had ever been here would be wiped clean, except for the natives who had fallen defending their land.

Jara had shown him where they were buried. Twelve were lost, far fewer than what he feared could have happened and would have happened if he and Laura hadn't intervened. They had helped turn the tide of the battle, sowed confusion among the enemy, giving the natives a chance to use their own weapons and their familiarity with the forest to whittle down the opposition numbers.

So much death and destruction, all over greed.

It disgusted him.

Yet he could understand it. Most of the world lived in extreme poverty, and it was something most in the Western world couldn't comprehend. Yes, America had its poor, had its desperate, even had its homeless, and it was tragic that in a country so wealthy, so many could fall through the cracks. But outside that Western world, the vast majority lived in poverty few Westerners could understand. And when desperate people were given an opportunity to change their lives from wondering where their next meal might come from, to never being hungry again, they couldn't be blamed for jumping at the opportunity, for fighting for that winning lottery ticket.

Nandini pointed toward the water, excitement on her face. "Professors!"

Acton spun to where she was pointing and peered at the sight of at least half a dozen boats approaching. And cursed.

"Did Tommy get help?" asked Mai.

Acton shook his head as he picked out the weapons clasped in the hands by those on the loaded decks. There were at least 50 or 60 armed men approaching, and muzzle flashes followed immediately by the clapping of weapons fire sent Acton into action.

"Everybody down!" He shoved Laura and Mai to the ground then joined them, placing himself between them and the boats. The natives scattered into the forest and Acton eyed the weapons piled nearby. He scrambled over and tossed AK-47s back, enough for everyone, even if they didn't know how to fire. He then began throwing ammunition as Laura and Jivi explained how the weapon worked to the others. With the last bit of ammo tossed back, he scrambled to join them.

"Into the trees! Everybody take cover, then start firing when they hit the shore. We have to make them think twice, otherwise, this is over."

The first boat ran up onto the beach, the troops pouring out like a poor man's D-Day. Acton leaned out from his cover and took aim, firing a single shot. A man dropped and Laura fired from the next tree beside him, then Jivi. Man after man dropped, but there were just too many, the other students too terrified to fire their weapons, too unsure of themselves. Two more boats hit the shore.

"Everybody fire or we die!"

Finally, more of the weapons they had joined in, but most were missing their targets, merely causing the enemy to duck. A barrage of fire opened up from the shore as the new arrivals hit the ground and took aim, shredding the trees they were hiding behind. He took a peek, getting off several rounds, then reloaded.

They weren't winning this.

Jara fled into the forest with the others, the horrifying clatter of the Outsiders' weapons filling the air. He glanced over his shoulder then stopped. Laura and the others weren't with them. "Everybody wait!" His brothers skidded to a halt, turning toward him. "They're fighting for us! We can't let them die! What would the gods think after they blessed them and brought them to us?" He jabbed his spear back toward the fight. "We need to help, even if it means we die, for if we do, we will have died with honor, instead of fled in cowardice."

He didn't wait for anybody to say anything, he merely sprinted back toward the fight. He heard something behind him and checked over his shoulder, a smile spreading at the sight of his people racing toward a danger they knew they couldn't defeat. He directed them with his arm to spread out in either direction, and as he emerged from the trees onto the sandy beach, he hurled his spear then ducked back to find cover, never taking his eye off the weapon as it sailed through the air. It impaled one of their enemy in the shoulder and he smiled with satisfaction at the scream as dozens of spears and arrows sailed through the air, more of the enemy felled.

And that's when the unthinkable happened.

Acton's eyes bulged at what he saw, and he turned to the others. "Fall back, now!" He grabbed Mai and hauled her with him as Laura grabbed Jivi. Everyone turned and sprinted deeper into the forest as the screech of an RPG raced toward them. "Everybody down!" He pulled Mai to the ground then threw himself over her as the RPG impacted a tree behind them. The explosion was deafening, and another screech signaled a second incoming projectile. "Keep your heads down!" Another explosion rocked the forest, breaking the spirit of the natives that had come to help them.

They would have never experienced an explosion, they would have no concept of it, and if the effects of an AK-47 were shocking, an explosion from a rocket-propelled grenade had to be dark magic. They fled back into the forest, terrified, but he didn't begrudge them their decision. They couldn't fight these people.

This battle was already lost.

He had no doubt they were here for the gold. He had noticed their yacht was gone, so someone had obviously left to get help and succeeded. The question was, what would they do when they discovered all of their fellow gang members were dead? Would they seek revenge, or take their spoils of war and leave?

He feared the former, and that meant they had failed in their attempt to save these people.

Jara stood, his mouth agape, his arms hanging heavy at his sides as he stared at the ball of fire spreading out from the trees, then just as quickly folding back in upon itself. He had no idea what it was, but the aftermath of disintegrated trees left little doubt this was a weapon far more powerful than the strange sticks the Outsiders had used before. These new Outsiders had weapons that he couldn't possibly imagine, that he couldn't possibly understand the need for. The strange sticks he could understand. Something that could fire invisible arrows could be used for hunting. But why would you ever need a weapon that would disintegrate the animal?

There was only one reason for a weapon like that, and that was to obliterate, to kill, to destroy your enemy. It was evil, and there was no way they could fight evil without the help of the gods. He stared up at the sky and beseeched them for an explanation as to why they had abandoned his people, and he gasped at the sight of six angels descending from the heavens.

The gods hadn't forsaken them after all.

Dawson assessed the situation below. A large group of hostiles had landed on the beach and were pressing their advantage. Once they were in the trees, rooting them out would be much more difficult. "One-One and Zero-Seven, you're with me on the left flank, the rest of you take right."

A string of "rogers" replied as he adjusted his chute. There was no point dropping in on 50 or 60 armed hostiles—they would just end up shredded in the air. Langley had reported the new arrivals on their way to the island, and the pilot of their G650 had poured on every extra ounce of juice he had to get them into position for their jump out of the specially modified aircraft. Equipped with a custom hatch in the underbelly, it allowed them to jump without worrying about getting caught up in the engines or wings.

He flared his chute and hit the beach, spinning around and pulling in the billowing fabric. He disconnected it from his harness as he rushed toward the cover of the trees, checking to make sure Niner and Atlas had landed safely. He activated his comm. "Zero-Five, Zero-One. Report, over."

"Three down safely over here, Zero-One," replied Spock. "It doesn't look like they've spotted us, over."

"Copy that, Zero-Five. Same on this end. Get into position then we'll put an end to this. Remember, we're here to prevent a genocide. If those men leave the beach and get into the trees, those natives won't stand a chance. Langley thinks the natives and the survivors are cooperating, so we've got people in the trees. If I know the professors, as soon as they hear our M4s, they'll come running to help. Zero-One, out."

"They're sweet that way, aren't they?" said Niner.

Atlas agreed. "Very."

Dawson gave them a look. "Don't you two start."

Atlas jabbed a monster size thumb at Niner. "He started it."

"Tattletale."

Dawson rose. "Let's get in position, ten meters apart. Watch your arcs. We need to take out as many as we can in the first engagement."

Niner and Atlas became all business. "Yes, Sergeant Major."

Dawson hurried forward. RPGs had joined in with the automatic weapons, and his concern for his friends grew. They were almost in the line of fire now, and things were about to get dicey. He pointed at a tree and Atlas took a position behind it. He continued sprinting forward, pointing at another for Niner, then covered the final ten meters, ducking as sporadic gunfire continued to spray the forest, thankfully dwindling as the hostiles recognized no one was fighting back anymore. "Zero-Five, Zero-One. We're in position. Report, over."

"In position now," replied Spock. "Ready when you are, over."

"Copy that. Execute in three, two, one. Execute!" Dawson had already picked out his first target in his arc. Six men and six arcs, the targets divvied up equally, ensuring no wasted opportunities. He squeezed the trigger on his M4, sending hot lead toward their enemy, already moving on to the next target as five other weapons joined in. It was a shooting gallery, and if he weren't taking human lives, he'd be enjoying himself. But this was real life, not a video game, and though these were bad people hell-bent on killing friends of his and an innocent culture, and he was entirely comfortable with removing these vermin from the face of the Earth, he wouldn't take any joy in it.

He and his team were doing what was necessary, not what was fun.

The hostiles responded.

And the job became more difficult.

Acton skidded to a halt, as did Laura. The others soon stopped as they realized the professors were no longer with them. "Do you hear that?"

Laura cocked an ear. "Some more weapons fire. Different sound. Disciplined."

"Yeah, those definitely aren't AKs. I've heard enough M4s in my life to know that's what that is."

"Who uses M4s?" asked Mai.

Acton smiled. "US military for one, including Delta Force."

Laura's eyes widened. "Could BD and the others be here?"

"I don't know, but we have to find out. They couldn't have come here thinking they'd be facing those numbers." He turned to Mai. "You and the others go with the natives. We'll be back as soon as we can." He gave Mai a quick hug as did Laura, then sprinted toward the gunfire once again, Laura at his side. It didn't take them long to get close to the action and he held up, not wanting to surprise their friends in the heat of battle. And that was assuming it was their friends. It could be complete strangers here to help them, who had no idea who they were and what they looked like.

He crept toward one of the gun positions, then spotted somebody in full combat gear behind a tree, firing at those on the shore. Acton leaned out. "Friendly on your six!" he shouted.

The man's head turned slightly for a brief instant. "Is that you, Professor?"

Acton and Laura hugged each other excitedly at Dawson's voice. "Yes, it is. I'm here with Laura. The rest are heading back to the native's village where—"

"I'm a little busy for a chitchat."

"Do you have any spare weapons, or ammo for an AK-47?"

Dawson stepped back and unslung an MP5. He hurled it toward them then several jungle style mags. He pointed to his right. "Niner and Atlas are that way." He raised his voice. "Niner, friendlies coming in from your six! Give them your MP5 and some ammo!"

"Roger that, BD!"

Acton retrieved the weapon and ammo, handing them to Laura.

Dawson pointed to his right. "One of you take position behind that tree. Single shot. Conserve your ammo. You see a target that's still firing, take them out."

"Roger that," said Laura as she rushed into position at a crouch. Acton continued past her toward Niner, slamming his back into a nearby tree.

"Hiya, Doc. You know I had to cancel dinner and a movie with my woman to come save your ass once again?" He tossed the MP5 over and some ammo.

Acton checked the weapon. "I call bullshit on that."

Niner glanced at him. "What do you mean?"

"You've got a woman? I don't believe it. You can't have a woman."

"I can have a woman." Niner squeezed off a few rounds as did Acton.

"Oh, I'm sure you can," said Acton in a mocking tone.

"No, it's true, she's real." Niner fired again. "Like, we kiss and do other mommy and daddy things. Atlas, tell him."

Atlas' impossibly deep voice rumbled across the forest. "Tell them what?"

"That I've got a girlfriend."

"Don't believe him, Doc. He's still holding out hope that you're going to buy it, and he and your old lady are going to end up happily ever after."

Acton laughed as he continued to fire. "It's okay, Niner. It never hurts to dream, but touch my wife, and we might just have a friendly fire incident."

Niner groaned. "But I really do have a girlfriend. Her name's Angela."

"RPG!" shouted Dawson from their left. Acton peered out and spotted the weapon being raised from the deck of one of the boats and cursed. He opened fire, but it was too late, the grenade already screeching across the sand toward where he had left Laura with Dawson. The explosion tore apart the trees and Acton sprinted toward the aftermath. He gasped as he found Dawson and Laura lying on the forest floor, unmoving.

"Dawson and Laura are down!" he shouted. He rushed to Laura's side as someone came toward them.

"Friendly at your three-o'clock, Doc." He recognized Spock's voice as he took up behind a tree near Dawson's former position, resuming fire. "How are they?"

Acton quickly checked Laura for obvious injuries and confirmed she had a pulse. He patted her cheek and she groaned.

"What happened?"

"RPG. Are you okay?"

"I think so. Just give me a moment."

Acton scurried over to Dawson, who sat up on his own.

"I'm good, Doc, just had the wind knocked out of me."

"They're both alive!" Acton reported to Spock. He ran his eyes over the soldier then pointed at a large shard of wood sticking out of his thigh. "Have you been doing some redecorating?"

Dawson eyed the projectile embedded in him then cursed. "Pull it out, Doc."

"You do realize I'm not that kind of doctor, right?"

"I won't tell if you won't tell."

"We don't know how deep it is."

"We'll never know until we get it out."

Gunfire ripped through the area, three guns out of the battle giving their enemy a chance to regroup. Acton ducked as bullets sprayed over their heads. "Let me get you out of the line of fire." He positioned himself behind Dawson and hooked under the man's armpits, dragging him back about 50 feet then propping him up behind a tree. "You just sit tight. I'm going to get Laura." He turned but saw Laura already standing, taking cover behind a tree, firing at the enemy. He returned to Dawson. "Never mind, she's already back in the battle. I guess she's more of a soldier than you are."

Dawson chuckled. Acton ripped open the pant leg, revealing the wound. It didn't look too bad, but what was happening beneath the surface could be the proverbial iceberg. He pulled off his belt then placed it above the wound like a tourniquet and tightened it with a yank.

Dawson grunted.

"You okay?"

"I'll live."

Acton gently tugged at the fist-sized shard. "Tell me if you want me to stop."

"Just yank it like a band-aid, Doc."

"And that would be the exact wrong thing to do."

"I thought you said you weren't a doctor?"

"I might not be a medical doctor, but I'm also not an idiot." He gently pulled and the shard came away. He held it up, revealing nothing more than half an inch long had blood on it. "Just a flesh wound, you wimp." There was some minor bleeding, but nothing to be worried about if they could get him proper medical attention within the next 24 hours. Dawson loosened the tourniquet and watched to see if any blood flowed, and it didn't. He handed Acton his belt back then pulled a small medkit from one of the many pouches on his gear and treated himself. Acton wrapped the wound with some gauze, then rose as the battle still raged at the beach.

Dawson raised a finger to his ear. "Copy that. Fall back to my position, twenty meters, out."

Acton put his belt back on then helped Dawson to his feet. Dawson lifted his knee on his wounded leg.

"How does it feel?

"Like I'll live to fight another day. Thanks, Doc."

Laura and Spock rushed toward them then hit the ground, taking position behind a couple of trees.

"Status report."

"There are too many," replied Spock. "I saw a couple more RPGs being waved around. If we don't get some serious firepower into this, we're not winning it."

Dawson frowned and Spock pointed at the newly dressed leg.

"What's going on here?"

"Flesh wound, nothing to worry about."

Acton heard something in the distance. "What the hell is that?" He couldn't quite make it out as the gunfire continued from the beach, the M4s and MP5s silent as Dawson's team had fallen back.

Dawson cocked an ear then smiled as he activated his comms. "Bravo Team, return to your previous positions. We need to keep them on the beach, over."

Jara watched in dismay as the angels retreated and the evil Outsiders advanced. Those the gods had sent had failed, and it would appear the prophecy was about to be fulfilled. The evil of the Outsiders had reached their shores, and his people were doomed. He heard something, a thumping sound, similar to when a fly was caught in his ear. It was coming from out over the water. He peered into the distance but couldn't make out anything. Yet the sound grew as did his terror. The strange fire on the horizon continued, the black pestilence it spewed covering the sky far offshore, and from it, the sound grew louder.

In his experience, nothing good ever came from that direction, and his fear built. Finally, he spotted something. What, he wasn't sure. He shielded his eyes as he peered into the distance then gasped as he spotted two large birds heading this way. But these were no ordinary birds. They were massive. As they approached, they took form, and he realized that these were no birds at all, these were massive abominations created by the Outsiders, and as they approached, his heart sank, for the end of days were here, and tonight, he would be feasting with the ancestors.

Then the unimaginable happened.

Acton rushed forward and slammed against a tree, opening fire as two choppers arrived on the scene. Dawson was in communication with them to his right, Laura was to his left as everyone poured fire on the enemy, keeping them hemmed in on the beach. The first chopper opened fire, shredding apart two of the boats, the second joining in a moment later, focusing on the beach. The encounter lasted less than ten seconds before their enemy were throwing down their weapons and raising their hands.

One of the choppers backed off to provide cover as the other turned to face the now vanquished enemy, its PA crackling. "This is Lieutenant Colonel Kurichh of the Indian Army. You are all under arrest. Lay down your arms and return to your boats. You will be escorted back to Port Blair. Any attempt at escape will be met with a violent response."

The men scrambled from the beaches and back onto the surviving boats, turning them back toward the island to the east. One of the choppers left with them and the other landed on the beach as Dawson and his men emerged from the trees. Acton took Laura's hand and they joined them. The soldiers saluted the Indian officer as he hopped out.

The salute was returned. "I'm Lieutenant Colonel Mankeshwar Kurichh, Indian Para SF. Who here is Sergeant Major White?"

Dawson stepped forward, answering to his cover identity. "I am, Colonel."

"Sorry to have kept you waiting, Sergeant Major. We had a devil of a time getting here. Hard to do thirteen-hundred kilometers in one of these without making a few stops along the way."

Dawson chuckled. "I suppose it is, but you got here just in time regardless."

Kurichh turned to Acton and Laura. "I presume you are Professors Acton and Palmer."

Acton stepped forward. "Yes, sir."

"Report."

J. ROBERT KENNEDY

Acton suppressed a smile. "Sir, Professor Jannarkar had eight students with him at the dig site. Two drowned as a result of the tsunami, and one was sent with one of my people on a raft to get help. Professor Jannarkar was killed a couple of hours ago, saving his remaining students. The rest are alive and sheltering with the natives."

"So, you have two on a raft out there somewhere?"

"Yes, sir. I managed to retrieve the life raft from our yacht, so it's seaworthy, but I have no idea what they may have encountered out there."

"We'll keep an eye out for them. And the genocide?"

Acton's eyebrows shot up. "Genocide?"

"We were told a possible genocide was occurring here."

Acton exchanged a look with Laura who tilted her head slightly. "It would seem to fit the situation."

He agreed. "Yes, sir. These people stood to be wiped out, but that's been prevented. We believe twelve of them were lost, but they should still have a viable population to continue."

"Then I suppose we should get out of here before we overstay our welcome."

"Yes, sir." Acton pointed at the weapons scattered about. "The natives have indicated they don't want any of these left behind." He then directed Kurichh's attention to the pile of gold. "And we better not forget the cause of all this."

Kurichh's eyes shot wide, as did Bravo Team's. "You'll have to explain that, Professor Acton, when we're in the air."

304

"Of course, Colonel, but how are we going to fit everything in the one chopper?"

"I've got a heavy transport inbound from the island. They were just waiting for the all-clear." He pressed a finger to his ear then turned to face the water and pointed. "Here it comes now. I suggest you get the rest of your survivors. We're going to collect up everything we can, then leave these people in peace."

"We'll go get them," said Acton.

Dawson looked at him. "Do you want an escort?"

Acton shook his head. "No. The elders accepted Laura and I into their community, but the way you guys are decked out, might make them nervous."

Niner flashed a broad smile. "How could anyone be nervous around a face like this?"

Acton gestured at the smile. "Well, if you showed those pearly whites to one of these natives, they would take that as a hostile sign and gut you."

Niner's smile disappeared, his lips pressed tightly together.

Atlas eyed him. "If I had known it was that easy to get you to shut up, I would have tried that years ago."

A bird was flipped and Kurichh eyed the unprofessional exchange.

Dawson shook his head. "I apologize for my men, Colonel. They're not used to having company."

Kurichh laughed. "No need to apologize, Sergeant Major. Camaraderie is why I joined the military. Unfortunately, I had parents who insisted I go the officer route rather than enlisted." He tapped his rank insignia. "This limits one's ability to express one's sense of humor."

The transport helicopter was approaching now, its rotors overwhelming any conversation, and Acton shouted over the din. "We'll go get the others now!"

Spock cocked an eyebrow then pointed at the forest. "If I'm not mistaken, that's them."

Acton and Laura turned, and they both waved as Mai and the others emerged from the trees, everyone racing across the sand, crying and cheering. Mai threw herself into Laura's arms and he wrapped his around both of them, breathing a heavy sigh of relief that their ordeal was almost over.

And that was when scores of warriors emerged from the tree line, every one of them armed with a spear or a long bow. At the center of the frightening sight was Jara, standing beside a man whose colorful headdress and belt indicated he was the leader.

"Prepare to repel!" ordered Dawson. "Remember the ROEs. Shock and awe only." His men immediately spread out, raising their weapons.

But Jara was smiling, his teeth revealed. Acton reached out and gently pushed Dawson's weapon down. "Tell your men to stand down."

"Are you sure, Doc?"

"Trust me."

The chief stepped out, Jara by his side, then raised his bow, stretching back on it, aiming directly toward them. Jara reached out and slowly pushed the man's arm toward the sand. The chief tossed the bow and arrow to the ground then dropped to his knees, burying the weapon.

Acton took the hunting knife he had confiscated off of one of the gang members the night before and raised it over his head. He dropped it onto the beach before kneeling beside it and burying it as well. The natives then turned and disappeared into the jungle, leaving only Jara. He smiled broadly at them and waved, then he too turned and disappeared.

Dawson stared at Acton. "What the hell just happened?"

"That, my friend, was the proverbial burying of the hatchet."

"What does that mean?"

"I would take it to mean that we can go in peace, but we shouldn't come back."

The transport chopper that Kurichh had called off the moment the natives appeared was cleared to land, and made its approach, once again drowning out any conversation. Acton stared at the beach and the aftermath of 36 hours of hell. So many had died here, all over a pile of gold that still sat nearby, something of no interest to those who lived here, but worth killing over outside of this small oasis.

Laura took his hand and he put an arm around Mai, who leaned her head against his chest. As the engines powered down on the new arrival, he looked at her. "How about we go find Tommy?"

Bay of Bengal

Tommy and Amit lay in the bottom of the raft, exhausted. Amit's wound was still bleeding, though slowly. He needed proper medical attention soon. Tommy had long since given up paddling. His arms were like dead weights on his sides, but the sail continued to flap, and they continued to be propelled forward, even if the pace were excruciatingly slow. They would eventually make it to safety and get help for their friends, but he feared it was too late. Those boats would have arrived by now. So many men, so many weapons. Tears filled his eyes as he pictured Mai and the professors slaughtered mercilessly by those desperate to get their hands on the gold he had found in the hold.

He cursed at himself. If he hadn't found those rotted and rusted strong boxes, none of this would have happened. It was his fault they were all dead. He was the one who came outside and raised the gold bar in the air like a fool. He had been an idiot. Why hadn't he just left it inside, out of sight, then called the professors over to show it to them discreetly? Nobody would have ever known about the gold. They could have come up with a proper plan, but no, in his excitement at having found something of importance, he sought the spotlight, and now so many were dead because of it.

If Mai and the professors were also dead, if those he loved the most were gone, it was because of him, and he had no desire to live in the world that he had created. If it weren't for Amit, he would sink this raft and go down with it, but he had a responsibility to his friend who was just as scared as he was, and innocent in all of this. Amit still had his family, still had those who loved him and whom he loved. He had to keep going for him and for his loved ones, even if everyone Tommy cared for in this world were gone.

He heard something in the distance and pushed up on his elbows to see what it might be. It was coming from behind them, and when he spotted what it was, bile filled his mouth. The criminals were returning, four boats heading directly for them.

But there was something else.

A military helicopter was behind them. It made no sense. Then it did. He shook Amit. "Something's happening!"

"What?"

"You have to see this!"

He helped Amit into a seated position and his friend's eyes bulged. "Are they going to shoot at us again?"

"No, look at the chopper."

Amit stared, puzzled. "What am I seeing here?"

"Remember those friends I was telling you about?"

Amit nodded.

"Well, I have a feeling this has something to do with them."

The boats sped past them but the chopper hovered nearby, its PA system activating. "Thomas Granger. I have a message from Professor Acton. 'Don't be an idiot. You will be rescued shortly.'" The helicopter then banked, chasing after the boats it had been escorting.

Tommy dropped on his haunches, his shoulders shaking as he laughed and cried, for the message meant many things. His and Amit's ordeal was almost over, Professor Acton was alive, and so were Professor Palmer, and most importantly, Mai. For if they weren't, Acton would never have delivered a message like that, it would have been serious in tone. He felt a hand on his arm and he looked at Amit.

"You can stop worrying now. It's over. You saved us."

Tommy sighed heavily, wiping his eyes dry with the back of his hands. He sat cross-legged beside his new friend. "What do you plan on doing when you get home?"

Amit thought for a moment. "First, I think I'll take an extremely long shower."

Tommy laughed, taking a whiff of his own pits. "Yeah, me too."

"Then I think I'm going to eat as much of my mother's butter chicken as I can, then depending on how bad things are out there, try to help in any way I can. What about you?"

Tommy smiled. "After that shower, I think I'm going to hold my girlfriend for as long as she'll let me, order a Detroit style pepperoni pizza, then figure out how I'm going to collect on that debt you owe me."

Amit laughed and Tommy joined in, and for the first time since Mai had whispered in his ear to lower the gold bar he had raised triumphantly over his head, the weight he had been carrying of guilt, responsibility, horror, and grief, lifted, if only somewhat.

For the dead were still dead, and he would have to live with that for the rest of his life.

Port Blair, Baratang Island
Andaman Islands, India

Acton stepped from the chopper then helped Laura and Mai down, the groundcrew urging them toward a nearby tent. The devastation they had witnessed as they flew across the Andaman Islands toward the capital of Port Blair on the eastern coast was horrifying, but there was life down there, plenty of it, and judging by the number of ships in the area from various navies of the world, help was arriving.

Everyone ducked into the large tent to find it set up as a field hospital. They were given the once-over and a clean bill of health. Dawson's leg was properly treated, he and the others having stripped out of their combat gear in the helicopter to avoid questions about why American Special Forces were here.

"Tommy!" cried Mai.

Acton spun and spotted Tommy coming through the door, helping Amit. He and Laura both rushed over with Mai as two medics took charge of the young Indian man, his arm bandaged.

"What happened?" asked Acton as the four of them hugged each other.

"We were attacked by some gang members on your boat. Luckily, they ignored us on the way back. At least six boatloads of them. Did you see them?"

Acton chuckled. "Yeah, we saw them."

"What happened?"

Acton squeezed the young man's shoulder. "How about this? I'll tell you all about it when we get on a plane out of here, and then you can tell us all about what happened with you. I'm just happy you're safe. Now, why don't you two get reacquainted. We've got some phone calls to make."

Tommy smiled then walked away with an overwhelmed Mai clinging to him, a tall though perhaps not so tall tale or two about to be told.

Laura pulled out her phone. "I've got a signal. Who should we contact first?"

Acton pursed his lips. "I know you want to call Hugh, since Dawson said Hugh was the one that contacted Dylan. But if I don't call Greg first, I'm never going to hear the end of it, and at least Hugh is on the other side of the Atlantic."

She laughed then handed him the phone and he began to dial when Dawson and the others walked over. He pocketed the phone.

"Thanks for saving our necks once again, Sergeant Major."

Dawson shook Acton's hand. "One of the many reasons I joined the forces was to see the world. And now, I can honestly say I've seen a part of it that almost no one ever has, so I'd say it was a good day."

Acton smiled. "You did more than that. All of you did. If it weren't for you, that little piece of the world that you were privileged to see today would have been wiped out. You saved a civilization, and you should all be very proud of that fact."

"We all did, Professor." Dawson glanced over his shoulder at Niner. "Anything from the peanut gallery?"

Niner sighed. "I had a string of one-liners ready, but the Doc ruined the mood."

"Sorry about that, Niner," said Acton. "I guess you're eager to get home to your girlfriend, 'Angela.'" He used air quotes around her name.

Laura gave Niner a look. "Girlfriend? I'm a little hurt. I thought I was the only one in your heart."

"Sweet Cheeks, you'll always have a place in my heart."

The entire Bravo Team groaned and Laura shook her head. "Word of advice, Niner."

"What?"

"If this so-called Angela is actually a real person and not inflatable, don't call her Sweet Cheeks."

Niner raised a finger. "Good tip. I'll write that down when I get back. Any others?"

"So many others. I suggest sticking with babe, dear, my love. Pretty much anything else out of your mouth will probably be offensive."

Heads bobbed among the team.

"The woman's absolutely right," rumbled Atlas. "Pretty much anything that comes out of your mouth is offensive. How about we just go with the general rule that you don't talk anymore?" Niner opened his mouth to reply and Atlas slapped a hand over it. "Starting now."

On board the Norham Castle

Southeast of the Andaman Islands

September 6, 1883

After the hell of the volcano and its aftermath, the voyage to the Andaman Islands was uneventful, Sampson's log entries again routine. The crew had spent the past days conducting repairs, then scrubbing clean every surface. Morale was high, despite the fact they were bypassing Burma, a far more exciting port of call than the Andaman's, though for now, most were content to have just survived the disaster so far away now, there was little evidence it had ever occurred.

He could chuckle about it now, about how he was convinced they were witnessing Armageddon, how he was certain it was the end of times as foretold in the Bible, and how he would never see his family again. But many had died. He had lost three to the wave, and over a dozen were completely deaf. Yet many more had lost their lives, and they had all borne witness as they passed by the devastated islands, hit by massive waves and rocked by repeated earthquakes.

He couldn't imagine the horror that must have consumed their final moments, helpless in the path of nature's fury.

He closed the log and placed it in his desk, locking the drawer with a key he kept around his neck. He had maintained a detailed account of everything he saw, including entries that might prove embarrassing later, though he didn't regret them. Far too often, the ship's logs were dry affairs, ignoring the humanity, and instead merely relating the facts. He was guilty of it his entire career, as he was today.

September 6, 1883. 1:15pm. All is well.

"Land ho!"

He smiled. He looked forward to setting foot once again on dry land, a land free of the corpses scattered about the beaches behind them. Smithers knocked, poking his head inside the open door.

"Thar be land, Cap'n!" he cried in his best pirate imitation.

Sampson laughed. "Have you been in the drink again, Doctor?"

Smithers faked a hiccup. "I swear I haven't touched the stuff since I felt the sun upon my skin."

Sampson smiled and rose, joining his friend and the rest of the crew on the deck as the Andaman Islands came into view. And as their sails billowed above them, carrying them swiftly toward the end of the most frightful leg of travel he had ever experienced, he finally let himself relax, the tension in his shoulders easing at the sight of the Union Jack flying proudly ahead.

They would soon be resupplied, the men would have a brief reprieve, then they would be on to India where they would deliver the gold in their hold, refill it with tea and spices, then return home.

Never to return again.

At least for him.

"Something's wrong, Captain!" shouted the lookout, pointing ahead.

Sampson tensed as he headed for the prow with Smithers and peered toward the shore.

And his heart sank as the water rapidly receded from the coast. He turned, as did the others, and closed his eyes, beseeching the Good Lord to care for his wife and children, for this was indeed the end. They had escaped the eruption, the hurled hellfire, the thick ash-laden rains, the tidal waves, and more.

Yet there was no escaping this wave, easily one hundred feet high, rushing toward them.

Goodbye, my love.

THE END

ACKNOWLEDGMENTS

A thought occurred to me earlier today, that I believe I have written about before, though not in this context.

Pink elephants.

For decades, I had nightmares about pink elephants. The specifics of the particular nightmares I can't recall, I simply remember waking up at least several times a year for my entire life, having a nightmare about a pink elephant.

A few years ago, I finally asked my parents if pink elephants meant anything, and my mother immediately knew what I was talking about. Apparently, I had one as a toy when I was very young, and I hurt myself (I think I cracked my head on the side of a table or something while bouncing on it).

This explained a lifelong mystery, and I haven't thought about it since, until this morning, when I realized something. I haven't had a single nightmare about pink elephants since I found out the secret.

This got me thinking about childhood traumas, and how they can impact us into our adult lives without even knowing why. Because I asked that simple question, I had my nightmares explained, and what was some mythical being in my subconscious became just a toy, not worthy of fear.

I wonder how many of us have similar things haunting us, that could be solved by talking. I fear with what is happening in the world right now, in twenty or thirty years, we'll have an entire generation of adults, who were young children today, traumatized by an experience they don't remember.

Troubling that we will be dealing with this for possibly generations.

As usual, there are people to thank. My dad for all the research, Brent Richards and Ian Kennedy for some weapons info, Fred Newton for some nautical info, and, as always, my wife, daughter, my late mother who will always be an angel on my shoulder as I write, as well as my friends for their continued support, and my fantastic proofreading team!

Also, a special thank you to an old friend of mine I haven't seen in years, Rajni Kurichh, who provided the names of the Indian professor and his wife, as well as his students. You'll recognize her last name as that of the Indian Special Forces Lieutenant Colonel who arrived on the helicopter. He is named after her late father, Mankeshwar Lal Kurichh. Thanks for your help on this one, Rajni!

To those who have not already done so, please visit my website at www.jrobertkennedy.com, then sign up for the Insider's Club to be notified of new book releases. Your email address will never be shared or sold.

Thank you once again for reading.

Made in United States
North Haven, CT
20 July 2023